The Trouble on Regency Road - Text copyright © Emmy Ellis 2020
Cover Art by Emmy Ellis @ studioenp.com © 2020

All Rights Reserved

The Trouble on Regency Road is a work of fiction. All characters, places, and events are from the author's imagination. Any resemblance to persons, living or dead, events or places is purely coincidental.

The author respectfully recognises the use of any and all trademarks.

With the exception of quotes used in reviews, this book may not be reproduced or used in whole or in part by any means existing without written permission from the author.

Warning: The unauthorised reproduction or distribution of this copyrighted work is illegal. No part of this book may be scanned, uploaded, or distributed via the Internet or any other means, electronic or print, without the author's written permission.

The Trouble on Regency Road

Emmy Ellis

Prologue

"*Get out of my face, you little cow! I bloody hate you, I do.*"

Ivy backed away from her angry mother who'd sprawled on the sofa, a blanket over her skinny body. Legs trembling, her heart doing that pitter-patter thing, filling her chest with fear and anxiety, Ivy wanted to run, far away, and never come back. But where would she go? She didn't have any other family, and friends were a distant memory, something she'd only had during the first few months at school until other kids' mummies told them she was smelly and 'not a nice child'. Maybe Ivy stealing food from their lunchboxes wasn't nice, but she was hungry the majority of the time, and the free school dinners didn't stay in her tummy all day, did they. If she took a sandwich or an apple, she could eat it for her tea later, something to stop the hunger pangs.

Mummy said things like, "Well, you get your food at school, so why the fuck do you need more, you greedy bitch?"

The teacher said they should eat three times a day and, "Is that your tummy rumbling, Ivy? Did you have breakfast this morning?"

No, she hadn't. Never did. She wished for the colourful cereal boxes, or the bread for toast, or even a bag of porridge oats, but the cupboard remained bare except for pasta and things Ivy couldn't cook. Too small, she was, and burning herself wasn't a good thing, the teacher said that, too. Mummy warned she must never go near the cooker until she was at least thirteen.

That was ages away.

Ivy stood in the hallway, staring into the living room. Mummy was drunk again. She gulped from a bottle with clear liquid in it, coughing after, and that'd be from the cigarettes. She smoked a packet or more a day, and sometimes, she had a homemade one wedged between her skeletal fingers. The smell of those wasn't very nice, and Mummy tended to be meaner after them. More violent.

Ivy waited for Mummy to fall asleep, snoring, and wandered into the kitchen in search of food. Half term meant no school dinner, and her stomach cramped from hunger until she all but doubled over. She found some rice, but the label said you had to cook it on the hob, so she'd best steer clear of that.

More searching brought no results, so she'd have to make the rice, no matter what Mummy had said. She would never know what Ivy had done if she washed the pan up after.

She filled the kettle, struggling a bit with the weight of it now the water was up to the top in the little plastic gauge on the side. While it boiled, she managed to light the gas ring, although the puff of blue flame that billowed towards her at first couldn't be right. She'd listened to the hiss of the gas for ages then struck a match, her hand unsteady, and put it near the cooker top. Maybe she shouldn't have waited so long. Mummy always lit it straight away.

She'd burnt some of her fringe.

Rice in a pan, she left it to cook and poked around in the little freezer box in the top of the fridge. There might be peas or something in there. But only Mummy's pizza called to her in its enticing red box, asking her to eat it all up, but she couldn't bring herself to do it, no matter how much her tummy growled.

She'd be in so much trouble if she ate it.

She thought of the other children at school and in the street. They'd be having a nice meal now, she'd bet, and pudding for afters, maybe a lovely trifle or pineapple upside down cake. Custard, Angel Delight, or a strawberry yoghurt.

Later, disturbing her forage, a funny smell had her turning to the hob, and she peered into the pan. The rice had boiled dry. It was cooked, light and fluffy, but had caught at the bottom. She grabbed the tea towel to hold the saucepan handle with, like Mummy always did when she made her own dinner, and carried the pan to the sink. She placed it on the draining board, and a hiss crackled where there was water underneath.

Another funny smell. Smoke. Similar to Mummy's cigarettes.

Ivy glanced down. Flames devoured the tea towel, crawling up towards her hand, and she dropped it, backing away. It landed on a pile of washing on the floor, slinking all over it and munching it up. She eyed her pan of rice and grabbed it, reversing out of the kitchen, her eyes so wide they hurt, her chest tightening.

She shut the door. Mummy wouldn't see what she'd done then.

Ivy sat on the stairs and ate the food by scooping it up with her curved fingers. It scalded her skin, but that was all right. Better to have blisters than hunger.

Mummy shot out of the living room. Ivy jumped, the pan going flying. It came to rest on the hallway floor, contents spilling onto the grotty carpet. She'd eat it off there once Mummy went away, when she shouted and ranted and slapped Ivy's face.

"What's that stink?" Mummy pushed open the kitchen door, and a blast of heat came out, shunting her backwards down the hallway. She rushed forward and closed it again, fumbling with the phone on the rickety table by the front door. "Fire. There's a fire." She gave their address and slammed the phone down. Stared at Ivy. At the pan. "You've been cooking. You stupid bitch! Look what you've done!"

She gripped Ivy by her hair, opened the door, and launched her out into the front garden. Ivy landed on the path, her knees and palms stinging from the grit digging in, and a couple of neighbours chatting on the pavement whispered things. Things Ivy had heard a thousand times. That poor kid. Should we do something? Look at the state of her mother—again.

Ivy, crying, managed to stand, watching Mummy for signs of a more vicious attack.

Mummy advanced.

The last thing Ivy thought as a clenched fist smacked into her nose was:

I don't want to be here anymore. I wish the fire had burnt *me* all up.

Confession

I hate to say this and never thought I would, but Sherry, my wife, is getting on my nerves. Always watching me, she is. She thinks I'm having an affair with all the women I do odd jobs for. Blimey, she's my life, always has been since the day we met, but no matter how many times I tell her that, she's just not having it. I'm thirty-seven, not seventeen, and messing about isn't my thing. Still, she'll see sense in the end, and at the moment, there are more pressing things to be thinking about. Like those people who keep walking down Regency Road, strangers, and that isn't normal. Who the hell are they, and what are they doing around here? – Billy Price

Chapter One

Billy sat in his favourite black leather armchair, the one at the back of the living room. He got a good view of what was going on outside then. Not that he was nosy or anything, and people-watching wasn't a crime, but lately, there had been some unknowns about.

Billy didn't like unknowns.

Especially because he was on the dole and did jobs on the side, the cash-under-the-table kind or money planted in his palm during a friendly handshake. He'd got himself all worked up that they were there to keep an eye on him, creeps from the social sent to spy. He wouldn't put it past them, and they'd catch a fair few residents if they watched for long enough. Most people around here were workshy when it came to legitimate jobs. Moonlighting occurred more often than not.

An old man walked along the opposite side of Regency, coming from the right. The streetlamp lit him up for the splash of time he went past. He had a black suit on, a white shirt with a dicky bow, and that was just bloody weird. Who put those on if they weren't going out somewhere posh? Even then, Billy doubted he'd ever have that sort of thing around his neck. Ties didn't agree with his Adam's apple. They tended to chafe and leave a red mark.

Sherry would think it was a love bite.

He got up and walked to the window. Sherry, on the sofa reading her Kindle, glanced up, and he sensed her gaze boring into him, the steely kind that had blades in it. Christ, did she think he perved on old men as well as the women?

A flush bruised his cheeks at that thought. Six months ago was the last time he'd perved on Delia, the woman on Mulberry Lane, who'd stood on the corner behind his house, touting her wares. He'd watched her on the quiet for years, but cheating on Sherry wasn't his bag. Looking didn't hurt, though, and only him and DI Yeoman knew Billy had done it. He was one of Yeoman's narks and filtered information to the copper. That was why he was so intent on knowing who the strangers were. Yeoman might need to know.

Billy sighed, remembering Delia in her cream leather jacket, standing beneath the streetlamp. No more watching her for him. She was dead now, and it was weird to stare out of the rear bedroom window and not see her there.

Poor cow.

"What are you doing?" Sherry asked.

"Just nosing out." He shucked off the irritation her question brought in the form of scrunched eyebrows and the need to snap. His every move seemed to be monitored lately. Couldn't a bloke peer through his window now, all innocent, like?

The old man crossed over and disappeared around the corner, going left. Billy lived at number one, so the fella was either on his way to

Mulberry Lane or one of the other streets down that way. The thing was, Billy had seen him before, earlier, around seven, going *up* Regency. Had he visited someone?

Probably.

A prickly sensation crawled over the back of Billy's neck, and he scratched it. That incited a shiver, one that wended down his spine, a river of ice, then shot up again. He couldn't work out why, but it was like a sixth sense warned him of something, or whispers of knowledge told him secrets, ones he couldn't hear.

He frowned and went back to his chair, crossing his legs at the ankles.

"Make me a cuppa, will you?" Sherry asked.

She'd taken to ordering him about these days, maybe to see if he still cared enough about her while supposedly shagging everyone else. He reckoned in her mind, if he made her a coffee, he gave a shit. Weird how the female brain worked. Weird and bugging. He didn't know how much more of her accusations he could take. He'd never cheated on her, so why had she believed the rumours? It had started with that bird he'd fixed a pipe for and escalated from there.

He pushed up from of his chair, holding back the huff waiting to come out. It wouldn't do him any good if he let her see he was naffed. There'd be snipes all evening, maybe even an argument to round it off, and he was tired of it. Just one night of peace, that was all he asked for.

In the kitchen, he put the kettle on to boil and had an idea. If he rushed out the back and climbed over the fence into the alley, he could go into Mulberry and see where the old boy had gone. All right, not normal behaviour, but something about the fella niggled him. Saying that, some time had passed since Billy had seen him, so who knew where he was now.

He opened the back door quietly so Sherry didn't ask, yet again, what he was doing. The grass, wet from a recent downpour, soaked his socks, but he paid it no mind. A quick vault over the fence had him standing in the lane, opposite Halfway House, the place where men stayed after a stint in Rushford Prison.

Shit, maybe the bloke lived there.

No, it was well past nine o'clock, and they had a curfew. Emma Ingles, the woman who ran the place, had some kind of keycode the lags used to get in and out. She'd know if someone wasn't back in time, although in the past, so he'd heard, that system hadn't worked and she'd had a new one installed.

Billy glanced up the lane, thinking he'd spot him heading to The Tractor's Wheel at the far end or perhaps visiting Cost Savers, Zuhaib Wasti's little convenience shop. Nope, just a few people standing outside the pub having a fag, their smoke visible beneath the lights on curved golden stalks hanging over the door.

Billy ran over the road and stood at the end, peering down the side of Halfway. The old man was in the distance, presenting his back, standing beside a lamppost, his arms stretched upwards. Eerie laughter floated to Billy, and it instigated another chill.

What's he bloody doing?

The fella punched the air, jumping up and down in some mad jig. He let out more laughter and strode off, past Elderflower Mead and Vicar's Gate, eventually going out of sight. Billy returned to the kitchen, his head stuffed with questions. Who *did* that in public? Who acted like they'd won the lottery while by themselves in the dark?

Fucking weirdo.

He sorted Sherry's coffee and took it in to her.

She gave him an evil glare, one of the many he'd received since the rumour emerged. "The back door squeaks when you open it. What were you in the garden for?"

He was tempted to lie and say he'd dumped some rubbish in the wheelie bin but instead chose a different route. "Do you want me to create a calendar on my phone and write down every movement I make? That'd save you asking then." He plonked her cup on the coffee table a bit too forcefully, and some fluid sloshed out onto the coaster.

"No need to be funny. How would you feel if you'd heard I'd had a good poking from someone?"

"I wouldn't believe it because I *trust* you." He moved to his chair, guilt bothering him for watching Delia, and slid his trainers on. The wet of his socks made itself known, cold and unpleasant.

"Where are *you* going?" Sherry's mouth dropped open.

"Out." He stomped over to the living room door. Fuck, he wanted the clock to roll back, to a time when they hadn't argued.

"To your woman?"

"Seriously, pack it in. I haven't done anything, but d'you know what? I may as well, seeing as I'm being accused of it." He shouldn't have said that, it'd give her more cause for concern, but fuck it, too late now.

He marched down the hallway, checking his keys were in his pocket, and left the house. For a moment, he stood there to catch his breath, which always quickened any time Sherry started on him. Shucking off her latest nag, he ambled up Regency. A pint in The Tractor's wouldn't go amiss, and it'd calm his anger a bit, soothe the ragged edges, or maybe he ought to have a tonic water. He always felt better after one of those.

Except he stopped outside Phil Flint's place, three houses knocked into one posh gaff. Phil had bought it off the proceeds of selling drugs for years, but he'd stopped that malarkey once Val, his girlfriend, had moved in. Val used to live in Mulberry, a prosser like Delia, and now rented her house out to a rum pair of fuckers with a million kids. Or it seemed like they had a million anyway. Phil had sold his drug patch to Terry, the landlord at The Tractor's, and now lived a reasonably legal life.

It was easy to do when you had a hefty bank balance.

Billy knocked on the door, seeing as the living room light was on. He needed a bloke to talk to, someone who'd tell him what to do, like Noah from the care home used to. Not only with the Sherry business but the strangers. Yeah, Phil would have answers.

Val stood there in her pink fleece pyjamas. She was a lovely sort, and you wouldn't think she'd opened her legs to all and sundry once upon a time. Her ex-husband, Steve, had run off years ago, leaving her with a nipper to take care of, and she'd turned to the profession in desperation.

Billy didn't judge her.

"Everything all right?" she asked, concern twisting her forehead into lightning-bolt lines.

Billy nodded. "Yeah, just needed to see Phil a minute."

"Come in then." Val stepped back.

Billy entered the large foyer, too fancy for him, but each to their own. He always felt uncomfortable here, the knowledge that he was a constant grafter with no grandeur in his future highly prevalent. The interior screamed money and rubbed it in that he'd never have vast amounts of it. Still, Phil had earnt it, albeit from the poor sods hooked on his gear, so who was Billy to be jealous? You reaped what you sowed, so the saying went, but if that were the case, why wasn't he rich, too? He worked damn hard and deserved a break.

"He's in the kitchen." Val smiled. "Go on through."

He bobbed his head and made his way there, entering and wincing at his nasty wet feet inside trainers that would need drying upside down on the rad overnight. He'd been too hasty in getting away from Sherry, that was the problem. Hadn't thought.

Phil squeezed brown sauce on top of cheese on toast. "Hello, mate. What's up?"

Billy must have his worried face on. Val had spotted something wasn't right, too.

"I just need a chat." He sat at the table. There was always a biscuit barrel on it, and he took the lid off and nicked a Hobnob.

"Help yourself." Phil raised his eyebrows as if appalled, but he was only messing really. "Just need to take this in to the missus, then I'll be back." He left, carrying the cheese on toast on a china plate etched with lilac flowers.

Billy fancied some of that grub. Sherry had ballsed up the dinner. Who burnt tuna pasta bake? She'd left it in the oven too long while reading. She always had her nose stuck in a book, those rude romances, and he reckoned that was where the trouble had started. She thought he should be more like her 'book boyfriends'. Well, he was Billy, always had been, and sweeping her off her feet and flinging her on the bed in a mental fashion wasn't in his nature. He bought her flowers on the odd occasion, but imagine doing that now. She'd think it was a guilt gift.

Fuck's sake.

Phil came back and, instead of flicking the kettle switch, he took a bottle of gin out of a cupboard and some tonic water from the fridge. Billy always drank tonic water on its own, but tonight, yeah, that called for alcohol.

"You wouldn't rustle me up some of that cheese on toast, would you?" he asked.

"Christ." Phil poured the drinks and handed one to Billy. "Because it's you…"

"Cheers. I'm starving. Sherry burnt the pasta."

Phil opened the oven and put two pieces of toast under the grill. "Make your own fucking dinner then, or better yet, take her out for a meal once in a while, even if it's only to The Tractor's. They've got two courses up there with a drink thrown in for a fiver each."

"That's a tenner all told. Money's scarce. Not had many private jobs in." Yet he'd been willing to sink almost three quid on a pint this evening. *Hypocrite.*

Phil sliced some cheese, Cathedral City, the expensive stuff Billy could only gaze at in the supermarket.

"I wonder why…" Phil was a sarcastic shit when he had a mind. "Women probably don't want you round there with your pawing hands, and men reckon you'll use your sausage where you shouldn't on their wives."

Billy grunted. "Not funny."

"You've got to laugh or you'll go mad. Look, think about it. Christmas isn't far off, is it. People are tightening their belts, starting the shopping early. All those presents, see, getting into debt for them an' all. I remember some skint Christmases as a kid. Gary used to get well arsey about the cheap stuff we got. He always was an ungrateful wanker. All right, they were knockoffs from the back of my old man's van, but it was the thought that counted."

Gary was Phil's younger brother. Like Delia, he was dead. Hanged himself from the banisters in Halfway, didn't he. Blimey, that had been a mad time, people being bumped off all over the place. Even Yeoman, the copper investigating it, lost his wife.

"Times have changed for you, though," Billy said.

"Just a bit."

"Bet you could afford to shop at Harrods with your bank balance."

"Maybe." Phil turned the bread over and placed cheese on top. He shoved it back under the grill. "So what's up, pal?" He swigged some gin.

"Have you noticed people walking up and down the road a lot lately, at night?"

"Can't say I have, no, but then we're not like you. We actually shut our curtains when it gets dark."

Billy could have been offended but wasn't; he was used to Phil sounding like an unfeeling twat, and anyway, he'd never told Phil *why* he kept the curtains open, so it wasn't like he meant to put his foot in it. "Well, here's the thing. There have been a few strangers about. They walk from my end up Regency, then come back about an hour later. Tonight, though, some old boy didn't come back for *two* hours."

"You need to get Sherry in the sack to relieve the boredom, mate, because you're clearly at a loose end. Isn't there anything interesting on Netflix?" Phil plated the food. "Do you want brown sauce as well?"

"Tomato."

Phil squirted some on and brought the plate to Billy. He sat and handed it over.

Billy grabbed a slice. "Ta. Yeah, I'd do that with Sherry, but she won't let me anywhere near her. Says I could have one of them infections."

"Right… Seems to me you've got deep shit to sort out, fella. Your relationship doesn't sound too healthy to me. You two used to be solid."

"I know." Billy bit a chunk of toast, and his stomach thanked him for it. He thought about what Phil had said regarding cooking. "Listen, if I start making dinner for her, she'll either think I've really been with other women or it's a slight on her burning the bloody pasta. I can't win."

Phil laughed. "Offer to do it anyway. And just have it out with her, a proper chat. Clear the air then eat some Hobnobs."

"Eh?"

"Doesn't matter, you wouldn't get the reference. So, the strangers. What do you expect me to do about them? You know I've stopped all that lark. No more sending heavies to give people a punch, no more drugs. I'm clean. I run my car showroom—well, the manager still does, I just go there to look willing every now and then. Prefer to spend my days with Val. We've got a lot of years to catch up on."

Billy swallowed. "I dunno, I just thought it was weird, that's all. The only people who walk down Regency live here or are from the estate. The folks we don't know, that's dodgy."

"A new family might have moved in. You could be seeing them all one by one." Phil drank some gin. "Might even be that mad couple who rent Val's old place."

"No, it's not them, and if it was new residents in Regency, we'd have seen the removal van."

"*You* would have, you nosy fucker."

Billy hadn't got the answers he was looking for, but he did get two things out of this visit. A full belly and the knowledge he was a snooping-through-the-window bastard who needed to get some action back in his life.

Work, home, Sherry moaning. Was that all he was prepared to have?

Probably. It was better than what he'd had before.

Confession

What you see is not what you get. I'm a professional, and the things I create have come in handy with what I'm doing. I have many faces but own only one, the nose and mouth and cheeks I was born with. The eyes...sometimes I keep them as they are, other times I hide their colour. It depends on the hair. Blue is nice with blond, green with red, brown with brown, grey with grey. I have wrinkles then I don't. I have fair skin then I don't. It's all in the person I'm supposed to be. And I'm many of those, too. –
Mask Maker

Chapter Two

Mask resisted having a drink in The Tractor's after he'd left Regency Road. It wouldn't do to have people seeing the blood specks on his white shirt. He should have put a plastic cape on really, the sort he used for his work, but that would have hindered his movements. Stopped his arm swings being so swift, the flourish of his flicking wrist.

Everything had gone to plan otherwise. The stupid cow had believed every one of his faces, the voices, the fake sincerity in his eyes.

Until the lie had been revealed.

Her expression when he'd shown her his gnashers… Worth every bit of planning, every bit of hard work.

She was alive, but her life wouldn't be as enjoyable now. He'd taken things away from her, *and* the ability to tell anyone who he was. Frightened her into keeping her mouth shut. She'd have remained quiet on who he was even if he hadn't taken the things away. He was *that* good at scaring. And besides, she had a secret of her own, one she wouldn't want him telling anyone.

Silence is golden.

She was as old as the hills, gnarly fingers, sparse white hair, wrinkles even L'Oreal's face cream couldn't prevent. She still had her own teeth. He knew that because he'd knocked a few out with the end of his meat cleaver. They'd fallen to touch her tonsils, and she'd choked, coughing one out.

It had hit him on the cheek. He'd picked it up and placed it in his pocket, a little keepsake.

He entered his home in Griffin's Holt, far enough away from the women he hated but close enough to pay them visits. Griffin's was the last street off the comb that made up the estate, and behind his house were fields that, if you walked for long enough, took you to Cobbs Moor. He'd discovered something about Fay once while on Cobbs, and she'd discovered something about him. Maybe he'd go there in the car, have a pint in Drinker's Rest. A congratulatory bevvy where he could toast his own magnificence.

It paid to let people think you'd forgotten what they'd done. It made telling them you hadn't all the sweeter.

Mask stripped off his soiled clothing and put the suit and bow tie in the washing machine on a hot cycle. The shirt, he soaked in the washing-up bowl in cold water with a liberal sprinkling of salt. In his boxers, he went upstairs to the bathroom and stared at himself in the mirror over the sink. An old man peered back at him, blood spatter on his cheeks and across the bridge of his nose. Some had landed on the short grey hair, but that was okay. It wouldn't go funny when he washed it because it was human.

He took the shower head down and turned the tap on. A nice douse in water, some shampoo added, and he massaged the hair and face, cleaning them of all the blood. He rinsed it off and patted dry, then removed the full head mask with its neck skin that gave the impression of reality. He always winced when the glue separated from his skin.

In his studio in one of the spare bedrooms, he placed the mask on a polystyrene head and styled the hair, leaving it to dry naturally. He'd disguise himself tomorrow, too, repeating the process all over again. There were other people to see, others to keep quiet.

After all, they might know his secret, too.

Chapter Three

1991

"Come on, you lot, out we go," Fay said.

Various groans mooed out of downturned mouths. The kids in the care home didn't want to go out today, what with it being cold and dreary, a deluge of rain on the horizon, but exercise was good *for them, and just because it was the weekend, it didn't mean they could lounge about.*

"It's only a short walk on the moor." She chivvied a straggler through the doorway and stepped into the courtyard.

"Can't we just play here?" one asked. Ivy Reynolds. Of course it would be her.

Fay reined in her temper. "No, we need more than just a game of rounders or a kickabout."

Fay didn't like Ivy. She always had a snotty beak no matter how many times she was told to use a tissue. The child had come to Loving Arms two months ago after the social had finally taken her away from her abusive mother, the father buggering off somewhere when Ivy was six months old. Ivy had a look about her, sly, and she tried to get other children into trouble. Fay didn't hold with that sort of nonsense, especially not from an eight-year-old.

"But, Miss Williams," Ivy wailed.

Oh, shut up, you moaning little cow.

"Enough." Fay chopped the air with a flat hand. "We're walking, and that's final."

She led her troop of six children out of the grounds and onto the moor. They had wellies on, so any sploshes in boggy puddles were permitted so long as they didn't get their clothes dirty. The janitor, Oliver Elford, also did the washing, and he wouldn't be pleased at trying to get mud stains out of the fabric.

They headed towards Drinker's Rest, and if she was feeling generous by the time they got there, she'd buy them all a Coke or lemonade, perhaps a packet of crisps if they were lucky. Ivy didn't deserve any, the whinging brat, but Fay couldn't be seen being mean to her.

Those were the key words. Couldn't be seen.

The wind whipped them this way and that, buffeting the group along the scrubby grassland. Fay had always thought there should be more trees, but they were dotted about in ones, their trunks single stems, no leaves to be seen. January was a wicked bitch this year, digging her chilly claws into everything. Some of the kids' faces were wind-chapped already, and she felt sorry for them.

Not Ivy, though.

She could remain out here and die of hypothermia for all Fay cared.

The pub came into sight, and she ploughed on, the children pushing against the wind, their coat hoods whipping backwards amid squeals. The sky, an ominous grey, darkened somewhat, and she pondered on how soon the rain would come.

A few splats landed on Fay's cheeks.

"Oh no, it's gonna piddle it down," Billy Price said.

God, she loved that boy. Such a joy to have around, and she dreaded the day he was fostered or adopted. Fay had put the kibosh on numerous attempts by perfectly suitable families over the past year, wanting to keep him all to herself. Billy didn't seem to mind being at Loving Arms, especially because she cuddled him and read him a story each night. He loved anything by Lewis Carroll, as did she, so they were suited.

She fancied he was what her own son would have been like had he lived.

"Let's go and have some pop in the pub then, shall we? It's quicker to get there than it is to turn back and go home," Fay said.

Cheers went up, and Ivy seemed particularly excited. It took the shine off Fay's suggestion, and a sour spread of hate swarmed through her system. Ivy was just like Fay's cousin, who was a snake, a slithering slip of a girl who'd done anything to get her own way.

Including killing Fay's baby boy.

She brushed the tear that fell and marched over the uneven ground to the pub, her gaggle of charges behind her. Inside, she shepherded them to the largest table with the instruction that they weren't to mess about and to sit nice and still until she returned.

At the bar, she ordered lemonades and a tonic water—Billy preferred that—and a mixture of crisp flavours, making sure to have a ready salted in the bunch. The barman put them on a black plastic tray.

Fay paid—she'd get the money back from petty cash later—and joined the children, placing the drinks on the table then pushing the packets of crisps off the tray so they landed in the middle of the circle of glasses.

Everyone snatched at their favourite flavour, as she'd known they would.

Ivy, as usual, was too slow.

"You didn't buy enough for me," the child sniped, her wind-pinched cheeks turning even redder.

Fay glanced at the tray with the packet of ready salted on it, held up too high for Ivy to see. "Oh, silly me, here's yours." She handed Ivy the crisps.

"I hate ready salted." Ivy's bottom lip poked out, and she folded her arms in temper.

I know, that's why I bought them.

"Well, considering you didn't get much of anything at home with your mother, I'd have thought you'd like whatever and be grateful for it." Fay smiled at her, although her instinct was to glare.

Ivy picked up the crisps and opened them. "I don't like them, but I'll eat them anyway."

Hmm, same as what I do. I don't like you, but I look after you anyway.

Confession

Things have been going okay since Lydia died. Life settled down after I attended her funeral and played the part of a grieving husband, but any love I'd had for her was long gone. She was a drug addict, a killer, and I can't hold a candle to her anymore. I've sold her house, given the proceeds of it to her parents, and moved to Griffin's Holt, a three-bed with a reasonable mortgage. Not too shabby. But I did get life insurance. Lydia must have taken it out on herself and not told me. Funny, because I thought she didn't love me come the end either. – Morgan Yeoman

Chapter Four

Morgan tooted the horn outside Shaz's house. His DS pissed him about every work morning, taking her time. No wonder she used to be late into the incident room before he'd insisted on picking her up. It was the eyebrows. She'd be drawing them on, no doubt.

Out she came, her red-from-a-bottle hair flying. The wind was a bugger today.

She flung herself into the car and belted up, smelling of lemons and jasmine, or whatever the hell her perfume was. Something off that market stall she liked digging bargains from. They had a tub full of stuff, end-of-line items, and Shaz, spying the sparkly packages, pounced on them all. Bloody magpie.

"Morning." She fiddled about inside her bag.

Morgan grunted. "More like afternoon." He eased away from the kerb.

"Oh, come on, I'm five minutes late. Plenty of time to get to work. We're not meant to start until half eight, and it's only five past now." She pulled out a bag of Scampi Fries and opened them.

"You're eating them for *breakfast*?" Morgan held back a gag. "Chuff me, Shaz, they stink."

"I'll stop eating them when you let me know you want a snog."

He shook his head. After Lydia had died, Shaz had made it clear she was interested in him. While that wasn't a bad thing, he still wasn't ready for a relationship, especially with someone who troughed Scamp fucking Fries any chance she got.

"Whatever." He drove towards the station and pressed the button to open the window a tad. "Seriously nasty."

"Oh, behave, you moany old sod."

They laughed, and he revisited Shaz's offer. Yeah, they got on well, and she understood his foibles, his moods. What she *didn't* understand, didn't even *know*, was that he'd covered up for Lydia after she'd been forced to slice her friend's throat and, once the case was over, he'd burnt Lydia's bloodstained pyjamas in the back garden, plus the carrier bag he'd put them in.

He doubted Shaz would keep quiet about that. While she turned a blind eye to his rough ways with criminals and witnesses, she'd keep them well and truly open if he confessed his wife was a murderer and he'd aided and abetted.

Still, Lydia was dead, as was the man who'd made her use the knife. Goat, a little prat of a fella she'd hung around with as a teenager, and later, purchased cocaine from.

Morgan slid the vehicle into a space in the car park and shut his window. He got out, waiting impatiently for Shaz to suck all the scampi crap off her finger and thumb, then she finally got out, too.

"You on a go-slow today or what?" he asked her.

"Bog off."

She'd clearly only had one coffee.

Morgan engaged the locks and walked into the station, going up to the front desk. Graham Vale stood behind it, filling out some form or other.

"Got anything for us, Gray?" Morgan scratched his temple, hoping there was nothing of significance they had to handle today.

"Nope."

"That's what I like to hear." He trotted to the incident room and held his breath. Jane bloody Blessing would be in there, perched behind her desk, peering over the top of her monitor at him, with either a look of disgust or one of triumph.

Jane had confessed she liked dressing all in black and going out into the night, shitting certain people up. She'd always publicly kept quiet about Morgan's way of behaving, his way of gaining info, yet it was nothing compared to hers.

She used a damn knife.

She felt he needed to keep his activities less obvious and find out whatever he needed with a better approach. Her hypocrisy wasn't lost on him. The times she'd berated him for how he went about, well, he'd lost count.

Nigel Stansford, the other member of the team and the expert in drawing up profiles, gave

Morgan the thumbs-up. "There's been a sighting of Martin Olbey in Shadwell."

Olbey was a man of interest in the last big murder case. He was the middleman between two killers and had absconded from Halfway House partway through the investigation.

"Shadwell?" Morgan sighed. "I'd say contact DI Bethany Smith there, but she's left the force. No idea who the new DI is now. How did you get the info?"

"Someone called Fran sent me an email. Seems Olbey ran a red light and knocked some old duffer over, and she recognised Olbey's face on CCTV—hit-and-run. No registration number, though, but the make was a Ford. She's looking into it further."

Morgan shrugged. "He'll have changed his name by now, got fake documents off someone he met in Rushford. Still, so long as this Fran's dealing with it, saves us a job."

"DI Morgan Yeoman, I'd have thought you'd have wanted to go over there and find him yourself."

"No, Jane Blessing, I don't. Look, can we dispense with the full-name bullshit now? It's getting boring."

She'd always done it to him, and he'd done it back, but a dig was a dig, and he was tired of playing games with her.

"Okay, Yeoman." She smiled over her monitor, but behind that seemingly sweet stretch of the lips lurked something other than sincerity, a barb most likely, one she was holding back. "Can I have a quick chat?"

No.

Shaz swanned in. Where the hell had she been? Probably gassing to Gray to pass the time. She went into the kitchen off to the side for her second shot of coffee. She needed two to get going of a morning.

"Go ahead, say what you've got to say." Morgan nodded to Jane.

"In your office." Jane stared hard.

Fuck. She's probably been out with her knife again. "Fine."

He strolled in there and sat behind his desk. Rain pattered on the window behind him, an irritation on top of the one due to walk into his domain any minute.

Jane slipped in, and he could see how she'd be stealthy, hiding in the shadows, her slim figure nothing but a slender stick in the darkness. She walked light-footed, so if she crept up on anyone, they wouldn't cop on until she was right up their arse.

She closed the door and sat opposite, crossing her legs. Jane favoured leggings and tight T-shirts. All the better to move about in, my dear.

"Guess what I did last night." She gripped the armrests.

Morgan sighed. "I dread to bloody think, but I'm sure you're going to tell me."

"I scared Terry."

Oh, for fu— "What, the landlord of The Tractor's?"

"Yes. The drug squad aren't doing anything quickly enough for my liking, just like they didn't with Phil Flint. *Years* Phil was left to do what he did, and now he's got away with it. D'you know, I think he used to pay someone in the drug unit to look the other way and told Terry to an' all. Well, I let Terry know the police are aware he runs the drug patch now. He wet himself. Literally."

"I might if I had a blade to my neck. Christ, woman, did you at least change your voice? He knows what you sound like, we're in the pub often enough."

"I'm not thick, Yeoman. Yes, I changed my voice. He was putting some crates of empty beer bottles in his yard. He dropped them when I stepped away from the corner."

"I should think he did. Land on his foot and break it again, did it?"

"Maybe. He did say, 'Ow. Not my other one…'"

"Don't do that anymore, please. Terry is off-limits. People are already watching him, but he's like Phil, bloody clever at not getting caught."

"I know." Jane shrugged. "I just fancied a night out, that's all. Not as if the telly is interesting at the moment, is it."

You wave a knife about because the telly's shit? Fucking hell, and I thought I was bad. "Most people have a meal or a few drinks, go to the cinema."

"I'm not most people."

He opened his mouth to say something cutting, but his mobile rang. Gray's name popped up on the screen. "Looks like we have a job. Hang on." He swiped to answer. "Yep?"

"Bit of an odd one for you," Gray said. "A woman rang in, says she's a carer for a Fay Williams, aged seventy-five. You might want to get round there—twenty-one Regency Road. There's been an incident."

"Want to elaborate?"

"A bit of knifework was involved in an attack. Williams has been in hospital but is home this morning. The carer didn't think to ring it in until just now, and the hospital haven't reported it to us yet. Probably snowed under. The carer panicked when she found her yesterday evening and took her straight in. She had an emergency op there and then and was released once she'd been observed for eight hours."

Morgan's guts rolled over, and his mind went to Jane. She'd been out with her damn knife last night, but why would she visit a woman who wasn't on their radar?

"It's a serious crime, so your department," Gray said, stating the bloody obvious.

"Okay, we're on our way." Morgan ended the call and waved at Jane to get up. "I need you in the incident room."

"I gathered." She walked out, her cheeks pink.

Probably pissed off I had a go about her visiting Terry. Tough. I don't need her fucking things up for the drug squad.

Morgan entered the incident room. Shaz had made herself a coffee and lounged at her desk, feet on top of it, leaning back in her chair and cradling the cup. You'd think she was at home the way she closed her eyes and settled in for the duration. Nigel was on Terry's Facebook page, so Jane must have put that idea into his head to go nosing. She was verging on not knowing her place, but she knew too many things about Morgan and had already insinuated she'd get him in the shit for it. Best to keep quiet.

In front of the whiteboard, Morgan cleared his throat. "Right, we've got an episode involving a Fay Williams, twenty-one Regency." Handy. He could go and have a word with Billy Price, see if he'd noticed anything. "It was an attack at home, so I want you looking into her, please. A carer was mentioned, and Fay is elderly—seventy-five. Might not be on social media, but then again, age is but a number, and anyone can work the internet if they're shown how. A knife was used. She's been in hospital, so once I know what's what, I'll let you in on it. Come on, Shaz."

She grumbled and got up, taking her cup with her to the door. Morgan led the way to the car and drove them to Regency Road, parking near twenty-one. Shaz had finished her coffee on the journey, so at least she'd be amenable now.

On the pavement, Shaz beside him, Morgan glanced down at number one. Billy's van was outside it. Good.

A brisk tap on the door of twenty-one, and a young woman answered, blonde, late twenties, a touch of makeup on, none of that plastered stuff that scared little girls into thinking every woman turned orange when they grew up.

Morgan held up his identification. "DI Morgan Yeoman and DS Sharon Tanner. We're here about the attack on Fay Williams."

"Yes, come in. I'm her carer—Louise. I've been assigned to stay with her until she's better. I'm not the same one who found her last night, by the way. Fay hasn't said much, and you'll need all the luck in the world getting anything out of her."

She led them to a living room with its old-lady furniture, the three-piece suite the sort with antimacassars on the arms and not much comfort from the thin flowery cushions. Fay Williams sat in one of the chairs by the window, staring out as if she needed to see her attacker if he came back. Presuming it was a he.

Bandages swathed her hands.

Morgan introduced them, and Louise said she'd make some tea.

"Fay likes it in a pot," she said. "Cups and saucers, too, although she'll need a straw now."

Morgan frowned at that. "Um, none for us, thanks."

Louise smiled and walked out.

Morgan concentrated on the old woman. "Fay, I'm Detective Inspector Yeoman, and this is my partner, DS Tanner. We're here to talk about the attack."

Fay didn't move her gaze from the window. A tear dripped down her cheek, but she didn't attempt to wipe it away.

"Do you remember what time they arrived?"

Fay nodded.

"And what was that?"

She ignored him.

"What did they look like?" *Maybe she's too shocked to talk.* "Can you recall that, Fay?"

Louise bustled back in, tea things on a tray. The kettle must have been recently boiled for her to have made it so quickly. She placed it on the coffee table. "Didn't you get told?"

Morgan turned to her. "Told what?"

"Fay can't speak." Louise poured milk into the cups.

"How come?"

"Oh, she had her tongue cut out and her fingers chopped off, although where the fingers and tongue are now, I don't know."

Morgan whipped his head round to look at Fay, and as if to prove the point, she opened her mouth and presented him with the gaping hole containing a quarter of a tongue at the back.

He spotted stitches and almost retched.

Shit. How were they supposed to find out what happened? Fay had no way of speaking and no fingers with which to grip a pen, so she couldn't write it down.

We're up the familiar shit creek. Bollocks.

Confession

I love Billy, I really do, but things aren't right anymore. The rumours are so rife, I don't know what to believe. Some say he wouldn't touch anyone else even if he was paid to, and others say he'll take whatever's on offer if it's served on a plate. Men say the former, women the latter, so is that the blokes sticking up for him and the women seeing him for what he really is? A cheat? Well, whatever he is, our relationship has gone to pot, and if he hasn't been near another woman, the state we're in is all my fault. I never was any good at holding on to something. Those I care about always slip away, and if I'm not careful,

I'll lose Billy, too, the one person in the care home with me who loved me as I am. – Sherry Price

Chapter Five

Sherry stood in Billy's usual place at the window, staring up Regency. She had to crane her neck to get a good view, and it cricked painfully, but she was sure that was Yeoman's car parked outside the old biddy's place. God, she shouldn't think of her as that. Fay had cared for Sherry at one time. Billy was always up there, asking her if she was okay, fetching and carrying. A carrier bag of things from Tesco or some of that nice cheese off the market man.

Billy said she'd treated him like her own, more so than the other kids. That was true. Sherry had witnessed it for herself. When he'd aged out of Loving Arms, she'd still come to see him in the bedsit he'd found, then two years later in the house he and Sherry now shared. The council had given it to him, a two-up, two-down with just enough room to swing a cat.

She supposed he was paying Fay back for everything she'd done for him, watching out for her now she was old. Sherry didn't feel she needed to do that. She wasn't at Arms for long either of the times she'd stayed there, and Fay was slightly prickly with her. Helen was always nice, though.

Why was Yeoman at Fay's?

"Billy, you might want to come and have a look at this," she called to him.

He was in the kitchen, sorting the sausages for their breakfast sarnies. She thought it was a dig at her for burning the pasta yesterday. Her fault for being too engrossed in a billionaire romance book.

"Hang on," he said.

Frustration bubbled, never far away where Billy was concerned these days. It was like she was constantly on her period, always arsey, tetchy. It didn't help that her monthlies were up the swanny anyway, preventing them from having kids. Mind you, Billy didn't want any, and she wasn't one hundred percent about it, so it was just as well really.

"Hurry up," she snapped. "You might be needed up the road."

He came in holding a black-and-white-checked tea towel. She'd been surprised and annoyed at his offer to cook this morning, suspicious even, thinking he was sucking up to her for something he'd done last night. Like, he hadn't really gone to Phil's and had been up to rude things with some woman. She'd tormented herself with it the whole time he'd been out. He'd come back and kissed her cheek, smelling of melted cheese, and that was just weird.

"What's the matter?" He dried his hands in the kitchen doorway.

"Come and see." She pointed up the street and moved so he could take her place.

Billy pressed his cheek to the pane. "Yeoman's coming out of Fay's."

"That's what I mean. What would he be doing there?"

"He's walking down here." He dropped the tea towel on the sofa and went out into the hallway.

Sherry followed him, her stomach in knots.

Billy slipped his shoes on. "Fuck, forgot to put them on the radiator."

What?

"Something's off," she said. "I can feel it." She wasn't sure if she meant Fay or Billy mentioning the rad.

"What, like you can feel my so-called affairs? Watch the sausages. They're in the oven, almost ready. Best not to burn them, eh?"

He walked out and closed the front door. His dig about burning food brought tears to her eyes, and she fisted them away. She'd been the one to criticize constantly lately, but it seemed the tables had turned and Billy was giving it back to her.

No more than she deserved.

She returned to the living room and opened the window a crack so she could hear any conversation, hiding behind the thick velvet curtain, out of sight. Billy stood in front of their door, and he waved at Yeoman, who crossed the road and hurried towards him. Shaz Tanner stayed at the other end, speaking to Fay's next-door neighbour.

Something *had* happened, so Billy's mean retort was unjustified.

"Got something for me?" Yeoman asked.

Billy glanced over his shoulder at the window, probably to see if she was eavesdropping, like she had when DS Tanner had come in once to ask her a few questions about the night of Delia Watson's murder. Sherry had had one ear on the convo with Tanner and one on Billy and Yeoman's.

Billy had said he liked watching Delia out on her corner, and Sherry's world had crumbled even more. It added to the weight of the rumours, the ones about the kitchen sink pipe woman.

Her husband turned back to Yeoman. "What's going on?"

"Fay was attacked. She had her tongue cut out, her fingers hacked off." Yeoman shook his head. "Who the bloody hell would want to do that to an old lady?"

"Fuck knows. Is she okay?"

Yeoman nodded. "She was taken to hospital, kept in until this morning—they shunted her out too early if you ask me, but eight hours is apparently okay. Seems to me the killer purposely prevented her from telling us who did it. No tongue to speak, and it's not like she can write anything down with stumps."

Oh my God!

Sherry felt sick. Billy thought of Fay as a second mum, so this was going to hit him hard. She needed to stop her griping and be there for him, a proper wife, not some harpy.

"I'll nip up to see her in a minute," Billy said.

"Did you notice anything off last night?"

"I did as it happens. I was standing at the window. We've had a few strangers down here this past week, and it bothered me. Some old man in a suit and bow tie went up towards Fay's end, then came back two hours later. Now, hear me out, I know people have folks coming and going, but it's not that usual down here. Mulberry, yes, because Wasti's shop, the laundrette, and the pub is there, but not Regency."

"I know what you mean. Only people from my street come down it as far as I've seen. Not there enough to take much notice." Yeoman scrubbed his chin. "How many strangers?"

"Well, there's the old man, a woman with brown hair and a burgundy leather jacket, and a bloke in his thirties," Billy said. "They're all average build, around five-eight or nine, and the weird thing about the woman is, she had a flat chest."

Yeoman snorted. "Thought you said you only perved on Delia."

Sherry's eyes stung.

"I did, and it wasn't perving per se, I was just making sure Delia was okay out there on her own, but you notice if a woman hasn't got any tits whether you're interested in them or not, don't you."

"Fair enough. What time did you first see the old man?"

"Around seven."

"Makes sense. Fay was found about half past nine. A different carer, the one who puts Fay to bed."

"I didn't see anyone at her house."

"Do you stand at your window all night or what?" Yeoman chuckled.

"No, I went to have a natter with Phil. I stood out here for a minute or two, then knocked on his door. Had a gin and some cheese on toast."

I knew I'd smelt cheese.

"So you didn't see Fay being taken to hospital then?" Yeoman asked.

"No, and Val wouldn't have. As Phil pointed out, they shut their curtains at night."

"Why would he say that?"

"Doesn't matter. He was just being sarky, saying I'm nosy, but it's not that at all. I don't close the curtains because—"

"I know. No need to tell me. It came up on your nark check, remember."

Sherry's heart went out to Billy. Just before he'd been taken to Loving Arms, he'd been playing in the living room on the floor at home, zooming his cars about. Someone had burst in with a gun and shot his mother in the kitchen, and Billy vowed he'd never have the living room curtains shut again. He always wanted to see if someone was coming. She'd even had to take the nets down the other day because he said they obscured his view.

"I followed the bloke," Billy blurted.

"You what?" Yeoman palmed his short hair.

"I went into the kitchen to make a cuppa for Sherry, and something about him got to me, you know how it is, so I jumped over the fence and went to find him."

I knew he'd been outside. Why didn't he just say?

Sherry's heart grew heavy. He never used to lie, even by omission. She was to blame for him keeping stuff to himself. He probably thought she'd think he'd had a quick fumble with someone in the garden, pressed up against the wheelie bins.

"Anyway," Billy went on, "he walked down past Halfway, Elderflower, Vicar's, and I couldn't see where he was after that because it was dark."

"Okay, that's good, we have a direction."

"But he was acting all weird."

"How do you mean?"

"He stopped under a streetlamp and punched the air, like he was pleased about something."

"Perhaps that he'd attacked Fay?"

"That's what I just thought."

"There'd have been blood on him." Yeoman sighed.

"So *that's* what was bothering me." Billy slapped his thigh.

Yeoman narrowed his eyes. "What was?"

"He had blood on his white shirt. I didn't take it in as blood at the time, just specks or whatever, and I was stymied by his bow tie, but now I know what happened to Fay…"

Sherry's body went cold. Had the man really meant to murder the old girl, not just attack? Did he think he'd bumped her off—she could have fainted from the pain and he'd thought she was dead. Was there another killer on the loose?

She staggered back and flopped onto the sofa, shocked.

The smoke alarm bleated.

Shit. She'd burnt the fucking sausages, and this time, she couldn't even blame a book.

Confession

I don't miss the old times, the way everything seemed so full and busy, nattering on the doorstep or out on the path, the neighbours passing on snippets of their day, me doing the same. I've had such a brimming life, been lucky in that respect. A childhood most would kill for, my parents loving and kind, then my first marriage to Jim, such a thoughtful man. The two children I had with him, one of them turned into a decent human being, and the other... I don't like thinking about that man and who he's become.

My daughter, Sarah, visits every week. Sometimes, I forget who she is—well, more than sometimes. She's a stranger, asking me if I'm okay and calling me Mum. Him, on the other hand… He's there, in the recesses of my mind, loitering. It's no fun getting old. And living in a care home knowing you have a mean son out there isn't either. – Catherine Smith

Chapter Six

"How are you today, Catherine?"

Liz, the nurse, popped her head around the door.

Catherine didn't know *how* she felt today, not after what she'd seen last night. She couldn't make head nor tail of it, and if she told her, Liz might say she was imagining things again. After all, little kids weren't allowed to just wander through the care home, were they, and especially not in the middle of the night.

'Help me…'

That was what the girl had said, standing at the bottom of Catherine's bed in her flower-patterned nightie. Catherine had sat up, staring, blinking to come to grips with what she was seeing, but the child disappeared, and that was the end of that, the residue of a dream she hadn't quite woken up from.

"The same as always," Catherine answered. It was advisable to say that. If she said she wasn't on top form, worrying about kids in her room, Liz would hover around her all day, launch an investigation into how someone had got in.

It was all stuff and nonsense Catherine couldn't be doing with.

She just wanted to sit by the window in peace and stare out beyond the courtyard and grounds at the moor. Pinstone was over the way a bit, where her children lived, and most days she remembered what Sarah's home was like, a four-bed detached on the posh estate. She imagined her inside it, laughing and getting on with life, happy, the children keeping her busy, almost adults now, the pair of them.

Living inside her head was preferable to living here, although sometimes, what with her son and his behaviour, it was better not to remember.

"That's good." Liz came in and sat on the end of the bed. "Soon be Christmas, won't it. A couple of months, and we'll decorate the tree in the main living room."

Catherine didn't want to know about Christmas *or* the main living room. It meant Sarah, her husband, and the grandchildren would come, spoiling their day by having to leave the house and come here. Sarah said they didn't mind, that it wouldn't be Christmas if they didn't see her, but surely staying at home and enjoying it there was better.

The weight of being Sarah's mother sat heavy on Catherine's shoulders. If she wasn't here, alive, there wouldn't be a problem.

She sighed.

"That's a big one," Liz said. "Anything wrong?"

Only you, keep bothering me. Please leave me alone.

"No, I just want to be by myself, that's all."

"All right then, as long as you're sure."

Of course she was sure, she knew her own mind.

Most of the time.

Liz walked out, leaving the door open, as she always did. And, as *she* always did, Catherine pushed herself up out of her chair and shuffled over to close it. Being alone meant just that, not an open door where anyone passing could peer in, asking her banal questions.

Funny how she'd loved that while younger but it grated now.

She returned to her chair and pulled a blanket over her legs. Her son had bought it for her one of the days he'd wrangled his way in to see her. Sherpa something or other, that was what he'd called the fur. On the other side a blue tartan brought it home she was old.

Elderly people had tartan blankets.

She threw it off her and reached for the other one, a pink velvet Sarah had given her. It matched Catherine's dressing gown.

She stared through the window, thinking of her daughter who'd done so well for herself. She was a solicitor, her husband the same, and they went on lovely holidays abroad, on a cruise once, if memory served her right. Her son, though… What was he up to? He'd been mysteriously absent for a while, same as he had all those years ago, and Sarah had said he'd gone away to work. Highly unlikely. Catherine knew who and what he was, didn't have any doubt he'd probably been caught for his behaviour again and was shipped off to Rushford.

Nasty boy.

She focused on the moor, thinking of that time almost twenty years ago when coppers searched it, coming up blank. Catherine had an idea back then that her son was involved with that awful business, but she'd kept her mouth shut, as some mothers tended to do. If she'd said something, *she'd* be tainted, too, and Sarah, but in the end, her closed lips had been for nowt. Everyone found out what he was anyway, and yes, Catherine and Sarah were tarred with the bristles of his wicked brush.

Catherine hated him for that.

Movement out there snagged her attention, and she squinted, wishing she'd put her glasses on, but they were on the other side of the room on her bedside table. It'd be a kerfuffle getting up to fetch them.

What was *that*? Light-coloured fabric, billowing in the wind. And was that a *person* out there? Whoever it was stood just outside the courtyard gates. Catherine peered harder, and oh, it was the little girl from last night.

"What on earth are you doing here? And without a coat on, too."

Catherine stood and stepped closer to the window, resting her hands on the sill between two photos of Sarah.

The girl turned and ran over the field then onto the moor, heading for Pinstone.

Catherine remained there for a long time, until the child reached a bend in the hedges that separated the moor from Pinstone, close to the river.

God, I hope she doesn't fall in.

Confession

I've been scarred from working at Loving Arms. All the goings-on there back in the day have left their evil mark. I used to cook for all the kiddies, see, and lived in, same as Fay and Oliver did. We were a happy family up until that *happened, and afterwards, we became fractured, sharp splinters, hurting each other every time we attempted to get close again. It takes a toll, something as bad as that occurring. And it also takes a lifetime to forget it.* – Helen Donaldson

Chapter Seven

Helen frowned at the knock on the door. While she was only sixty-one, her hips played her up something chronic. She was on the NHS waiting list to get them fixed, but they said it'd be a fair while yet. Replacements, that was what they'd told her, one at a time so she wasn't incapacitated as much after the operations.

She shuffled into the hallway, still clutching the spoon she'd been using to make her tea. The rap had come as she'd squeezed the bag against the inside of the cup, and now, if the caller kept her talking, she'd have that horrible scum on the surface where the bag was in there for too long.

Helen sighed about that and reached for the Yale lock, then remembered she needed to draw the two chains across first, and the bolt at the bottom.

Security was important when you lived on your own, and the past had taught her to be secure.

She popped the spoon in her apron pocket. It was baking day, and she always took a batch of shortbreads up to Fay once they'd cooled. Helen fancied making a beef stew, too, with choux dumplings, better than the puffy ones, she found. The children used to love them.

I'll take some dinner to Fay as well, save her cooking.

Helen sorted the bolt and chains and opened the door. A brunette woman stood there, trim of body in a fitted, light-blue skirt suit, a cream blouse with ruffles at the neck, a bit over the top, but there you go. Court shoes, now there was something Helen couldn't trot about in anymore, a nice navy patent with a lovely gold band across the toes.

"Can I help you?" Helen asked.

"Hello, I'm from *The Pinstone Star*, here to do an interview about your time at Loving Arms. Katie Violet, crime reporter."

Oh. Fay had mentioned having reporters round, two of them, a brown-haired woman and a young man, but she hadn't told them much. She'd said reliving the past was an awful thing, like going through it all over again, and doing that didn't change it, didn't make their splinters go away.

"I'm a bit busy today," Helen said. "Baking, you know."

"We can chat while you bake, I don't mind." Katie smiled.

Aww, she looked so kind, so nice, and while Helen didn't want to talk about back then, it was inevitable people would still revisit it from time to time. Especially a crime reporter. Nothing much had been going on in Pinstone since those terrible murders six months ago, so perhaps stories were thin on the ground and the old tales needed dredging up to sell papers.

"Okay, but only for an hour. I have a nap about ten as I'm awake at five. Can't seem to forget I don't need to be up to make breakfast for the kids." Helen allowed Katie inside. "Go through into the kitchen. I was just making tea. Do you want one?"

"That would be lovely, thank you."

Helen frowned at Katie's voice, high-pitched. Door closed, she followed the woman down the hallway, wondering what questions she'd ask. Helen couldn't tell her anything she hadn't already told the police and that journalist years ago, so what Katie hoped to achieve was anyone's guess.

In the kitchen, Helen stared at the cup of tea. It already had that terrible scum on the top. She sighed, poured it down the sink, and started again. Drinks sorted, she took one to Katie at the table then got a bowl out ready to make the shortbreads. She'd do the stew after and let it cook in the oven for a couple of hours.

"I don't know what you want me to tell you." She drew her scales over and reached for the flour.

"Everything," Katie said. "Absolutely everything."

Someone else knocked on the door, but Helen ignored it. One guest at a time was quite enough, thank you.

Chapter Eight

1991

It was bedtime, always a fractious half an hour beforehand, gathering the children together for their hot drink, all of them seated around the battered, well-used wooden table in the large kitchen. If not for Ivy sitting there scowling, it would be a precious scene, heartwarming, Fay and Helen caring for the kids together, their ragtag brood of unwanted souls who needed guidance and to know not everyone would treat them badly. But Ivy was sitting there scowling, and Fay wanted to slap her spiteful little snot-nosed face.

I'm a hypocrite.

"What's the matter, Ivy?" Fay asked, calm as you like. Polite, nice. It was a strain to act this way with her, but she'd have to do it regardless.

Ivy thumped the table. "I wanted cocoa, not hot chocolate."

"Same thing if you ask me," Billy piped up.

"I didn't ask you, poo head." Ivy poked her tongue out at him, her eyes scrunched tight with malice.

Billy's face fell, his placid expression retreating, a mask of confusion coming to the fore and crumpling his features. He must wonder why Ivy was such a cow to him when all he'd ever been was kind, trying to help her settle in. Goodness, that boy had suffered a terrible tragedy, a masked man bursting into his home one dark night, killing his mother, then leaving. Billy had discovered her slumped against the kitchen cupboards, her blood streaking the doors and floor either side of her, half of her face blown away. The man had shot her in the eye, a shocking thing to do, yet Billy still found it in himself to be gentle with others, while Ivy…

Well, she was a bitch.

"Please don't be rude to Billy." How Fay kept her voice even and her hand by her side, she didn't know. Her palm itched to connect with Ivy's sallow, freckled cheek.

"He's your favourite." Ivy messed about with her drink, poking a finger into it.

"We don't have favourites here," Helen chipped in from where she stood at the sink. *"Everyone is loved the same."*

"No, they're not." Ivy narrowed her spiteful eyes at Fay.

"What's all this then, a family argument?" Oliver the janitor came in and swiped his drink off the side.

Fay liked it that he thought of them as a family. That was her take on it, too. While the kids didn't have one with their relations, they could have one here. She tried so hard to include Ivy in that, but the girl insisted on being difficult.

"Of course not," Fay said. *"Ivy is tired and acting up, that's all."*

"She must always be tired then." Oliver sipped some cocoa. *"Because she's got something negative to say on any subject."*

He glanced at Fay for a moment, his gaze hooded, eyes darkening, and she sensed he didn't like Ivy either. Or perhaps that was wishful thinking, the hope she wasn't some wicked person for disliking a child. Yes, it must be, as he looked his usual self now.

"I could always be a proper father and sort you out," he said to Ivy. "Tan your backside."

"We don't condone that," Helen was quick to say, her face showing her alarm, "and you know it."

"Just a warning." Oliver grabbed a pile of fabric napkins and a couple of tea towels from the wicker wash basket by the door. "I'll take these into the utility and bring my cup back when I'm finished."

He left, closing the door, and Fay rather thought he'd got the hump. Ivy's cheeks had reddened, and some of the bluster seemed to have gone out of her. Perhaps that was the way to go with her, threaten her with a smack. Her mother was an abusive sort, heavy-handed, quick to strike. Ivy was probably scared of getting the same treatment here.

Something to bear in mind.

And if that were the case, you'd think she'd behave herself.

Helen handed out her homemade shortbreads, perfect rounds with fine sugar coating them, better than any Fay had eaten from the shops. Biscuits were a treat the children were allowed prior to bed—so long as they brushed their teeth afterwards.

Ivy had learnt since the pub/crisp incident and nabbed one first, and Fay decided that from now on, she'd walk around the table so they could take one at a time, not become this rabid mass of broken human beings, desperate to get there first, because until now, they'd always had to fight for what they received. She'd taught them all better than that, but they must have been so used to being hungry, their instinct kicked in.

Ivy frowned. "I want one with pink icing on the top, like last night."

Fay looked at Helen, who had moved to the cupboard, no doubt to get the icing sugar out. Helen was always so accommodating, ready at a moment's notice to give the children what they'd missed out on.

Fay shook her head at her. "No icing tonight." She gave a tight smile. "Be grateful for what you have, not griping about what you want."

And my God do you always want, you wretched girl.

Ivy ate, sullen, and by the time everyone had finished the biscuits and their drinks, Fay was ready to commit murder.

"Come along. Teeth, wash, then bed." She clapped to emphasize the point.

Chairs scraped back, the noise awful on the grey flagstone, as was the push of them beneath the table. At least they'd taken that lesson on board. The children scampered off, and Helen collected the cups and plates.

Fay glanced at the clock on the wall beside the Welsh dresser. Ten to eight. She'd go and check on everyone soon, read Billy a quick story.

Oliver came in and popped his cup into the bowl. "I'm off to bed early."

"Night," Fay and Helen said.

He didn't answer, still in a huff with Helen.

Fay all but fell onto one of the more comfortable armchairs beside the huge fireplace, her feet aching, her back sore. It had been a day, the children boisterous after school, needing to expend some energy. She'd taken them into the courtyard and encouraged them to draw grids with chalk for hopscotch.

"Ivy really needs a placement with fosters or an adoptive family." She sighed. "She's not doing too well here."

Helen placed a washed-up cup on the drainer, bubbles oozing off it. "I noticed. She doesn't fit in like the others. She has no idea how to manage herself in a family environment. It isn't surprising, considering where she came from."

"No." Fay stared out through the window above the sink, past the night-washed courtyard and onto the moor beyond. She'd go and have a walk out there soon, alone, giving herself time to clear the terrible thoughts in her head. They were constant lately, a whirlpool of wickedness, and she knew once Ivy was gone, they'd vanish back to the recesses where she'd shoved them before.

It was Fay's cousin's fault, this dislike of Ivy.

Hatred, if Fay were totally honest.

And who could blame her for feeling the way she did? People with Ivy's attitude were bad to the bone, and no good would come of her. She'd grow into a spiteful, entitled little madam, and more fool the people who took her on.

Still, Fay would lie, tell any prospective new parents that Ivy was an angel.

Anything to get rid of her.

She got up, sighed again, and rubbed her lower back. "I'll do the first check of the evening then. Thank you for the biscuits. I do love your shortbreads."

"Most welcome, you know that." *Helen smiled and continued cleaning the cups.*

Fay left the kitchen and walked into the foyer with its winding mahogany staircase and cheery daisy-smattered wallpaper. All was silent upstairs, and she prowled the long left-hand landing where the children's bedrooms were, checking inside each one to make sure they were in bed. Billy was already sparko, so no story for him.

She left Ivy until last, and the bratty moo was bouncing on her bed, smirking at Fay.

"Get in bed," *Fay snapped in her no-nonsense tone, one she'd only ever had to use with another devil child who'd left here a year ago, thank goodness.*

The boy had settled well with his fosters and turned himself around.

"I hate you," Ivy spat out and continued bouncing.

Fay had had enough. Ivy was the bad apple in Fay's perfect orchard, and this behaviour had to stop—now. "I said, get in bed, and if you don't, I will ask Mr Elford to come up here and smack your bottom just like he suggested. It will hurt, believe me, and you won't be able to sit for days."

"No…" Ivy dropped onto the bed and scrabbled under the covers.

Fay thought that would work, saying she wouldn't sit for days. Ivy's mother used that line, it was all in Ivy's file, and the girl had indeed had trouble sitting with those terrible stripes from the belt. Shame it hadn't taught her to act nicely.

"I'm going to tell Helen what you said." Ivy peered over the top of her blankets.

"I don't think you will, and Helen won't believe you. We all know what a nasty girl you are, how you lie. And besides, I shall deny it."

Ivy's big eyes watered.

Fay ought to feel sorry for her, she would if it were any of the others, but she couldn't bring herself to warm to the surly, recalcitrant child.

"No point in crying. You're playing with the wrong person here." Fay held the doorknob,

intending to shut Ivy inside, grateful she wouldn't have to see her face until morning.

"Please don't tell Mr Elford," Ivy whispered.

Fay paused. "Why?"

"Because I want him to still like me."

What? Oliver didn't seem to like her*. What was she talking about?*

Fay closed the door and leant against it. The stupid girl got right under her skin, and if she wasn't careful, she'd act out those horrible thoughts she had.

It was imperative she find this bitch a home.

Before I lose the plot.

Confession

The days will be so much more difficult now he's paid me a visit. I didn't think he'd ever come for me, but he has, biding his time, waiting until I'd felt safe. He came here in his disguise, some old man who claimed to want to put me forward for an award, all those years I spent caring for the children. There's no award, unless you count the badge of his madness I'm now forced to live with: no tongue, no fingers, missing teeth. He took them with him, placing them in a plastic sandwich bag and sliding them in his suit pocket as though it was normal. He said I mustn't tell a soul it's him, and I wouldn't anyway, even if I could. I've remained quiet for so long already. He also knows my

secret, and if I were to say anything about him, it would have been years ago. Why has he decided to deal with this now? Why, after so many years have passed? I don't understand, and I can't even ask him if he comes back. –
Fay Williams

Chapter Nine

The painkillers were wearing off. The agony in Fay's mouth and hands was worse than when she'd given birth, which had been hours of teeth-gritting delirium, her son taking his time about coming into the world. Then he'd been there, a sudden warm gush between her legs, and the relief, the sight of his face, had chased that pain away.

She'd had him for three short weeks.

They'd been beautiful weeks, and she'd spent ages staring at him while he slept, his dark hair an inky halo, his nose a tiny button, and his lips, moving while he dreamt, perhaps of suckling at the teat. When he opened his eyes, they were the darkest blue and seemed to hold the preciousness of his soul in their depths.

It was a sin that he'd been taken away from her so soon. She'd imagined him growing up, turning into a toddler, one who waddled on unsteady, podgy legs, dimples in his knees. Then an older child, studious and caring, and on to a teenager, with a quick temper brought on by hormones and him just as quick to rein it in and say sorry. And lastly, a wonderful adult. She'd planned to teach him to be a gentleman, although not someone to be walked over, like she had been. A fellow opposite to his father then, who'd pretended to be kind, then fled the moment he'd had sex with her twice.

Then she'd missed her period.

It was such a shocking thing in those days, to have a child out of wedlock, but she'd done it, shunned by her friends and neighbours, her parents, their evil looks scoring her skin as if they'd scratched her with their ragged, bitten nails.

And apart from her mum and dad, they'd come, those hypocrites, to her little one-bedroom mouldy house, to offer their condolences when her angel had gone to Heaven. She'd let them in, of course she had, sucking up their platitudes, when all the while she'd conversely died inside, wanting to claw their crocodile-tear-filled eyes out, give them pain to pay them back for snubbing her for the four months they'd known about her pregnancy.

She hadn't been able to hide it for long, her bump sprouting at five months.

Their casseroles and cakes had sat in her stomach, rock-like, but she wasn't well-off and couldn't afford to put them in the bin, much as she'd wanted to. So she ate, gagging on every mouthful, wishing her baby were here for her to nurture. And her breasts, by God, they hurt with his loss, mourning him along with her, drying up along with her.

The evil in her heart and mind had flourished the moment she'd found out her son was dead. Over the years, she'd managed it, kept it caged.

Until Ivy.

Shitty fucking Ivy.

Fay stared out of the window, thinking about being turfed out of the hospital so quickly. They didn't keep anyone in for a length of time these days if they could help it. She couldn't very well ask to stay in, could she, what with no tongue, and plead with them to keep her safe, away from *him*. He was a dreadful man, out to shut her mouth as well as Helen's. Fay worried about Billy, because he'd been there that night, too, the little boy in that terrible state he was in, ushered to his bed.

'Back to sleep now, my love. I'll be up to check on you in a minute.'

There was no way she could warn Billy. Or Helen, who'd be along later with the weekly shortbreads. God, how Fay wished she could turn back the clock to before it had happened, baptise her thoughts into good ones instead of the despicable ones that had soured her brain and heart.

As though she'd conjured him, Billy strutted by the window, his head bent, hands in pockets. A light tap on the front door, and Louise walked past the living room to open it. She'd been in the kitchen, polishing Fay's baby's christening gifts from Nan, so many silver trinkets that she'd allowed to go beige over time, hidden away in the spare room Louise was staying in. Louise would have them looking good as new, she'd said, and perhaps Fay could display them on the living room windowsill so she could look at them often, remembering the times she'd had with her son, cherishing them.

Louise was a lovely girl, and she meant well, but Fay didn't want to display the fucking things. She didn't want the reminders. There were enough of those in her heart and head.

"Hello, Billy, come in," Louise said, all cheery as usual.

"Is she all right? I've just heard what happened."

Poor Billy. He sounded distraught. It hurt Fay's chest to think of him upset.

"She'll be happier once she's healed. You know what she's like, never one to let anything beat her."

If only you knew. It's a façade.

"That's good to hear," Billy said.

"She'll be her usual self in no time."

It was strange to listen to them talking as if she couldn't hear them. She wanted to shout that *he* hadn't popped her eardrums with the tool he'd whacked her teeth out with, and she knew what they were saying, she wasn't dead yet. But that would be cruel, the Fay who belonged in the past, the Fay who was a bitch to her cousin.

And to Ivy, and all because the child looked and acted like said cousin.

Ivy had a reason to behave that way, the abuse in her life bringing out the worst in her, but Fay's cousin? No, she didn't have any excuse.

Fay was only happy on the outside. She'd learnt to be that way, to act, to pretend nothing was wrong. From the moment *it* had happened at Loving Arms, she'd played a part, a shocked woman traumatised by the events of the lightning-strewn, rain-lashed night, and oh my goodness, what are we going to do?

She'd taught herself to lie in order to survive.

'I get paid to give people new faces so theirs aren't seen. Just like this one,' he whispered last night, his mask close to her face. He pointed to his wrinkled skin and laughed.

She shivered at the memory of his breath on her cheek, coming through the mouth slit between the fleshy fake lips. It had the faint aroma of pickled onions about it, and she'd never eat them again, not after that. Once her tongue had healed, she had an appointment about her teeth—the hospital had sorted it for her. He'd knocked the front ones out, and oh God, she'd thought she'd choke on them, death by enamel.

Billy appeared in the doorway, his face showing his concern, but now he wiped it away with that beautiful smile of his. "Are you okay?" He blushed. "Sorry, that was a stupid thing to say."

She shook her head and managed a smile so he'd know it was fine. He could be mean to her and she wouldn't mind. Anything to have her pretend son near.

"Is there something I can do for you?" He came over and knelt beside her chair, took one of her poorly hands in his, careful not to squeeze it.

Fay stared at the hand, swaddled in pure-white bandages, the ends of her finger stubs sewn up in an operation underneath, and wondered whether Helen would get hers chopped off, too. There wouldn't be any shortbreads then, and wasn't that a shocking thing to think?

Selfish, that's what I am.

She nodded—yes, there was something Billy could do for her. But how could she tell him, warn him? What he needed to do was stay safe, alert, and never let a stranger into his home like she had, no matter whether they seemed genuine or not. Those reporters, they'd been *him* in disguise, those masks he'd bragged about covering his face, him talking in different voices, tricking her into thinking he was young, old, and also a woman, for Pete's sake.

She raised her other bandaged hand and brushed it over Billy's cheek, telling herself he was her boy, but that wasn't the case at all. Her son would be older than Billy. Her eyes stung, but she held the tears back. She didn't want him to end up like her, he wouldn't be able to do his odd jobs, and he didn't deserve this treatment just because he might have seen something while he was small.

Fay groaned. It was useless. She couldn't say a damn thing to help him.

She rested her head back, closed her eyes, and wept.

Chapter Ten

The morning had zipped by with Morgan and Shaz speaking to the neighbours in Regency, although a couple of them hadn't answered their doors. Uniforms were in the other streets, checking whether anyone had seen an old man walking past their turnings. There was just Phil and Val to go now, and Morgan said he'd deal with that. He sent Shaz back to the car to rest her feet, ones she'd been complaining about for the past hour. Anyone would think she'd been standing on them for days.

Morgan chuckled and knocked on Phil's door. While he didn't believe for one minute Billy had anything to do with Fay's attack, he needed to strike him off the list just the same. He wouldn't prompt Phil for Billy's alibi but see if he offered it. Best to do that. Putting words in people's mouths could come back to bite you on the arse.

Val stood on the threshold, looking lovely and happy. Morgan smiled. It'd been ages since he'd seen her. She'd stopped being his nark when she'd given up the game, although she did phone him on occasion to let him know a few bits and bobs, free of charge, things uniforms needed to know: some bloke stealing a car, another robbing the granny in Vicar's Gate, a third spray-painting racial abuse on Mrs Ives' door in Elderflower.

Bastards.

He missed his weekly visits to Val's old place. She was easy to talk to and a genuine sort. Her son, Karl, lived in a flat in Vicar's, still away from the crowd he'd latched on to in college, thank God. Boggin, the main kid, was a pain up the police's arse, always gobbing off, shouting abuse in the town when pissed. Little dickhead.

"What on earth's going on?" Val said, a hand up to her neck, covering the sparkling diamond pendant Phil must have bought for her.

She had nice nails, acrylics like Lydia used to have, and Morgan was pleased. Val deserved the best, a few treats.

"Phil in?" he asked.

"Yes, but you know how it is with him now. You don't need to speak to him about anything anymore."

Morgan wasn't about to argue the toss. "Not that, no, but there's something going on regarding Miss Williams at twenty-one."

"Taken ill, has she?" Val moved out of the way so Morgan could go in. "Only, I saw a car out there last night. Someone was helping her into it. Fay had blood on her face. Did she have a fall?"

"No, she's not ill as such. Phil in the kitchen?"

"Yes, go through, you know where it is. He's making lunch if you want a sandwich." She winked.

"Only if he makes one for Shaz an' all. I'll never live it down if she knows I ate and she didn't."

"I can hear you offering my food to a pig," Phil called good-naturedly.

Morgan smiled. Never in a million years would he have thought he'd like Phil Flint, but damn it, he did these days. Now Phil wasn't supplying drugs, he was an amenable chap, and Val had worked wonders in softening up the former hardman. Gone were the days of wishing he could nab Phil, and instead, all Morgan wanted him to do was look after Val and treat her kindly. If Phil kept his nose clean, Morgan would forget what the man had done in the past. He shouldn't, but he would.

Morgan didn't tend to toe the proper line.

"Get buttering the bread then." He entered the kitchen and shut them in.

"That's ominous." Phil nodded at the closed door, knife held midair.

"As is that blade you're holding. I'll have some of that ham." Morgan pointed at the packet on the side, the breaded stuff Lydia used to favour. "Shaz will have cheese, grated. And pickle, if you have any. Branston."

"Blimey, what is it with people coming here and eating lately? This isn't a ruddy café. But yeah, we have Branston. Karl likes it with chicken roll. It's in the fridge. Do the honours, will you?"

Morgan got the pickle jar out and handed it over. "Just asking this, because we've done the same with nearly every other resident, so don't go getting lairy and defensive. Where were you last night between seven and ten?"

"Here with Val, although Billy nipped round and filched some cheese on toast, not to mention a gin, the cheeky bleeder. I'm fucking feeding the five thousand." Phil continued making the sandwiches. "Why, what's happened?"

"Someone went to Miss Williams' and attacked her. She's got a tongue and all her fingers missing. I didn't ask about the thumbs."

Phil paused in spreading Branston. "Bloody hell. That doesn't sound like one of my old lot, if you know what I mean."

"Of course I know what you mean, but it's best we pretend you didn't engage in that sort of shit, even while we're alone. So the MO isn't familiar to you, fine, that's what I wanted to know."

"Why would anyone want to rough up an old dear?" He grated some cheese over the pickle.

Morgan chuffed out a funnel of air. "It's more than roughing up. It's a message, that's what it is."

Phil sliced the pile of sandwiches in half.

"You're cutting all of them at once." Morgan frowned.

"Yeah, so?"

"You might get Branston on mine from the knife."

"Want to make it yourself?"

"I wouldn't mind. Put Shaz's in some cling film."

"Christ, want me to eat it for her an' all?"

Morgan nudged Phil out of the way and prepared his own lunch. "Anyway, back to it being a message."

"I get it. You lop a tongue out to stop them blabbing, everyone knows that." Phil put a sandwich on a plate and covered it with clingfilm. Probably Val's.

Nice that he didn't want it to go stale if they talked for a while.

Morgan ran a hand over his hair. "What would an elderly woman know, though?"

"Ah, I forget you're not originally from around here, are you. Fay used to run Loving Arms, a care home for kids."

"I know, Billy said yonks ago. He was there, wasn't he, but I asked him earlier if anything untoward had gone on, and he said if it did, he couldn't remember."

"There's bound to be a few little bastards who walked through those doors. She probably gave one a rollocking and he's come back to get her."

"Bit off, waiting so many years, don't you think?" Morgan munched on one half of his sandwich. Bloody lovely. Better than the processed ham he bought. It was always wet in the packet, too.

Phil shrugged. "I dunno, things fester, go through your mind until you can't stand it anymore. Or it could be like David Ives, a prisoner unable to get his revenge until he's let out of Rushford."

Morgan had helped put Ives away for murder, and yes, it was plausible this was another lag on the warpath, but again, why wait so long if it was to do with Loving Arms? Unless something triggered him recently and he went off the rails. Whatever, Morgan would go round to Halfway and speak to Emma Ingles, see who she had staying there at the moment.

"Have you got a to-go cup I can borrow?" Morgan asked.

Phil gaped. "You what? You're taking the piss, aren't you?"

"Nope. Shaz will need a coffee by now or she'll turn into a mean little creature."

"Just slap a sign over our door and call us Costa. Fuck me." Phil grabbed a cup and plonked it on his fancy coffee machine. He pressed a button. "I want this back. It's part of a set. Odd cups make me go funny. There has to be eight, six for the mug tree, two spare, so if one breaks, you've got a replacement for the tree."

"Slightly obsessive, but whatever makes you happy." Morgan stuffed more food in his mouth. Swallowed. "Lurpak." He nodded at the butter. "Nice."

"That's why we have it. Here." He thrust Shaz's sandwich at him. "You can go off people, you know."

"I know, but best not to go off me. I'm aware of things."

"A forced friendship, that's what this is." Phil grinned and added single cream and two sugars to the cup. "There. Now bugger off."

"Cheers. Keep your ear to the ground, will you?"

"Yep."

"I'll see myself out."

"Best you do, else I'll feel like a ruddy butler as well as your lunch skivvy."

Morgan laughed and waggled the sandwich at Val through the living room doorway as a wave on the way out.

"Oi, where are you going with that cup, Yeoman?" she called.

"Calm your tits," he said. "You'll get it back."

He walked up the road and got in the car, handing Shaz her lunch. "You can't say I don't think of you."

"God, did you get Val to make it? Rude or what. Not that I'm complaining. Bloody gagging for a coffee." She sipped then closed her eyes for a couple of seconds. "Nice."

"No, Phil made it."

"You're joking." She turned her head to stare at him.

"I'm not. He even did you Branston."

"What a legend. Hard to believe he's the same person, isn't it."

"Hmm. As long as he stays how he is at the moment, that's fine by me. Listen, once you've finished that, we'll go and see Emma Ingles. Phil made a fair point. This could be another David Ives. Man stuck in prison, coming to sort Fay out for whatever she did to him. She worked at Loving Arms, remember."

"Not every kid in care is a psycho."

"I didn't say they were."

"I mean, look at Billy."

"Like I said, I didn't say they were, but it's an angle, and we'll follow it. Actually…" He phoned Nigel in the incident room. "Right, I need you and Jane looking into all children who have been in Loving Arms and are now adults, ones Fay Williams would have known. Check when she left there—and find out why, and where she went to work afterwards. She could have stayed until retirement age, but I want to know what's what."

"Right. Are you coming back in?"

"Not at the minute. We've questioned Regency, uniforms are doing the others. No bugger saw anything except Billy Price and Val. He clocked an old man going up Regency towards Fay's, then coming back again two hours later, blood on his shirt. Dodgy, so maybe the old boy worked with her at the care home and has held a grudge all these years. Val just saw the carer taking Fay to hospital. We're off to see Emma Ingles, for obvious reasons."

"Okay, see you when I see you."

Morgan drove off down to Phil's and got Shaz to hand over their precious cup. Back on the move again, he thought about the job he'd just set for Nigel and Jane. So many people must have passed through Loving Arms, and God knew where they were now. The place wasn't a home for children anymore but the elderly, Cobbs Moor Residential, so still a facility that catered to those in need, but talking to any of the residents and nurses wouldn't help them in their enquiries, unless someone involved with the children's home was still there as an employee.

He parked outside Halfway House, and they walked up the path. Morgan always found it difficult to look at the alley between Halfway and number one, the home that used to belong to Olga Scrivens, someone who was killed along with Delia, Goat, Lydia, her best friend Alice, and a bloke called Steve. Gary Flint's hanging was a by-product of the killing spree.

Was it really half a year ago it had all happened?

Emma pulled him out of his musings by opening the door. She was used to the police knocking, so why was she so jittery? She'd been the same ever since those murders, not her usual easy-going self at all, and she always stared at them to begin with, a smidgen of fear in her eyes, as if she thought they might be someone else.

"Oh, hello," she said, her shoulders sagging.

"We just need a word." Morgan smiled.

"Oh God, has one of the residents done something?"

"Not as far as we know."

She took them to the large kitchen out the back where she prepared meals for those living there. She offered a laundry service, too, and looked after the men well, despite what they'd done to find themselves in Rushford. Prior to this post, she'd been a social worker down south, so the story went, although she never spoke much about that, just enough to give him the gist.

She closed the kitchen door.

"Everyone behaving themselves?" Morgan asked.

"Yes, I have a lovely lot this time. All younger lads who made a mistake. You know, constant petty crimes as opposed to the bigger ones. No murderers at present, thank goodness." She gave a nervous laugh.

"Are you all right, Emma?" Shaz stepped closer to place her hand on Emma's arm.

"Of course. Why wouldn't I be?" That had sounded far too sharp.

Shaz lowered her hand and moved back. "Just asking. Doesn't hurt to be kind."

"I apologise." Emma reddened. "I'm not feeling myself at the moment."

"Anything we can help with?" Morgan raised his eyebrows.

"No, but thank you for asking. Was that everything?"

"Nope. Do you know if any of the lads were in care at all?" Morgan stared out at the multiple washing lines Emma had striping her garden. Lots of male clothing flapping about in the cold wind.

"No, all from good homes from what I can gather. They just got in with bad crowds."

"What, all twelve of them?"

She shrugged. "It happens. I'm just glad I have *them* here and not—" She bit her lip.

"And not...?" Morgan cocked his head.

"Not anyone dangerous. I almost left this job, you know, back when Martin Olbey and the like were here. Seemed I had a houseful of nasty people."

"You did. Heard anything from him?"

"No."

"He was seen in Shadwell recently, so he's close. Be on the lookout."

She shivered. "I will."

"If we could just have a list of your current residents."

Emma walked off into her office beside the big living room that everyone could use if they wanted to get together. She returned a couple of minutes later with a printout. "Here you go. As I say, nice lads. They just need a second chance, that's all."

"Cheers."

Morgan and Shaz left her to it, and he drove off, wondering why Emma had become a nervous ninny. Maybe she had personal issues. It wasn't his place to pry. He should know how it felt to hide what was going on in your private life. Only Shaz was aware of Lydia's nasty behaviour, and even then she wasn't privy to the fact she'd been hooked on cocaine.

Christ, the fucking webs we weave, every strand a lie.

Confession

I'm a wreck and have been since Oliver Elford whispered those words to me in my kitchen, the ones that told me my ex-husband, Derek, knows where I am. There was a comfort in hiding behind this name, a woman nothing like the former Fiona Denham, but now most of my new self is gone, the empty jigsaw spaces filled with the worst parts of Fiona. The nerves. The fear. The knowledge that if Derek comes here, I'll be dead. He never could abide anyone disobeying him, and I've been the worst culprit. I left him without a word, and now he wants me back. – Emma Ingles

Chapter Eleven

Emma closed the door behind Yeoman and Tanner and sucked in a huge breath. She shook from head to foot. God, this life, she wished it wasn't so complicated and frightening, still, after she'd spent so much time away from the south.

Just before they'd turned up, she'd had another wretched call. The voice was the same as all the others, his tone one she wished she could forget but never would. Even when he hadn't known she was here and she felt free, safe, she'd heard him, his wicked whispers, his evil shouting, so many spiteful sentences in her head, swirling, roiling, sending her mad for a moment until she scrubbed them from her mind.

They had returned full force, along with his calls. She'd had to slam the phone down because of the police arriving, so he was sure to ring back. She'd cut him off mid-sentence, and he wouldn't have liked that. He'd take it as a slight, especially because he'd asked her a question and would have wanted an answer.

In a fit of desperation last week, she'd told one of the lads here she was getting funny calls, and as he lived in a bedsit on the ground floor, he'd offered to always pick up for her, no matter the time of day or night. Bless him, but she'd declined. Derek wouldn't care that this was a home for those in need until they got a permanent address, he'd imagine it was a boyfriend, a young man she'd left him for, his mind too warped to accept anything else. He'd say she was one of those cougars or whatever they were called, and mutton dressed as lamb, assuming she chose tarty outfits now, when she didn't, *she didn't*!

How had he found her? How did he know her new name? How had he even met Oliver? And why had Oliver passed on that message anyway? He'd always given her the willies, but it was more to do with the crime he'd committed than the man himself. Child abuse. He'd fiddled with a Pinstone girl, and the next day, she'd shopped him to the police. A long investigation had followed, and Oliver was found guilty, sent away for years. He'd been freed, then went back to Rushford for a robbery, and here he was again, on the outside, a menace to all the little ones.

Why would a pervert know Derek?

She'd never asked Oliver that, and he'd moved out a month after he'd said what he had: *Derek sends his regards*. Such a dreadful set of words, ones that had chilled her to the bone.

She must leave here, let her boss know what was happening, despite Derek warning her not to in one of his horrible calls: *If you go, I'll follow you again. I'll find you, always.*

She'd get another new name, start again somewhere, maybe farther north. Scotland would be nice. Cold but nice. Somewhere in the wilds, a Highland retreat. Yes, she'd look into that soon. There had to be halfway houses there, too.

The phone rang again, the jangle loud, and she stared at it hanging on the wall. Terror flushed through her, and her cheeks heated. But it might not be him, just a family member of one of the lads, or her boss, or a probation officer, even someone from social services, seeing as Ian in number seven's Universal Credit hadn't gone through yet. They rang the communal phone sometimes instead of the different line in her office.

Ryan poked his head around his door. "Want me to get that? It might be me mum. She said she'd phone."

She shook her head. "No, it's fine, thank you. I'll call you if it's her."

She waited for Ryan to go back into his bedsit then reached for the phone. Put it to her ear. Listened to the breathing she knew so well. Ragged. Harsh.

"Emma Inglessssss…"

"Yes," she whispered.

"I'm coming to get you."

Confession

I've suffered greatly since the loss of my brother, someone the locals called Old Man Cossack. Not a day goes by where I don't think of him. A heart attack, they said, although I'm more inclined to think it was the cocaine he took on a regular basis. I hate Phil Flint for that. I wonder if Val, my old next-door neighbour, knows what her precious boyfriend used to get up to? Mind you, Val isn't any better when it comes to flouting the law. She sold herself, all of us down the lane know that, and with a little boy at home, too. Some people are so vile, aren't they? –
Florrie Dorchester

Chapter Twelve

Florrie stood in front of the grave in Mary Magdalene Cemetery, her hands trembling, the bouquet's rose petals shivering, more than likely from the wind, not her trembling fingers. It was always an emotional trial coming here, not only to visit her brother's last resting place in the newer section, and her husband's close by, but that of the tiny mite in the old part, tucked away in the far corner as though he no longer mattered.

But he did, he always would.

She sighed, once again thinking of the past, as she usually did while laying flowers on his grave. She bought him daffodils in the spring and roses the rest of the year, white ones for his pure soul, the boy she'd loved yet had been accusing of killing. Her cousin, Fay, had been distraught, of course she had, but Florrie had suffered as well—from the sting of the accusation and the loss of the baby. No matter that the police and doctor had cleared everyone of any wrongdoing—Fay had insisted on blaming Florrie for her son's death, but that hadn't been the case at all.

Florrie had loved him that night, cuddled him, sang him lullabies.

Up until the early seventies, she'd tried approaching Fay, wanting to ask if they could talk, if she could give her side of events, the true one, not the version Fay had created in her grief-addled mind, but no, Fay wouldn't listen, and Florrie had retreated, keeping away and attempting to put the past to bed.

The baby appeared in her dreams, though, too quiet, too still, his lips blue.

Pretending it hadn't affected her had been fine for years, a mantle she'd draped over herself as a form of emotional protection—until Fay moved into Regency after she'd left Loving Arms. Yes, Florrie knew where her cousin had worked, but only after it had been splashed in the news in the nineties, Fay in the top-right corner in a grainy photo, a black-and-white visual, her face splattered with terror and, perhaps, guilt.

Fay knew more than she'd let on to the reporters and the police, Florrie would bet, but only because of what had happened to Fay's baby.

"There you go, little lad." She placed the roses down then got on with using a dishcloth and some hot soapy water from a Thermos to clean the headstone.

Odd that it was so grubby. Fay came here a lot and tended to it well—Florrie had seen her on many occasions. Maybe she couldn't keep maintaining it now. Florrie had hidden once, behind a fat-trunked yew, the low sprawling branches heavily laden with leaves, their stretching arms disguising her. Fay had walked to this very spot and knelt, sobbing as though her heart hadn't already broken a thousand times with each visit.

Tempted to show herself, to offer some support, Florrie had taken a step forward, treading on some fallen twigs, and Fay's head whipped around. Heart setting up a clunking rhythm, Florrie had hidden again, unable to stand the look on Fay's face.

It was wrecked by mourning, but culpability also played a part in the way it twisted her mouth into an ugly grimace.

"Such a shame she accused me," Florrie said to baby Frankie.

Funny, they all had F names. Fay, Frankie, herself, and Florrie's brother was Fred.

She finished cleaning, popping the cloth and the Thermos in her shopping bag beside the other bunches of flowers. There were two more graves to stop by, Fred's and her husband's, then she'd visit the market. The cheese man was there this week, and she wanted some Brie to put on Jacob's Crackers, maybe a few Ritz.

The second and third flower bunches deposited and the headstones washed, she walked out of the cemetery and down the ginnel that led to town, the cobblestones slippery beneath her fur-lined ankle boots. The heavens had opened for a short spurt on her way here, nothing a brolly couldn't handle, but it had left a hazard on the ground, a parting gift from a downpour that had bounced off the streets as though wanting to get back into the clouds. She'd be careful then, always was.

In town, she headed for the square, the voices of shoppers and stall owners luring her in. It was crowded despite the weather, folks wrapped up in their padded coats, scarfs around necks, gloves on, a multi-coloured crowd drenched in the drab grey of late autumn, eager to buy their things and be away home. Florrie had forgotten her gloves, but she'd remember next week. The air bit at her skin and wrapped around her arthritic knuckles.

Yes, she'd remember.

She weaved through the throng to the cheese stall, where Wilf Atticker, known as Mr Cheese, stood ready to wrap his wares and pocket the money in his blue-and-white-striped apron pocket. He lived in Elderflower Mead with his wife, Dolly, who churned the cheese in their new conservatory out the back.

The things you found out while shopping. People liked to natter, didn't they.

Sherry Price handed over a fiver at the veg stall opposite, her face pinched in that way when something's gone wrong and you can't keep it hidden no matter how hard you try. Shadows under her eyes, her cheeks drawn.

There was talk of her Billy having affairs, but Florrie paid that no mind. She was a regular in The Tractor's on quiz and bingo nights, and never once had that man's eyes or hands strayed. Maybe the rumours were getting to Sherry, who stuffed a bag of potatoes in her rucksack then hauled it onto her back.

Florrie turned away and ordered her Brie, a nice big triangle, and slid a tenner between ready-wrapped blocks of cheddar, a corner poking up.

"Nasty weather lately," Wilf said.

"It is."

"I'm surprised you're out, what with your Fay."

Fay? What did *she* have to do with Florrie going to the bloody market? And she wasn't her Fay anymore. They may as well be strangers the way they avoided one another, and if they were close by in the market or the shops, or in Wasti's, they pretended the other didn't exist, noses in the air, shoulders stiff, lips in thin, tight lines.

Aye, definitely strangers.

Florrie slipped the Brie in her bag. "I don't know what you're on about."

Wilf nodded over at Sherry and plucked the tenner out. "She's just told me Fay was attacked.

Had her tongue and fingers cut off by all accounts."

Florrie's heart did a little dance. Attacked? Who could have done that? God, she hoped no one thought it was her. It was common knowledge there was bad blood between them, more of a steady trickle now compared to the flood in the sixties, but still. "Blimey, that's awful." It was—*if* it had happened to someone else. They said karma was a bitch, didn't they, and she'd caught up to Fay now.

About time.

Wilf handed her the change. "It's terrible, but you know what others are saying, don't you."

Of course she didn't. This was the first she'd heard of it. "Go on." She shuffled closer, under the awning. Some drips of water had fallen and drizzled down the back of her neck, bringing on a shudder.

"Well, a couple of old women piped up after they'd heard what Sherry said, and they reckon it's to do with that thing at Loving Arms. You know, where Fay worked. It was a bad business, that, and some people feel she was more involved than she made out."

Florrie was one of the 'some people'. She'd never believed Fay was innocent, but then she knew things others didn't, so she was bound to have suspected her cousin. "I see."

Florrie may dislike Fay, but she wasn't a grass, and she'd never tell on her. Didn't Florrie walking round with the invisible label of 'baby killer' strapped to her forehead prove that? Family loyalty tied you, although she wished she'd opened her mouth and said something when Frankie died. Maybe she'd have had the courage to speak her fears about Ivy as well then.

"Hmm," Wilf went on. "Unless it was one of them attacks on the elderly. Some people like to hurt the vulnerable."

Wasn't that the truth. Fay was a dab hand at it.

Florrie hefted her bag straps higher up her forearm, settling them at the bend of her elbow. "Well, it's no concern of mine." She puffed her chest up. "She washed her hands of me years ago, and there's no way I'm nipping round to Regency to offer her a helping hand after she accused me of what she did." She almost tittered at 'helping hand'. Fay with no fingers was a delight.

She knew what she'd just said would spread, Mr Cheese passing it on, and that was why she'd said it. Saved her having to explain that to Fay if she got down off her high, deceitful, murderous horse and asked for assistance.

Wilf tapped his large front teeth. "I wouldn't either. Being blamed for a kiddie's death is bound to make you want to avoid her."

He nodded her a good day and moved on to another customer, a lady who glanced at Florrie sharply, as if what Wilf had said referred to Florrie *actually killing* a baby. She hadn't, but that wouldn't matter to some fishwives, which had been evident over the years.

Florrie scuttled off, chased by the spectre of a murder she hadn't committed, pushing through the crowd this time, not being polite about it. She passed the jar stall and contemplated stopping to grab some piccalilli, but that man who always gave her the shivers was there, a large jar of pickled onions in his hand. He was a regular in The Tractor's and always sat in the corner with a pint of real ale, watching the door as though he waited for someone he knew to come in. He'd been a young man when the Loving Arms thing had happened and settled in Pinstone, becoming part of the fixtures and fittings.

Shame. Florrie wished he'd fuck off back to where he'd come from. You got a sixth sense about people, didn't you, warning you to stay away, and he had shifty eyes and the look of a troublemaker about him.

She walked on, foregoing her piccalilli, thinking she maybe had some dregs at the bottom of a pot at home. Her memory wasn't so good on things like that these days, but it was sharp as a tack about the past.

Odd how that happened.

On purpose, she went along the other end of the comb on the estate so she could glance down Regency on her way past. Wouldn't hurt to see if Yeoman was about. She could get the gossip from him, see if it were really true.

Sadly, his car wasn't there, so she trudged on into Mulberry.

"Ah, I'll get my piccalilli from Wasti's," she muttered, one foot out, ready to cross the lane.

A kid came past on his bike, cutting her off, yelling, "Don't you know talking to yourself is the first sign of madness?"

"Don't you know you're meant to have manners and respect your elders?" she shouted back.

That boy would come a cropper one of these days, the despicable ingrate. He was one of the lads belonging to the nasty couple living in Val's old house. Despite the ginnel between their homes, the racket that came out of their place was enough to prompt her into paying out for double glazing. She'd used some of her savings, and the man was coming next week to fit them. She only hoped the rain held off that day, and God knew how cold she'd be with great gaping holes in her house while he put the new frames in. Perhaps she'd go down to one of the other neighbours and beg an armchair and some company. Cheryl was nice.

She ambled over the street and entered Wasti's, the heater above the door drenching her in recycled warmth, and headed straight for the jar aisle. She knew where everything was in here. Wasti hadn't moved anything around from the moment he'd set up shop. He didn't hold with confusing his customers, so he'd said.

"Afternoon, Florrie," he called from behind the counter.

"A shit one, that's for certain," she said.

"Have you had a bad day?"

She curled her hand around the piccalilli jar and clutched it to her chest. Was there anything else she needed? Better to get it now than have to come back out, especially if it tipped down again. "It isn't the best day I've had, no, but I'll get over it."

She browsed the other aisles to jog her memory. Oh, the crackers, that was it. She picked up a packet and went to the counter, placing her items on top.

"Why is it bad?" Wasti prodded at his till. "Anything I can help you with?"

"I heard news I'd rather not have." She pursed her lips and eyed the cigarette cupboard with its closed shutter. She could just smoke a Bensons now, but she'd given up two years ago on the account of her wheezy chest.

"Ah, Fay." Wasti tutted. "Sherry was in here earlier and told me all about it."

Why was that young woman going around spreading other folks' business? She of all people should know the damage chitter-chattering did. Well, if Billy was up to no good in the women department, Sherry deserved all she got now.

Florrie slackened her mouth, swearing she tasted the smoke from a fag. That was what sensory recall did for you. "Yes, Fay, although that's nothing to do with me. Her, I mean. I don't have anything to do with *that* woman."

"I know. She says so every time she comes in. Four pounds and ninety-two, please."

Now why would Fay do that? And God, Wasti's was expensive. Maybe she should have bitten the bullet and got her pickle from the jar stall despite the weirdo being there. Mind you, it was a double packet of Jacob's, so that might be it.

She gave him a fiver and held her hand out ready for the measly change that would go in her penny pot. She gave the contents to the Father Christmas float that came round every year, people knocking, holding up their buckets, carols wailing from a distorted speaker, *Silent Night* and the like.

A swarm of smugness overtook her. "Proves us falling out still bothers her if she feels the need to harp on about it."

"I've heard the same line every day for ten years." Wasti dropped coins into her palm.

"Sad baggage," she mumbled and dumped her things into her bag. "Anyway, I'm off."

"Try to have a good afternoon," he said.

"You an' all."

She shoved the door and marched down the lane, thinking of Fay grumbling about her every day. It had to be getting to her, more so in her old age, and that was telling. Florrie had found that the longer she lived, the more she examined the past and the part she'd played in various things. Slights, a bad word, her reaction to something someone had said…she picked them apart and wished she could have done it differently, especially regarding little Frankie.

Maybe Fay was doing the same, *her* nefarious parts in life coming back to haunt her. Good. She deserved having her tongue and fingers cut off. At least she couldn't spout nonsense at Wasti anymore.

That was a spiteful thing to think, but Fay had always thought her spiteful anyway, no matter that Florrie was usually more kind-hearted. Sort of. Yes, she'd become bitter lately, but that was loneliness talking. Fay was just jealous of all the attention Nan had showered on Florrie over her, that was all.

Come to think of it, there wasn't any mention of Nan killing Frankie, oh no.

She put the key in the lock and went to enter her house, but a burst of angry voices had her pausing. Them next door were at it again, the rowdy bastards.

"He's fucked off with my purse," the mum shouted. "Go and find him."

"*You* go and find him." The dad.

"Muuum, he's nicked my bike!"

"Oh, for Pete's sake, I'll skin him alive," the mum screeched.

Florrie shook her head and stepped inside.

The day for her double glazing couldn't come quick enough.

Chapter Thirteen

Mask had followed Florrie Dorchester from the market. He'd spotted her rushing off after he'd paid for his pickled onions, and she'd taken the route to walk past Regency. That was handy, he could see what was going on down there since he'd left Helen's. And wasn't that a shoddy statement about the police force these days? Two plainclothes coppers making door-to-door enquiries, and the woman, DS Tanner, she'd said, had come to Helen's on their second cuppa and hadn't batted an eyelid about him being there. Okay, he'd dressed up as Katie, the *Star's* crime reporter, but she hadn't queried him when he'd said he was her.

Useless bitch.

Luckily, Helen hadn't acted funny, and that was unusual, given the questions he'd been asking her. *Do you know Fay Williams well? And little Ivy Gibbs, tell me what you know about her. What about Billy Price?*

Her answers had been vague, just as he'd suspected, but he had another trick up his sleeve. He'd visit her again tomorrow as a different reporter, same newspaper, and see if a man could bully the truth out of her. He needed to know if Billy had talked in the end, words spilling out of him with some therapist or other. And then there was Billy himself to visit, asking him similar questions, the main one being: *Do you remember me?*

That may be difficult. His wife, Sherry, was always around, and Billy didn't seem to have any work on at the moment. Mask had planned to follow him to whatever address and collar him there in one of his faces, but he'd have to think of something else, some other way to get him on his own.

The wind pushed at his real skin. He'd nipped home after Helen's to take Katie's mask off, then, jittery and in need of fresh air, he'd gone to the market. He sailed past Regency now, nothing going on down there. Florrie disappeared inside Wasti's at the end of Mulberry, so Mask carried on, past Elderflower. Vicar's Gate was coming up, and he peered down that way. Police in uniforms at doors.

Oh dear. They were bound to get to his street soon.

He'd go to Drinker's Rest and spend the remainder of the afternoon and evening there to avoid them. Take a brisk walk over the field then onwards to the moor like he had all those years ago. Have his dinner. They had a lovely chicken breast with mushroom sauce, mashed potatoes, and buttered green beans.

That got him thinking about Olga Scrivens. He missed the veg she used to sell, her down the lane at the house next to Halfway. Such a pest she'd got murdered because you could get a carrier bag full for a fiver from her. Someone else lived there now, obviously, and they'd torn her greenhouse down—apparently, they'd patioed the back garden and installed one of those hot tubs. At least they'd put the veg in boxes on the pavement out the front, offering it for free. Mask had swiped some carrots and runner beans, a couple of large potatoes, and a turnip.

Hungry after thinking of all that food, he continued on, pondering the job he'd been paid for this morning. Someone wanted Belle and Beast whole head masks, and did he know of anyone who could whip up the costumes as well, love? Of course he did, and he'd get commission on the referral. That was how it worked in his professional circle.

As well as missing Olga's veg, he missed his time employed by the acting troupe that had played on stages up and down the country. He'd been the man who made the masks then, although they weren't of the quality they were now. Years of practise and new materials meant he had a thriving online business, no need to follow the actors around, and anyway, they'd 'let him go' when they'd arrived in Pinstone that time, and he'd had to find another job until he could save up to start with the masks again.

That was how he'd met Billy.

He pinched his nose to bring on pain, enough to steer his thoughts to that and not what had happened in the past. Billy wasn't sweet little

Billy anymore but a man, and Mask had seen him around often, though no flash of recognition ever glittered in Billy's eyes.

Some children shut out traumatic events.

Or maybe Billy was just ignoring him.

His street came into view, and he walked down it, incensed, as always, at Yeoman's big dog barking up a storm. It was a German Shepherd called Rochester, of all things, and the copper had employed a young girl to walk it twice a day while he went about his piggy business, but that never quieted the animal. He was only silent once Yeoman got home, and no matter how many times Mask pushed anonymous notes through his door, nothing had been done about the barking.

He'd break in one day and let the dog out, tell it to shoo and be gone.

In his house, he put his pickled onions in the cupboard with all the others, smiling of days gone by when his mother peeled shallots and popped them in vinegar, enough jars to last them months. She'd been a good mother, the best, the only person to see him in a shining light. Everyone else viewed him through a clouded lens, unable to understand his surly appearance and behaviour.

Some people just weren't prepared to see beneath the façade, much like Fay with Ivy. That child acted up out of desperation to be noticed, even he could see that, but Fay...oh, evil Fay, she'd taken it as the girl messing up her ideal family. A smack or two would have seen the kid right, a bit of punishment, some rules and order, but Helen wouldn't ever hear of it.

Mask had asked her about smacking earlier, and she'd been vehement that nothing like that had happened at Loving Arms. He begged to differ, although he'd kept that to himself. He was sure Helen didn't know what he'd got up to once the lights went out. Still, it was best *she* lost her tongue and fingers, too.

After all, he couldn't have her talking, his dreams had told him that.

So strange how he'd lived in Pinstone since *it* had happened, and Fay hadn't said a word to anyone about him being there that night. She may have told Helen, but she hadn't let that slip today either, yet that first dream... God, it had him sitting upright in bed, sweating, and the suggestion that they would eventually open their mouths on their deathbeds had pushed him into ensuring they never got the chance.

Florrie, though... He'd heard of the falling out between her and Fay before he'd come on the scene, but would Fay have broken her vow not to speak to Florrie so she could tell her about *it*? Florrie had always looked at him funny, so perhaps she knew something, too.

He'd pay her a visit as Katie and find out.

So much to do, and there were the masks to make for the customer as well.

How would he fit it all in?

Chapter Fourteen

1965

Fay didn't like to leave Frankie with Nan, but it was her friend's engagement party, one of the women who'd snubbed her during pregnancy, and she was desperate for some fun. Selfish of her to think of herself when her baby was only three weeks old, but Nan had insisted it would do her good, and so what if the 'friend' was a wolf in sheep's clothing, only inviting Fay along so she could rub it in her face that this was the way you did things: engagement, marriage, then *the baby, not the other way around. Fay, delighted Nan was paying her some special attention, had agreed. If Nan said she should go, she'd do it. She'd do anything to be treated better than Florrie and her brother, Fred.*

Florrie had come round to help, and Fay gritted her teeth about that. She'd never got on with her, mainly because Florrie was the favourite of the family, her brother a close second, and she was all sweetness and light in front of others but spiteful to Fay in private. Still, Nan wasn't as sprightly as she once was, and if she said she needed Florrie on hand then who was Fay to argue?

Mum and Dad had ceased speaking to her since she'd announced her pregnancy, and it was Nan who'd found the mouldy one-bedroom house for her to live in, paying the first week's rent to that nasty man who came round to collect it with his little book and ink pen, beady-eyed behind thick-lens glasses. Mum had turfed her onto the streets, see, and she'd run round to Nan's, pouring her heart out.

"Now then, your mother was a surprise for me, too, and she knows it, so why she's acting like this with you, I'll never know," Nan said. "It's all that church's fault, filling her head with nonsense. She

should never have married your Bible-thumping father. He changed her into a pious woman."

A 'surprise'. A polite term for an unwanted pregnancy. But Grandad had stuck by Nan and married her, and that made all the difference. Fay had no one. She was an outcast, someone to sneer down your nose at, and the 'friend' would probably do so tonight, despite the invitation. With a few gins inside her, Fay wouldn't care, so that was the end of that.

She twirled in front of the mirror in Nan's bedroom. The dress was a bit tight, she hadn't had time to lose the baby weight, but she wasn't after catching any man's eye, so what did a few rolls around her middle matter? Her old friends would snigger, of that she had no doubt, but she could ignore them and dance the night away.

"You look fat," Florrie said, leaning on the doorframe.

Fay blushed, anger taking over her previously happy mood. "You would say that. Thin as a rake, you are. You'd think all those cakes you eat would pack on the flab, but it will later on, you mark my words—then who'll be the one struggling to put a dress on? Anyway, it was worth it, because I have Frankie."

"People think you're loose."

"I don't care what they think." But she did.

"They say you're nothing but a whore. Still, never mind. Like you say, we have Frankie."

"I have Frankie," Fay gritted out. *"Not you."*

"I love him like my own."

Fay couldn't dispute that. Her cousin doted on the baby. "I know you do."

"Well then, shut your trap."

Florrie flounced off, and Fay stared at herself in the mirror again. She did *look fat. God. She straightened the fabric, holding her tummy in. That was better.*

She'd do.

Down in the kitchen, Frankie fast asleep in Nan's arms, Fay fetched a small bottle of gripe water a neighbour had given her.

"If he frets, give him some of this." She put the unlabelled bottle on the table. The neighbour had said she'd poured it in there out of her own.

"What's that?" Florrie barged in and sat beside Nan. She stroked Frankie's hair. *"Aww, he's so lovely. Look at his little face."*

A prickle of annoyance stabbed Fay's gut. "None of your business what it is. Nan knows."

"It's gripe water, duck," Nan said. *"Frankie's on bottles with us this evening, so he might get colicky."*

Florrie eyed the water, a strange expression cluttering her features. "Right…"

"Off you go then, our Fay." Nan smiled. *"Chin up. You're worth more than a million of them girls put together."*

Fay kissed Frankie's clenched fist and left the house on feet created from wings. Nan had made her life saying that.

Chapter Fifteen

Helen put the last of Fay's shortbread in the plastic tub and sealed the lid. Fay's portion of the stew and dumplings was in a bigger one, so she placed them both in her wicker shopping basket and hung it over the crook of her arm. It was only a short trot to number twenty-one, but with her failing hips, it took twice as long to get anywhere than it would if she didn't have the impediment. Still, it would be nice to have a natter with Fay, even though the poor woman couldn't talk. DS Tanner had been round and told her the terrible news.

Helen wondered if Fay would even be able to eat the biscuits and dinner. The police officer had mentioned missing teeth. And the tongue and fingers, gosh, what a horrendous thing to have happened.

Katie, that lovely reporter, had been so shocked, and Tanner had asked her not to put this news in the paper as they were keeping it on the downlow at the moment. Katie, nice lady that she was, had said she wouldn't dream of doing that if it meant hindering the investigation and she'd wait until she was given the go-ahead.

The awful circumstances of last night had frightened Helen, if she were honest. *She* was classed as elderly in some people's eyes, too, and what if there was an old lady killer going about? According to Tanner, nothing had been stolen from Fay's that the carer could see, but that didn't mean they hadn't pilfered her pension from her purse, did it? And there was all that money upstairs in a shoebox under the bed as well, only, Helen hadn't mentioned that to Tanner, just Katie.

The wind was being a pig and attacking her, and her journey along the street proved more difficult than usual. It was cold, too, and she should have put a coat on. Her cardigan fronts flapped open, the chilly air seeping between the buttons on her thin flowery blouse, and she shivered, blinking to see straight. The swift breeze had dried her eyes out, sneaking behind her tortoiseshell-rimmed glasses and wafting up to ruffle her grey-and-brown-striped hair.

At last, she made it to Fay's and knocked.

That pretty Louise answered, all smiles. "Ooh, come away in, out of the cold. It'll freeze your nipples off if you don't watch yourself."

Helen laughed. Louise was such a card, always there with a cheery word or two to brighten your day.

"It would if my nipples weren't inverted." Helen stepped inside into the warmth. "The wind has no chance of popping them out of their booby burrows."

Louise's giggle tinkled out, warming Helen further. When she got older, she'd ask to have Louise come and look after her, too.

Door closed, Louise's face scrunched, and she leant forward and whispered, "You know she can't speak, yes?"

Helen nodded. *So ghastly*. "I've brought her some dinner and her usual biscuits."

"Well, she can't manage them at the moment. The hospital said I need to puree her food. Her tongue, you see. It's got stitches. She had an operation."

Helen held back a gag at the thought of a surgeon sewing the stub of tongue up. "Poor woman. What will happen when you go home later? How will she manage?"

"Don't worry about that. I'm staying in her spare room for the duration. Well, until we can get hold of any family members to come and care for her."

Fay shrieked from the living room, and Louise rushed in there, followed by a struggling Helen who wobbled and winced at the sharp jabs of pain in her silly hips.

Oh no. Fay stood in front of her window, swiping silver trinkets off her sill with her bandaged hands. Louise went over and guided her into her seat, murmuring that everything would be okay once someone from her family arrived.

Fay shook her head, manic, and snorted, her face bright red.

"No," Helen said, more forcefully than she'd intended. "You mustn't contact her family.

There's only one person left, and that's her cousin, Florrie. They don't get along. She did have another cousin, Florrie's brother Fred, but he died."

Louise picked a blanket up from the floor and covered Fay's lap, patting it into place. "I see. A falling out, was it?"

"Yes, and it's irreparable, so please, don't get hold of her. Fay would hate that, wouldn't you, Fay."

Fay nodded, snorting some more, then tipped her head back, tears falling.

Oh dear, what to do? Helen felt like a spare part, unable to ease Fay's suffering, and that was all she had wanted to do in her life, help people to get over trauma and become happier. Look at how she'd fed those kiddies up, giving them cuddles and singing them songs. She didn't have nippers of her own. Her live-in status at Loving Arms meant no man gave her a second look when she went to the parties in the town hall anyway. She wasn't available, married to her job, and fellas sensed it.

"What can I do for you?" she asked Fay. "I have your biccies and a stew with those nice choux dumplings we used to have, remember those? But maybe another day, eh? I'll leave them with Louise here. Maybe pop it in the freezer?" She took them out and handed the tubs to the carer.

"Hayydomim," Fay said, the word just a strange sound.

Maybe it was the name of her attacker?

"Haydon? Is that who did this to you?"

Fay got agitated and said it again, this time with gaps. "Hayyd om im."

"I don't understand, love." God, this was just awful.

Fay crumpled her eyes up and gave it another go. "Hayyd fom im."

"Hide from him?" Helen asked, her eyes widening.

Fay nodded.

"Hide from who?"

But Fay was exhausted and closed her eyes. A soft snore came quickly. Perhaps it was the painkillers she must be taking.

Helen turned to Louise. "Why would I need to hide from anyone?"

Louise sighed. "I don't know, it sounded like mumbo-jumbo to me."

Helen nodded. "You're right, it was. I'd best be off. Don't worry about the tubs. I'll pick them up next time I'm here. Feel free to eat it if Fay can't."

Louise followed her out to the front door. "I won't allow this Florrie woman to come round here, not now Fay's put up a protest and you've explained, but just in case something happens to Fay…"

Helen's heart picked up speed. "W-what do you mean?"

"She's older than you, and a shock like this can sometimes…"

"Oh, I see."

"I'll definitely need to contact her family then." Louise opened the door. "Do you happen to know where Florrie lives?"

Helen nodded. "In Mulberry Lane, but I forget which number. And I don't want this coming back on me. I'm Fay's friend, and I wouldn't like her thinking I betrayed her."

"I understand. You stay safe now."

Helen stepped outside, and this time, the wind shoved her home, pressing on her back with insistent fingers. She almost stumbled at one point but righted herself, determined not to fall. All the while, what Fay had said swirled in her mind.

Hide from him.

Who, though? And, if Fay was insinuating he'd be coming for Helen, why? She'd never annoyed anyone as far as she knew.

"My word, this is all so upsetting."

She'd need one of her blood pressure tablets to calm her down. That and her stew, and she'd be right as rain. Or as right as she could be in the circumstances.

Chapter Sixteen

Catherine had a nap about an hour after seeing the girl. It had taken a lot out of her, worrying about her in just that scrap of fabric, and by the river, too. Had she slipped and fallen in? And Catherine hadn't thought to check, but did she even have shoes on? And how had she got into the care home last night, and why was she hanging around the gates? Perhaps she'd ask Sarah to do a bit of digging. It wouldn't seem odd if she did it. They wouldn't think *she* was mad.

Sarah was due any moment, so Catherine left her room, walking down the left-hand landing towards the stairs. A lift had been installed, so she stepped inside it, ever fearful of taking a tumble. That was one of the rules anyway: Always use the lift, never the stairs! It made sense, seeing as some residents were unsteady on their feet. Dodgy hips, painful knees, all a part of being elderly and useless, the human version of a clapped-out old banger.

In the foyer, she stopped to stare at the front door, dithering with rebellion, wondering if she should open it and watch Sarah's car trundling up the drive. No, Liz would have something to say about that. Another rule: Don't wander the grounds without supervision! All the rules had exclamation marks after them, which seemed condescending to Catherine, as though those who lived here were dense and that little strip and dot of punctuation hammered it home better.

!
!
!
Bugger off.

She moved through the big kitchen, where Cook stood at the stove, stirring a huge pot of chicken casserole. Catherine didn't like it. Cook left it simmering for too long, and the chicken broke up into strings. She'd do her sloppy mash with it, Catherine would bet, and over-boiled peas, the green leached out of them, bordering on mustard-yellow by the time they hit the plate.

Catherine missed preparing her own meals.

"Afternoon, Cath." Cook smiled in her usual cheery way.

Sometimes, Catherine wanted to punch her, and she mulled over whether that was where her son got his badness from. Her. Passed down through the genes. Or maybe it was being elderly that brought on these thoughts, the body and mind tired of so much that even a simple smile brought on rage.

Catherine nodded as an answer and walked through the utility area and round the corner into the main living room. All visits were there, something to do with another rule. She'd heard talk of it being because some visitors had abused their parents when visiting was allowed in the private rooms, giving them a slap or two or administering drugs to one lady to chivvy her along to Heaven. She'd had a hefty life insurance plan.

Appalling.

Other residents sat in armchairs, each with their own coffee table, private little clusters for chatting, although Catherine always heard what they were talking about. Everyone but her was half deaf and tended to shout.

She opted for the area by the window, more secluded, and settled down to wait.

Liz bustled in, pushing the tea trolley with its big silver urn, cups rattling on the shelf below, the saucers quivering. Catherine eyed the biscuits. As usual, dry Rich Tea and crumbly digestives. No custard creams or bourbons. The filling made a mess with some of her fellow home-dwellers.

She longed for a garibaldi or a fig roll.

Visitors appeared, drifting in, Sarah at the back of the queue near the door. Catherine's heart leapt at the sight of her, such a lovely woman who dedicated her life to getting justice for anyone who needed her. She'd wanted to go to court as the prosecution against her brother, but that wasn't advised. Still, her publicly stating that in *The Pinstone Star* had gone some way to cleaning off some of the shit his behaviour had flung at her.

"Mum! Lovely to see you." Sarah kissed Catherine's cheek.

She smelt of flowers and washing powder.

"Hello, love." Catherine smiled like Cook had, all balled cheeks, and she chastised herself for thinking uncharitable thoughts about her. "How are you?"

"Oh, so-so. Busy, same as always. Dave sends his regards."

Dave was her husband, a good, decent man. Catherine wished he were her son instead of *him*.

While Sarah chatted animatedly, Catherine studied her. If she concentrated hard enough, Sarah could be the child she once was, her older countenance vanishing to be replaced with a chubby face and no laughter lines beside her sparkling blue eyes. Catherine disappeared into the past, remembering Sarah at ballet, clumsy, out of step, but she went every week regardless.

"…and Fay Williams was attacked."

Catherine catapulted out of her memories. "What?"

"Yes, someone went into her home and did awful things to her."

Catherine had never liked Fay, having that baby out of wedlock, but that didn't mean she'd wish an attack on her. "What things?"

"I'm not sure I should tell you."

Catherine bristled at that. "I'm old, not precious about bad news. I've seen and heard a fair few things in my time, so this won't faze me."

"An old man went into her house. Cut her tongue out and her fingers off."

Oh. That was unexpected. "Why would he do that?"

"No idea. I'm so glad you're in here. If it's an elderly thing…"

Catherine nodded. For once, she was glad to be in here, too.

"Anyway," Sarah said. "What's new with you?"

"There's a girl here." Catherine smoothed her skirt over her thighs. "She came to see me last night. In my room."

Sarah snapped to attention. "What girl?"

"She was only little, maybe about eight or nine. She had a nightie on."

"That's not on. Did you tell Liz? Your room is private, only for you."

Catherine chuckled. "Liz would say the dementia's playing me up. But I saw the girl again this morning, out on the moor. She went along by the river. She was in her nightie, and I'm worried she fell in and drowned."

Sarah frowned. "I'll ask around about her."

Catherine nodded. She knew her daughter wouldn't pooh-pooh it. "It's not good for a littlun to be out there in this weather, is it. Without a coat. I don't think she had shoes on either but can't be sure on that one."

"Poor mite." Sarah bit her lip. "Um...I saw *him* yesterday."

Catherine didn't need to ask who that was. Her wicked son. "I'm sorry for you."

"Hmm. We didn't speak or anything. First time I've seen him since he came back, so I successfully avoided him for months."

"He should have stayed wherever he went." Catherine shuddered, entertaining the thought of him turning up here for a visit. She hadn't told Liz she didn't want to see him, that would mean questions, ones Catherine didn't want to answer, but maybe she should if it saved her worry.

Who said life got easier when you grew up?

Chapter Seventeen

Morgan and Shaz had returned to the incident room after seeing Emma Ingles, and the afternoon had dragged. There was a lot of info to catch up on before they could move forward. They'd typed out the neighbours' statements, and now he busied himself writing down the new info on the whiteboard as neither Nigel nor Jane had had the time.

Nigel had found all but two of the former residents of Loving Arms and was in the process of contacting them to see what their relationship with Fay was like. Billy had already told Yeoman a while back that Fay was like his mother, so he didn't anticipate any bad news on that score, and Sherry was no one to worry about. Nigel would chase the other two up when he had a moment to dig deeper. Maybe they were girls and had got married, their names changed in the process.

Jane had taken it upon herself to look closer at Fay Williams after she'd snooped on social media and found nothing—Shaz was giving that another go now, she liked falling down the rabbit hole. Jane had wanted to see if someone from Fay's past who didn't have anything to do with the care home cropped up, and she was online, still browsing.

So far, she'd discovered that Fay had lost a child when he was three weeks old in nineteen sixty-five, and she'd thrown herself into her new job at Loving Arms soon after, one she'd got on the strength of the authorities vouching for her—during her pregnancy, she'd gone to Arms to help out as a volunteer. Back then, things must have been different, less stringent rules when employing people, but apparently, she'd thrived at her job. She'd remained in their employ for forty-five years.

Seemed Florrie Dorchester, Val's old next-door neighbour, was Fay's cousin. That was a shocker, and Morgan had decided to nip there on the way home from work with Shaz. Florrie needed to be told Fay had been attacked. He wondered whether there was a bad seed in the familial bunch with a score to settle, and Florrie would be next to receive a sinister visit, although he didn't rate their chances. She was a fierce old bird and probably still had her late husband's walking stick in her house somewhere to batter them with.

"Um, Yeoman, you might want to come and see this." Jane popped her eyes above her monitor, eyebrows high.

He walked over there and drew a spare chair across to sit beside her. Not his favourite thing to do, being close to her, but work was work, and he had to get over his aversion to this DC. He stared at her screen. It had a saver on it, a tropical beach, the sand white, the sea turquoise, a palm tree captured as static when it might really have been mid-sway in a warm and gentle breeze.

He thought of Lydia running to Spain but clamped down on his mind going any further to her murder, to her eye hanging out, her body sprawled on a strange hotel bed, her neck bitten.

Stop.

"What am I meant to be looking at?" he grouched. "If you're showing me your next holiday destination, bully for you, have a great time when you get there."

"Hmm, it does look nice. It's in the Bahamas. On the bucket list, hence me having the picture. Something to aspire to. Cocktails and a suntan." She clicked her mouse, and a web page came up. "Read that. Only found two articles so far, but still, it's a start."

Morgan leant forward, elbows on his knees, fingers to his mouth.

CHILD GOES MISSING FROM LOVING ARMS!

Reginald Davies – Crime Reporter

Ivy Gibbs, aged eight, is a resident of Loving Arms. She went missing in the middle of the night two days ago and hasn't been seen since. Ivy is four feet tall and approximately three stone. She has long blonde hair and blue eyes. One of her back teeth is missing. She used to reside in Elderflower Mead prior to her removal from the family home.

Police are scouring the area, thinking she may have wandered outside and got lost. It's a dangerous task, as Cobbs Moor is flooded in places from the recent bad weather. There is a worry she may have fallen into a bog or ditch and drowned, the water hiding her from view.

PC Yarthing said: "We're increasingly concerned for Ivy's safety. It was a cold night, and the care home manager wasn't aware Ivy was missing until the child didn't come down for breakfast. Everyone in residence was asleep that night, the doors locked, so Ivy must have let herself out and taken the key with her. A stool was left beside the utility room door which she could have used to reach the top bolt. The iron gates in the courtyard were locked from the inside, so she must have squeezed through one of the gaps. If anyone has seen Ivy, please come forward."

There's speculation that Ivy could be a sleepwalker. According to our sources, many children are, especially those from abusive households who may have night terrors. Ivy's mother has been contacted, but she has no idea where her child is. Neighbours say the woman has been inside her home for a week, not answering the door to the postman, who has attempted to deliver a parcel twice. She's an alcoholic.

As PC Yarthing said, if you've seen Ivy, get in contact. The weather is frightful today and has been since the night she went missing. All her clothing was left behind except for the nightie she was wearing when she went to bed. It is white with pink flowers and has a pink bow on the neckline. Her slippers, wellies, and shoes remain beside her bed. Hopes are still high she can be found, but whether that's alive or dead remains to be seen.

Morgan frowned. "Right, so they're thinking she opened the door, took the key, and locked up once she went outside? Then she squeezed through the gate? Sorry, but if we were investigating that, I'd say someone *in* the house locked that door and gate *after* she'd gone. Stinks of an inside job to me."

"We're on the same page. Could have been Fay Williams." Jane wasn't asking, she was telling in her usual way.

"So why wait all this time to attack her for it?" Morgan pointed to the screen. "That says it happened in nineteen ninety-one."

"So the old man fits. Let's say he's the same age as her and they both worked there together. I should look up the reporter, Reginald, and see if he's still alive. You could do with talking to him."

Morgan shook his head, confused by the obvious lack of police awareness, and kept reading.

IVY IS STILL MISSING!

Reginald Davies – Crime Reporter

Ivy Gibbs still hasn't been found. A week has passed since her disappearance, and there are no leads. The moor has been searched, as has Loving Arms, and there is no sign of her. The wandering child situation has turned to her being abducted. With no body in the vicinity, that's the only other viable answer.

All employees of Loving Arms have been questioned, and none of them are persons of interest. If Ian Brady and Myra Hindley had not already been arrested and they weren't so old, we wouldn't be remiss in thinking this had something to do with them. The moor is a chilling parallel.

Fay Williams, the manager and main caregiver of Loving Arms, is distraught. She said: "I can't believe she's gone. Although she hasn't settled in here as well as the others, she's a pleasant child who would eventually benefit from the love we give here. I'll blame myself for the rest of my life if something's happened to her."

Helen Donaldson, the cook and carer, said: "Ivy just needs love, some special attention. I hope she comes back to us soon. She loves my iced biscuits."

A tragic event. Let's hope Ivy is found. Keep alert. Keep looking. Sheds, outhouses, bushes, garages, everywhere. She could be hiding and frightened. If someone has been acting suspiciously, they could have the child.

Can you let that linger on your conscience if you don't report them?

Morgan rubbed his eyes. They itched from tiredness. "Christ. Why go down the child abduction route *after* they'd waited a week thinking she'd just wandered outside? With the lock business as well, it's clearly dodgy. See if you can find the copper in charge of this, or this PC Yarthing fella, he'll do. I'll give him and Reginald a visit tomorrow—if they're even alive."

"What's up?" Shaz came over and bent to read the screen.

While she did, Morgan turned to Jane. "Got anything else?"

"Isn't that enough? Good grief. I'll look up any other articles about it in the morning. There are only so many hours in the day."

"Sorry, I'm desperate to find out why the hell Fay was attacked. Granted, it could well just be a chancer who knocked on her door and talked himself inside, but he's an old man, so that leads me to believe she knew him. Plus, no forced entry, so she let him in."

"I realise that, but having a pop at me isn't—"

"Hey," Shaz said. "I spoke to Helen Donaldson today. She had Katie Violet there."

"And you're just telling me this about Katie now? What the fuck was she there for?" Morgan sighed.

"Didn't think it was my business to know why so I didn't ask. Thinking about it, I should have, because she could've got wind of what happened to Fay, found out Helen was her friend, and gone round there to get the details so she could put it in the paper."

"Tsk." Jane shook her head. "That was silly of you. So they didn't mention this Ivy girl?" Jane asked.

Shaz bit her lip, then, "No. I asked Katie not to print anything about Fay at the moment, and she agreed. I believed her. She seemed full of sympathy."

"Right, we'll go and see Helen again tomorrow as well." Morgan glanced at the time on the bottom taskbar. "We're due at Florrie's, not that she knows it, and I'm not sitting here all night working this lot out. If it was a murder, yes, but it isn't, so home at the normal time for us lot."

"Glad you said that." Jane smiled. "I have things to do."

Shaz walked off to get her bag.

"Don't," Morgan whispered to Jane. "I mean it."

"Oh, shh, I was pulling your leg. I have ironing in my future, nothing menacing."

"Keep it that way."

"Maybe." She saved the web page to her favourites and hit the print button. "I'll do a few copies of these so we all have one, plus another for the board."

"Right." He rose, unsure about trusting her to give her clothes a good press tonight over going out into the darkness.

She waved him off. "Away to Florrie's with you."

He walked across the room, feeling like he'd just been given an order and *she* was the DI, not him. Cheeky cow.

Shoulders tense, he strode over to Nigel, attempting to shake off the need to round on Jane and put her in her place. "Just do the next one on your pad and deal with the rest tomorrow. Also tomorrow, I want a list of all the former employees at Loving Arms. I realise you haven't had the chance this afternoon. I want to know who worked there at the time of a little girl's disappearance."

"Little girl? Bloody hell. From the children's home?"

Morgan nodded. "Jane's printing the articles now. You can have a read. Anyway, we're going to question Florrie, then it's home. Clock off at five—no staying here with your head buried in your notes."

Nigel laughed. "But I've got a profile to do on the attacker yet."

"Do it at home with your curry or whatever and a nice beer if you have to, just not here. Scribbling notes in your pyjamas is preferable, eh?"

Morgan flapped his hand to beckon Shaz and walked out. No need to nip in and let the chief in on what was happening. The bloke only wanted to know the ins and outs if it was murder.

Suits me.

In the car, he released a long breath while Shaz delved in her bag.

"No scampi shit," he said. "You'll spoil your dinner."

"Blimey O'Reilly, pissy pants." She shoved them back inside. "Got in a tizz because it's Florrie we're seeing?"

"Maybe. She swears blind I used to shag information out of Val, no matter how many times I've told her Val's a mate."

"Florrie's all bark and no bite. Remember that time she was in The Tractor's after we solved a case and went there for a drink? Fucking singing karaoke. *I Pretend* by bloody Des O'Connor. She murdered it."

Morgan winced. "That's the only time I've seen her without a scowl, you know."

"Same. She's fierce, but I bet she's soft underneath."

"We'll soon find out."

He parked down the lane, saddened by the state of Val's old front garden. She used to keep it nice, but the new residents hadn't bothered. Lengthy grass, a bike on its side, half hidden by wet clumps of it, and an empty milk flagon on top of an unruly bush in the centre. Surely that was a breach of the tenancy agreement.

He shook his head, walked up Florrie's path, and turned to see what was taking Shaz so long. She was just shutting the car door, so he spun to face the house again.

Shaz's footsteps pattered. The scent of fish wafted. He whipped round to stare at her, spotting what she held.

"I only had *one*," she said and crumpled the bag of Scampi Fries and put it in her pocket.

"Jesus," he muttered and knocked.

The door sprang open almost immediately, Florrie standing there in a floral dress, an ostentatious yellow bow on the neckline.

"Are you here to do something about that unruly lot?" Florrie jabbed a thumb in the direction of her new neighbours, the scowl he'd mentioned firmly in place. "I tell you, they're a rowdy bunch of fuckers. They keep me up at night. Even them noise-cancelling headphones don't work."

"Aren't they a bit uncomfortable in bed?" Shaz asked.

"I have to sit up to sleep. I've got a dodgy chest and keep coughing if I lie down." Florrie heaved her tits up onto her forearms. The ends of the ribbon ruched against them. "Well? Are you going to do something about it?"

"What, your chest?" Shaz smiled.

Florrie's mouth flapped. "You know damn well what I'm talking about, young lady. *Them*." She flung an arm out, almost clipping Morgan's nose.

"Landlord first, see if they can sort it. Failing that, Environmental Health," he said. "Keep a record of all noise. Record it if you can."

"I'll go round and see Val. She's the one who let the reprobates move in, so she can be the one to get them out. It's a fucking liberty, their behaviour. And if you're not here for them, what *do* you want?"

"We need to come in," Morgan said.

"I don't think so. Say what you have to say out here. I haven't hoovered in a month of Sundays and don't want you seeing my manky carpet."

Morgan held back a smile. "It's about your cousin."

Florrie blanched. "I haven't got a cousin anymore."

"Fay Williams?"

"Oh. Her. Well, she's my cousin by name but not in my life, if you know what I mean. I haven't spoken to her since I don't know when. A while after that baby of hers died, which was in the sixties. Last I remember, it was maybe seventy-two I tried making up with her. Something like that."

"That's quite some time ago." Morgan straightened his jacket. "Look, whether you speak to her or not, we're here to let you know she was attacked last night."

Florrie sniffed. "Already been told by Mr Cheese, and *he* was told by that Sherry Price, a loose-tongued bint if ever there was one, her who hates being gossiped about but thinks it's okay for *her* to do it. She needs a kick up the arse about her Billy. He wouldn't do anything behind her back. He's too much of a gentleman for that, and I hear you have my so-called cousin to thank for it. She more or less brought him up, even though she'd have been classed as an older mum when he was a nipper."

What did being an older mum have to do with anything? "We're aware of that. So, are you going to pop round and see her?"

"What for? It's not like we can have a chat, is it? She's got no *tongue!*"

She stepped back and slammed the door.

"Fucking hell," Shaz whispered.

"By that, I'm taking it she wants nothing to do with Fay. And you said Florrie might be soft underneath. Hard as nails, that one. Rightio, let's go home."

He dropped Shaz at her place, gritting his teeth at the stench—she'd continued eating her disgusting snack, probably thinking he wouldn't notice if she surreptitiously took one out of her pocket and pretended to cover her mouth in a yawn while shoving the stinky thing in her mouth.

"Get out," he said at the kerb.

"Fuck me, rude."

"Yeah, well, those things are rotten. Save them to eat in the evenings. Stink your house out instead of my car."

She thumbed her nose and waltzed up her path, middle finger held up for all to see.

God, she'd be the death of him, but he laughed regardless.

The drive to his place didn't take long, and he parked on the street, greeted by the sound of Rochester's manic barking. Maybe whoever was sending him notes about it was right. There was him telling Florrie to contact Environmental Health, but *his* neighbour had the right to do about to him, too.

He'd look into what he could do online. Some sort of training.

He collected the mutt and drove to the Chinese where he used to live with Lydia. Li Wei, the owner, waved him off as Morgan opened his mouth to order. Yep, the man knew what he'd be having.

He'd sit on the bench for old time's sake and eat his food, then let Rochester off in the field behind for a run. Christ, the times he'd spent here, chewing his dinner and hoping Lydia wouldn't be in such a bitchy mood once he went back home.

He should have left her years ago, but hindsight always had a habit of chirping up to remind you of such things.

Well, hindsight could jog on. Morgan had a new life now, he just had to get around to living it.

Chapter Eighteen

Emma Ingles locked up for the night now it was past curfew, ensuring the main kitchen was also secured so no one raided it for midnight snacks. She'd learnt to do that early on in this job. Money for shopping and the like was only so much from the government funds, and it wasn't like she earnt a fortune to top it up. A man had come to fix the keycode issue she'd had with her security system, and now, if anyone went in or out, *everything* showed on her computer.

She'd asked him why it had stopped working properly, and he'd said someone had overridden it, allowing the resident who'd done it to come and go as he pleased without detection.

Martin Olbey, the hacker. She'd bet he'd been in her office and accessed her computer, changing the system's settings.

She went to her flat situated off the kitchen and turned the key in that door, too, intent on watching a bit of telly in her cosy living room in an attempt to forget the calls.

Like that would happen. They'd always be in her head, her dreams and nightmares, the same as Derek had been when she'd lived with him and again once she'd moved over two hundred miles to get away from him.

Buckinghamshire seemed so long ago now.

She had a warming shower and got into her purple pyjamas and fluffy slippers, wrapping her pink fleece dressing gown around her thin frame. She'd lost weight through worry, and that wasn't a bad thing. Derek didn't like skinny women. He preferred her with a bit of meat on her so no other man would glance her way. If he *did* turn up like he'd threatened, he wouldn't want her anymore.

She settled on her two-seater brown leather sofa and tucked her legs up beneath her, a nice cup of tea balanced on her knee—because tea was always a 'nice' one, wasn't it—her finger curled around the handle. TV on, she selected the Netflix app and browsed for a film, a light-hearted romance maybe, or a comedy to cheer her up. She couldn't remember the last time she'd properly laughed.

Tsk. Someone banged against the fence in the alley. Nothing unusual. Folks drunk from The Tractor's took that route home on their way to Elderflower, staggering all over the place, their passage unnoticed until they emerged at the other end where the streetlight was.

The wind moaned against the windows.

She found what looked like a good film and pressed PLAY.

Something tapped to her right, and she glanced over at the closed curtains, the light from a lamp on the sideboard splashing on the green-and-gold stripy fabric. This room overlooked the back garden, and there was a glass door with small windows either side behind the material.

Must be the wind again.

Although she had to wonder if it was Derek, standing out there on the crazy paving, his face pressed to the glass, hot breaths clouding it.

Stop it.

She listened to the opening credits music.

Another tap, followed by a succession of them.

Someone knocking.

Stomach somersaulting, she switched the TV off and put her cup and the remote on the side table. Up on her feet, she was anxious and automatically brought her hand to her mouth to bite her nails. Should she go and get Ryan, or the other lad on this floor, James? They'd help her if Derek had come, she knew it.

Or should she ring Yeoman, finally tell him what had been going on? Admit to how scared she'd been so he could help? She couldn't keep doing this alone, worrying every five minutes.

Indecision warring inside her, sending her heart into an uneven pounding, she crept over to the lamp and reached beneath the pleated cream shade to switch it off. She'd see outside better in the dark. Standing by the edge of one curtain, she pulled it back a centimetre and peered with one eye into the immediate blackness. A person-sized shape filled the door glass.

She gasped and let the curtain go.

"Emma!"

In her panic, she couldn't place the voice.

Who was that, and what did they want?

"Emma!"

She drew the curtain back again, a couple of inches this time to get a better view. Peered hard. The man had fair-coloured hair, blond or grey or white, she couldn't tell, shown by the light of a full moon now a bulbous dark cloud had shifted from in front of it. Derek's was black—unless he'd dyed it? Whoever it was shouldn't be there, and she guessed he'd climbed over the fence in the alley or at the bottom of the garden—there was no other way to get in.

Was that who she'd thought had banged into it but instead they'd clambered over?

"Emma, I need to talk to you. *Urgently.*"

His muffled voice didn't disguise who it was this time.

What did Oliver Elford want *now*? It could only be bad news, another stupid message from Derek designed to frighten her.

She could crack the window open. Whack him on the head with her heavy silver-plated candlestick she'd bought off the market if he came too close, stun him, then lock the window again. Ring Yeoman. Oliver had moved out after getting a flat in Vicar's Gate, so the copper might intercept him leaving on his way over here. Yeoman lived in Griffin's Holt, so not far.

"Please, Emma, I have to warn you about something. I can't do this anymore. I'm trying to be good after all the bad."

She picked up the candlestick. Unlatched the window. Held the weapon high so he could see it, choose whether he fancied his chances or not. "Do what? Terrorise me?"

"It's about Derek…"

"Of course it is." Anger beat a path to her mouth, and she spat out, "What about him?"

"He'll be here soon, so I have to be quick." He darted his gaze about as if Derek crept up behind him.

Soon? Tonight?

He glanced at the alley fence. Back to her. Whispered, "I was supposed to keep that quiet, but I was sitting at home and thought about it all… I had to let you know. He wants to take you back to Buckinghamshire."

Emma's belly muscles contracted, bringing on a dull ache. "How do you even *know* him?"

"He rang once, when I lived here, and I answered it."

She let out a long breath. That explained it. The communal phone.

Oliver breathed heavily. Was he nervous? Had he been sent here to distract her while Derek broke in and he was on pins and needles waiting for him to appear?

She stared with contempt. "You were stupid to speak to him. He's dangerous. Why do you think I ran away?"

"I didn't know that. He asked about you, what you looked like, and whether I'd watch out for you until he could get here. He said he wanted to surprise you by arriving."

"But that must have been months ago," she said. "Six, in fact." She'd never forget Oliver whispering those dreadful words in the kitchen. "Why didn't he come then?"

"I told him about the police always being here, you know, because of the murders. He said he'd wait—like, he'd waited long enough anyway, so a few more months wouldn't hurt. I had to keep an eye on you in the meantime, but then I moved out and I had to stay outside and catch you through the windows."

No wonder I felt as if someone watched me. "Why did you agree to it? What did you get out of it? Money?"

"No. He asked me my name, and the next time he rang, he said he'd had a private detective onto me and he knew what I'd done, what I was, and if I didn't do as he said, he'd remind everyone of it. That's all behind me now, it was years ago that happened, I was young and I paid my dues for it. All right, I went back into Rushford again for a stint, as you know, but it wasn't for *that*."

Emma couldn't feel sorry for him, not when he'd done what he had, but she understood his desperation to start again. A second chance. After all, she'd tried to do the same thing, and Derek had ruined it, just like he wanted to ruin it for Oliver, too. Regardless of what Oliver liked doing behind closed doors, and that he was only here to save his own skin, he was still here, warning her.

Didn't that count for something?

"Thank you," she said. "What time is he coming?"

"I don't know, but it's tonight. I have to go now. In case he's out there and sees me."

"How is he still in contact with you? You haven't lived here for months."

"I-I gave him my number, my mobile. I'll be changing it, getting a new SIM, because I don't want him bothering me no more."

"But if he's employed a private detective once, he'll do it again. He probably knows where you live now already."

Oliver's face fell.

"Oh, he does, doesn't he?" She sighed. "He won't let you walk away from this knowing what you do about him. He'll drop you in it. I know him, know what he's capable of." She made the decision to give him a lifeline. "Go to The Tractor's, get seen. Stay there until closing, and if Terry has a lock-in, be there for it. You can't let Derek blame you. He mustn't win." *I can't let Derek win.* "Go."

She slammed the window and snapped the curtain across, shaking at the enormity of what Oliver had said. Derek had told her time and again on the phone he was coming for her, and she'd ignored it, thinking he was just scaring her, when all the while, he'd had Oliver keeping tabs.

The sound of feet scuffing on the wooden fence filtered in. Oliver had taken her advice and left the garden.

Unless it was Derek vaulting it.

Oh God…

She looked out again.

No one there.

The smashing of glass in the main house came then, whipping her away from the window, and she rushed to her flat door. All the windows were double glazed apart from the one in the foyer. She remembered watching Martin Olbey through it as he'd walked up the lane the night he'd absconded. If Derek had broken it, he'd be inside by now.

She grabbed her phone, ready to ring Yeoman, shaking and wishing she had the guts to go out there and confront her monster of an ex, but she didn't, so she remained in place, frozen.

Confession

That bitch has a lot to answer for. She left me—how dare she!—and it took me a long time to find her. A PI helped locate her, even though he wasn't supposed to ask his friend in the Deed Poll offices if he could see if she'd changed her name. She had. Emma Ingles. What kind of name is that? No, she's Fiona, my Fiona, and it's about time she realises that. It's time to come home, wife. – Derek Denham

Chapter Nineteen

Derek climbed through the side window into the foyer. It paid to have Oliver on his side. The man had drawn him a crude map of the interior of the property, taking a picture of it and sending it via email once he'd moved out of Halfway and into his cosy little flat. He didn't live in the flat anymore, though, but Derek had found out the latest address.

He knew the layout of that house, too. Oliver was such a plank. Too trusting. Or maybe too afraid not to do whatever was asked of him. He'd walked around his home doing a video of it on his phone, thinking Derek just wanted to see what it was like.

Speckles of glass had settled on his sleeve, a few slivers. Inconvenient. They'd better not pierce him through the jacket fabric or he'd go spare.

He gripped his long knife, the one Wife used to cut his bread with, chop his chicken, his onions, all the things she cooked for him. She'd recognise it by the red handle with the black stripe. He'd sharpened it nicely, the edge wicked enough to do a fair amount of damage if she didn't behave and he had to stab her to show her he meant business.

A door swung open opposite, a splash of light brightening the foyer, a silhouette of a male in white shorts standing in the frame, his hand curled around the door edge. Muscled arms, a beefy shoulder. Strong jaw, the type boxers liked to punch.

Derek didn't have to think about it. He lunged forward, knife out, the blade sinking into the man's abdomen. He withdrew it and stabbed again, stepping back slowly to inch the knife free. Blood gushed, black in the limited light, a stream down his stomach, sinking into the waistband. The fella bent over, still clutching the door with one hand, his belly with the other. Groaning. Panting. Saying, "Fuck. *Fuck*!"

Derek buried the weapon in the busybody's neck, some resistance there, the steel jarring against something, perhaps the top of the spine, or muscles, tendons, he didn't much care.

Busybody gargled, reaching up to clutch the side of his neck and, oh dear, the knife happened to slice two prison-tattooed fingers as Derek eased it out. He slashed at them some more until the man fell to the floor, on his side, hopefully leaving this world in the same position he'd been in just before he'd entered it. Foetal, although this time he'd bleed out, his blood coating the tiles in a pitch-dark puddle.

Derek kicked him in the head.

Along the corridor beside the stairs, he also kicked the door to the kitchen, secured by a simple key lock, easily bashed in if he gave it a few more wallops. He imagined it was Busybody's head and that it burst with every connection, brains splattering.

Someone opened another door behind him, Derek picked up the sound of it, and he turned, waving the knife.

"Back the fuck off," he said to whoever stood there, them indecipherable, no light seeping out of the bedsit, just the parcel of illumination from Busybody's beyond.

"Shit. Right. I don't want any trouble, okay?" The person slammed the door, the noise of bolts being thrown across loud and scraping.

Derek kicked the door again, and it burst open along with the brain imagery in his desperate mind, to reveal the window Oliver had mentioned, and the moon-graced garden with its many washing lines.

Movement to his right, some other bastard coming to investigate, he reckoned, and they paused halfway down the stairs.

"Crap. Ryan?" They took another step.

"Piss off out of it or you'll get much of the same," Derek snarled and entered the kitchen, taking the key to Wife's flat from his pocket.

Oliver had stolen it months ago, getting a copy. He'd returned it to her bunch without her even knowing it had gone. You'd think she'd be more vigilant with criminals about, men who hadn't had a woman for years, and there she was, ripe for the raping, behind her flimsy door in her supposed safe sanctuary.

"Wife!" he barked.

"The police are coming," she shouted. "Get out, Derek."

"Not without you. I've been searching for *years*, woman. I always said you'd never get away. No one leaves me, *no one*."

He inserted the key, and Wife screamed.

Someone banged on the front door, the pounding insistent, maybe that kid who didn't want any trouble but was asking for it by doing that. He probably couldn't get out, forgetting his keycode in panic. Derek glanced over at the hallway door, a murky figure coming at him. He raised the knife, but the person darted at him, and another blade plunged into his face at an upwards angle.

Pain lanced his brain, and he screamed along with Wife, vowing to haunt her from the fucking grave. Follow her, torment her, until she took her own life and joined him.

Chapter Twenty

Florrie couldn't settle. She'd been thinking of Yeoman's visit, plus some bugger had smashed a window somewhere about ten minutes ago, the sound not unusual in these parts. Always people rowing, getting lairy with their fists and punching the glass, usually in the front doors as they weren't double glazed.

Hers would be soon. She felt quite smug about that. Imagine everyone down the lane admiring them, the shiny white uPVC, thinking she thought she'd gone up in the world. A few would say that to her face an' all—"Who do you think *you* are?"—but she'd just give them a gobful and send them on their sorry-arse way, the jealous prats.

Neighbours. Who'd have them.

On cue, 'them next door' started up, having a barney in their front garden if she was any judge. She hefted her large frame out of bed, annoyed Fay had been right. Florrie *had* got fat as the years had gone by, and no, she couldn't get into a bloody dress, not the fitted type anyway. She preferred the ones cruel people called tents. They hid a multitude of sins, like too many crackers with Brie and piccalilli. She'd stopped counting at twelve of them.

At the window, she drew one thick curtain across, plus the net. She'd have to give them a good wash in soda water before she put them back up in front of the new ones. Maybe she'd buy some off the market next week, pristine white and stiff with starch.

She stared outside. The mum and dad went at it, her with a frying pan, him with his hands up, defending himself. She took a couple of swipes, but he blocked her using his forearm. She'd break the bone if she whacked any harder. Looked like that pan was cast-iron.

Florrie opened the window. This was too good to miss. A muffled soundtrack wasn't as good as sharp tones, and they'd be sure to carry on arguing in a second.

"You fucking *shit*!" the woman said.

"Pack it in, Karen."

Ah, so that was her name. Florrie had often wondered.

"Pack it in? Pack it in? I'll chop your piddling cock off if you use it outside of our bedroom again. This is the last time, Ray. Any more of your dirty crap, and you're gone."

Karen and Ray, clearly having marital problems. So Ray was one of those womanisers, cheating on his wife, but Florrie reckoned *she'd* cheat on her if she were him, too. Karen wasn't a nice sort.

Now *his* name rang a bell, and come to think of it, his face did, too. Didn't he used to live in Elderflower? Yes, his mum was called Sheila, and her husband had fucked off and left her—so the story went, but others thought differently. What was Ray doing back in Pinstone?

Yeoman's car flew down the lane, taking Florrie's attention away from the squabbling couple and her thoughts. He parked outside Halfway and approached a small crowd of men out on the path, then they disappeared inside.

What was going on there then?

Karen and Ray stopped fighting to stare.

"You might want to go indoors," Florrie called out. "He's a copper."

"Knob off, you old crow, with your nosy beak in our business." Karen stared up. "Enjoying the show, are you?"

"No, I never do where you're concerned." Florrie tipped her chin up. "I've heard enough coming out of your house to give me cause to ring the social. Those kiddies of yours deserve better, *and* they need to learn some manners. Brought up like a pack of wolves, they are. One of them nearly knocked me over with his bike earlier. I'd have squashed my Brie if I'd landed on my bag."

"Just try it with the social and see what you get, and fuck your cheese." Karen raised the frying pan.

Florrie wasn't afraid of some scabby little bitch giving her threats. She had the perfect plan to get this bunch of scum out of the lane, and in fact, she'd do it now. No time like the present, was there.

She slammed the window and grabbed her dressing gown. Slippers on, she marched downstairs, picked up her keys, and walked out. She'd go to Phil's. Something needed to be done about this lot. Phil had killed Florrie's brother with that cocaine, so turfing her neighbours out for her was the least he could do.

"Look at her gadding about in her pyjamas," Karen said.

"Leave it," Ray warned.

"Don't you tell me to leave it."

"Get indoors. You're making a spectacle of yourself."

"What, like you did with old loose lips in the pub?"

Loose lips?

Oh. She must mean the ones down below.

Such a foul-mouthed woman.

Chapter Twenty-One

Catherine shivered at the sight of the child in her room again. One second Catherine had been lying there reading by the light of the low-watt lamp, the next, she'd caught movement.

She sat up slowly, not wanting to scare her, and smiled as best she could with trembling lips that seemed to have a mind of their own.

"Help me…" The girl hugged herself. "It's so cold."

Catherine didn't think so, but then she was in bed, wasn't she, with her big heavy duvet covering her. "What are you doing here, love?"

"What are *you* doing here?"

"I live here."

"But this is my bedroom."

Catherine shifted the duvet off her and kept her movements calm as she swung her feet to the floor. She stood, her heart thudding. Maybe she ought to press the alarm button beside the bed. At least then a carer would come running and catch the girl. "No kids live here."

"They do. *Lots* of kids do."

It was true, they had, but a long time ago now.

"Not anymore." Catherine took a step forward.

"Help me…"

Then she was gone, just like that, as if she'd never been there.

Bewildered, Catherine moved forward, checking her tiny en suite in case the child had zapped in there so fast she'd missed it.

No little girl.

Catherine frowned. "What in the world?"

Chapter Twenty-Two

Morgan stared at the body of Ryan Vittles on Emma's foyer floor. "What the hell has gone on here?" he asked the lad closest to him.

"Some bloke broke the window and got in. Stabbed Ryan, and when I came out to see what was going on, he threatened me an' all."

"And you are?"

"James."

"Right." Morgan glanced around.

Every resident was there, clogging up the crime scene, their trainers or slippers crunching the glass. Cameron Quinton, the lead SOCO, was going to have one hell of a job on his hands once he arrived. Too many people had tromped through here, someone treading in the edge of Ryan's blood puddle, trailing bleeding footprints, and with them shuffling around right this minute, the glass scattered to all corners.

"Give me a second." He phoned the murder in to Amanda Cartwright on the front desk, then messaged Shaz to get her arse off her sofa and come round because there was a 'problem' and 'make sure you put on protectives from my boot'. Phone in his pocket, he eyed the lads. "Okay, all of you back to your bedsits to get changed. I need your clothes and footwear in carrier bags—and write your name on the bags, and your room number. They'll need to be taken in as evidence, even if none of you went near Ryan or had anything to do with this."

One of them stepped forward from behind two others. "I...I've got blood all over me." He appeared about twenty-five.

"Okay, you stay here. The rest of you, do as I said."

They dispersed, leaving the lad with blood by the stairs and Morgan beside the body of a young man, someone Emma had sworn was on the right track now, and look at him, dead on the sodding tiles, stab wounds to the abdomen and neck, his fingers sliced.

Shit. Fingers. Did this intruder attack Fay Williams? Didn't he manage to finish the job here by chopping them off completely? No time?

"Emma?" he called out.

No response.

"Stay there, son." He pointed at the young man and walked through to the kitchen, and oh, fucking hell, another body by her flat door. He returned to the foyer, his guts going over, mind spinning. "What's your name?"

"Lenny."

"Okay, Lenny. Did you do that in the kitchen?"

"Yeah. He had a knife; he was going to stab me."

"Who is he?"

"I don't know. He's the one who shivved Ryan. I came down from upstairs, saw Ryan on the floor, and that bloke told me to piss off out of it, saying something like I'd get the same. I followed him, and he was going to break into Emma's flat."

"It's Derek." Emma, voice weak.

Morgan spun to face her, blocking any sight of Ryan. "Are you all right?"

She nodded.

"Self-defence then, understand?" Morgan said to Lenny over his shoulder.

"It was anyway, it's not a lie." Lenny sounded affronted.

"Didn't suggest you should lie." He had, but whatever. He'd heard bits and bobs about Derek from Emma, and it wasn't a hardship the man was dead. "Don't wash or anything, Lenny. SOCO will need to take photos of the blood."

"Yep."

"I watched it," Emma said. "I opened my flat door a bit and saw it all through the crack." She stared at Lenny, in that way where you're willing someone to really understand what you said beneath the words you spoke: *I'll back you up.* "Derek was after killing him."

"I didn't see you," Lenny said. "It was all so quick. I was more bothered about him sticking me or getting in your flat."

No conspiracy going on between them then. If there was, Lenny would have agreed with her. Emma must think a lot of Lenny if she was willing to lie for him. Maybe she had it right with this one and he wasn't going to return to crime once he left here.

"You can tell this to the uniforms when they turn up to take statements." Morgan sighed, thinking of another long night.

There was a shitload to sort out here, but he could leave it to Cameron if he had a mind. A soak in the bath and a series on Amazon had been the order of his evening until this, and he wished he were back home. The thought of Rochester barking at this time of night bothered him. The neighbours really didn't need the noise. Nothing he could do about it at the moment, though.

"I have to speak to you." Emma retreated into the kitchen.

Morgan followed, leaving the door exactly where it was for forensics.

"Oliver Elford came to warn me," she whispered.

"What, that Derek was coming? How did *he* know?"

She explained what Oliver had said to her earlier in the garden. "So he felt he had to do it. He had no choice. I didn't tell you half of what Derek is like, so you wouldn't understand how he can scare people into doing what he wants."

Morgan thought of Jane Blessing frightening people. "Did Oliver ever harm you when he lived here or after he moved out?"

She shook her head. "No, he just gave me the creeps, then round about the time of the murders, you know, Delia and everyone, he told me 'Derek sends his regards'."

"Is that why you've been so jittery lately?"

She knotted her fingers. "Yes."

"Why not tell me then? If you were worried Derek had found out where you were, we could have got you moved, another new name."

"I know, I just… I thought I could handle it until the phone calls started."

"Phone calls?" *Why the hell did she keep that to herself?*

"Derek's been ringing me, and Ryan offered to answer the phone, tell him to go away or whatever, but I didn't want him involved."

"He *did* get involved, though."

"What do you mean?"

"Looks like he came out of his bedsit after Derek smashed the window. He's been stabbed, love."

Her eyes rounded and filled with tears, and she clutched at her throat. "What? Where is he?"

He moved her along so she couldn't see past him into the foyer. "You don't want to see."

"Is he all right?"

"He's dead, Emma."

"Oh God..."

She crumpled to the floor and, damn him, he checked if she'd bodged the scene up by doing so. No, she was okay there, so long as she didn't move anywhere else.

"Were the lights on at the time of this happening?" he asked. "The foyer and the kitchen?"

"No, it was dark."

So someone had switched them on. Great. He'd have to let Cameron know.

"Morg?"

He moved away from a sobbing Emma to the door and stared through to the front. Shaz stood there on the outside step, gloves on, protective suit, booties. A copse of what appeared at first as birch trees stood behind her outside, but it was SOCOs standing side-on, their white suits striped by shadows from the branches on a tree in the garden, similar to the black slashes of birch trunks.

"May as well come in. Lenny, go in the living room, mate." Morgan led the lad there. "Now, don't go worrying. You won't go down for this."

"No, because I didn't do it on purpose. Like, I didn't plan to kill him."

"I know. Hang tight. I'll get someone to speak to you in a minute. We'll get the photos done, then you can get those boxers and slippers off and have a shower. You'll need fingerprinting. What knife did you use?"

"It's from the kitchen. I dropped it on the floor."

"Rightio." Morgan went back into the foyer and addressed everyone. "IC1 male here in the hallway, stabbed by IC1 male in the kitchen. A lad called Lenny, he's in the living room, stabbed the bloke in the kitchen in self-defence—Emma witnessed it." He spotted uniforms appearing in the doorway. "I need one of you to get a statement off Lenny. Photos and fingerprints need to be done ASAP so he can get the blood off. Can't be nice for him. It goes tight when it's dried. Offer counselling if you think he'll benefit from it. Emma needs to give her statement, as do the other residents, and get their fingerprints, too, because someone switched the lights on. Busy night, lads."

Everyone spread out, and Morgan took Shaz into the kitchen and stood beside Emma.

"What's happened in here?" Shaz asked. "Are you hurt, Emma?"

She gazed up at them from the floor, a small smile creeping through the tears. "Derek's dead. Oh, thank God, he's dead."

Shaz gave Morgan an 'ooer' look. "Okay…"

Morgan ignored her. She didn't know much about Derek. If she did, she'd understand.

"Emma, we need to nip off now Cameron's here. If you can go into the living room, you'll need to give a statement, including Oliver Elford coming here."

"What?" Shaz's eyebrows drew together. She must have had a wash after work as they were normal ones, just hair, none of that bloody pencil business.

"I'll explain on the way to his house. Emma, you must have his address?"

"A flat in Vicar's Gate, number three. That's what he gave me—I checked it with the council as well, so he wasn't lying." She wiped her face and glanced over at her ex. "Fucking rot in Hell, you bastard." Up on her feet, she left the kitchen and disappeared into the living room.

"Blimey," Shaz said. "Is she okay up top? I've never seen her act like that before, all venomous and shit."

"He was a wanker to her. I don't blame her one bit. She can stay here now, not live in fear."

"What the hell went on?"

"I'll tell you in the car. Come on." He walked into the foyer.

Cameron crouched by Ryan. "If he hadn't been stabbed in the neck, I'd say he'd have lived. Lisa will know for sure."

"Thought the same myself. I'll leave the scene in your hands. We have to follow up on a lead." Morgan strode out, signed the log with the officer stationed in the front garden, and took a deep breath of fresh, biting air.

Lisa, the ME, had parked at the kerb, so he waved at her and went to his own vehicle.

She got out and ambled to her boot, probably to get her bag. "Stabbing, yes?"

Morgan nodded. "Two of the buggers."

"Lovely. That's me sorted tomorrow then. And to think I got excited after work because I've cleared the morgue decks. Mind you, there's bound to be non-criminal deaths overnight."

"No rest for the wicked," he said.

"Oi, what are you trying to say?"

"I wasn't trying." He grinned, got in the driver's seat, and waited for Shaz to take her protectives off at the front door.

She dropped them into a bag the officer held out then made her way over, flopping into the vehicle, sighing while she was at it. "Right, why do we need to see Elford?"

Morgan glanced down the lane. A lot of the neighbours were out, gawping.

He drove off and related what Emma had said.

"Bloody hell, the sneaky little shit. I thought everyone already knew what he got up to in the past, that's why they give him a wide berth. No need to worry whether Derek spreads it about."

"Maybe Elford's thinking only the older generation know."

"I'm not old and I know."

"Yep, but I bet your nan or grandad mentioned it."

"Hmm. I've always known as far back as I can remember, but I suppose if someone like him comes up on the news, families talk. Stories get passed down."

"Yes, so if he thinks younger folks don't know, he's a bit dim in the head."

He turned into Vicar's and parked outside the flats. They headed over there, and Morgan knocked on number three. A bottle-blonde woman answered, must be about twenty, a scrawny kid on her hip. He needed a good bath, chocolate all over his mush.

"I haven't done nothing," she slurred.

Morgan bit his tongue, waiting for Shaz to correct her grammar, then, "Didn't say you had, did I? Is Oliver in?"

"Who?"

"Oliver Elford."

"What, the kiddie fiddler? Fuck is he. Like I'd let him near any of my kids."

"I was told he lived here."

"Used to. This is a temporary flat before you get a proper house. His post still comes here, so if you find him, tell him to put in a bloody redirection."

"Do you have the post?"

"Nope, it goes in the bin—the wheelie bin out there, because I won't even have his name in this place."

"Okay, thanks for your time."

She shut the door, and Morgan took his phone out to ring Emma. She didn't answer—her mobile was probably in her flat, and she wouldn't be allowed near Derek's body to get it—so he tried the communal phone at Halfway.

"Cameron Quinton."

"It's Morgan. Can you put Emma Ingles on, mate?"

The phone exchanged hands with a muffled bump and shuffle.

"Yes?"

"It's Yeoman. Oliver doesn't live in the flat anymore."

"Oh. He'll...he'll have gone to The Tractor's. I told him to in case Derek tried to blame him for...for this mess."

"Cheers." Morgan slid his phone away.

Two minutes later, they were in the pub, Terry holding court at one end of the bar with a load of cronies, while Heidi, his server, worked her arse off pulling pints. A scan of the area showed Oliver tucked in a corner, sipping an orange juice, which may or may not have gin or vodka in it. His eyes grew wide upon him spotting them, and Morgan held up a hand to placate him. Oliver relaxed and settled back.

Morgan and Shaz sat at his table.

"We know what happened," Morgan said, deliberately leaving out the fact that they also knew Oliver hadn't done it.

"Has he said it was me? Is Emma all right?"

"Emma's fine." Morgan lowered his voice. "But Derek's dead, so no need to worry about him anymore. We are going to need you down the station to give a statement, though, explaining what you've been getting up to. Tonight would be best."

"I didn't do anything but pass on a message." He looked shifty, as if he'd done a lot more than that. "All right, I gave him a key to Emma's flat an' all. I shouldn't have, I know that, but he was insistent, and he'd have killed me if I didn't, I know it."

"Right, I need your address, and don't palm me off with the flat in Vicar's."

Oliver blinked. "I thought you'd know it already."

"Why would I?"

"Because I'm your next-door bloody neighbour."

Chapter Twenty-Three

1991

Fay tended to the vegetable patch to the left of the courtyard while Helen and Oliver entertained the children. At forty-six, she winced with every bend and stretch, tilling the earth, which was waterlogged, but Helen insisted it needed turning over regardless. It was all right for her, she was only thirty-two and wouldn't feel the pain as much. Or Oliver would be better, only just twenty-eight, his birthday last week, and Helen had made such a lovely cake, icing it and piping his name on top in blue.

But Fay had said she'd do the garden, so she shouldn't complain. Ivy had been a particularly irritating cow all day, bored with no school, it being a Saturday, taunting the others to instigate a bickering session. If Fay went near her at the moment, she was likely to give her one of those slaps Oliver was so fond of mentioning.

Eight-year-old Billy, though, she'd love to spend time with him, but Ivy's comment about him being Fay's favourite had twanged a sensitive chord, one that stuck in Fay's throat, a wicked thistle, threatening to choke her. She had to be careful how she acted around him. If Ivy had noticed, the other children might, and Fay wouldn't want them to feel left out. She loved them, too, just not Ivy.

Poison Ivy.

She stabbed at the too-hard ground with the rake, the chatter and laughter from the children a balm to that thistle, chipping off the pointed tips of the thorns. She stopped and peered over her shoulder, leaning on the top of the rake handle for support. God, her lower back ached. The kids ran around, dodging Oliver who threw a small bag of beans at them—well, a little pouch containing dried peas Helen had sewn the other night. If the bag hit them, they were 'out'.

Ivy wasn't playing.

Of course she bloody wasn't.

Fay gritted her teeth and stared at her, letting anger shift up from her toes to her head, infusing her cheeks with heat. Ivy leant against the wall beside the door, the one that led into the utility room. She had a leg bent, her foot pressed to the bricks, her arms folded. Her scarlet jacket stood out, something Fay had bought her on purpose—so she could spot her amongst the others, causing trouble. Red for danger. Everyone else had grey or blue. Oh, except Billy, who had a fetching bright green. No guessing why he had a striking colour, too. Fay could also watch whether green and red were close together, Ivy picking on the sweet boy.

She was such a horrible child.

Fay returned to her work so she didn't get het up, go over there, and wallop Ivy with the rake, the spikes digging into her brain. Anyway, hopefully no one would have to put up with the wretch for much longer. Someone was coming for an interview on Monday for Ivy, a Welsh couple who wanted to bring her up in a lovely village, give her some peace and quiet, time to settle.

Ivy could take that bloody coat with her. Fay never wanted to see it again.

The prospective parents sounded ideal on paper and over the phone, but Fay had entertained scenarios of Ivy rampaging through the lanes in the silent valleys, her coat a crimson streak of menace, alerting anyone and everyone that she was coming, trouble and evil all rolled into one. If the couple decided Ivy was too much for them, she'd be coming back to Loving Arms. They were fostering her first, to "give her a try" and "see if we're compatible". No one would be compatible with that nasty brat, so Fay wasn't holding her breath for a happy ending.

She glanced at the sky and nodded to Helen.

"Come on now," Helen called. "Everyone inside. Looks like the rain's on its way back." She clapped and chased the kids towards the door.

More laughter.

It was good to hear. Those poor souls had the most dreadful lives prior to coming here. She hoped they were truly happy and it wasn't just a façade they pressed themselves into each morning, a suit of armour, pretending everything was hunky-dory when it wasn't.

Ivy was the last inside, and their gazes locked. The child stuck her two fingers up then vanished into the house.

Fay's temper rose. "Why, you fucking…"

She zipped her mouth closed. No. She wouldn't finish that sentence. Wouldn't let Florrie's mini doppelganger upset her.

She turned back to the veg patch, and a mulish mood came over her. Rake propped against the wall—sod the gardening when the ground was so unyielding—she walked out of the courtyard and into the grounds, thinking to stroll on the field for a while, perhaps around the edge to calm her nerves. Helen could manage the children for half an hour, giving them beakers of fizzy pop and the iced buns she'd baked this morning, an afternoon snack that wouldn't spoil their dinner, which was at six.

Head bent, hands in pockets, she set off, and the splatter of rain landed on her head. She glanced up—was that snow as well? And what was that? A figure coming across the moor? A man, she reckoned, going by the size and shape, maybe drunk from being in the pub and straying this way by accident. She'd soon tell him where to go, and if he got mouthy, she'd run back to the courtyard and shut the big gates with their iron poles, snapping the padlock into place.

At the end of the first edge, he came close, a young fella, early twenties. Nice enough to look at, blond, a bit of a big nose, but you couldn't get lucky all the time, could you.

"Seems like you need the grass cut." He gestured to the field.

Yes, they did, but the three of them had enough to do without getting the ride-along mower out of the storage garage and driving it up and down. Oliver was in the process of replacing all the plastic U-bends under the sinks in the bathrooms, and his next job was to exchange the old bath taps for new ones. Everything here was so dated and old. And why cut the grass in this weather anyway? If the predicted snow came, it would get covered up.

"We have a man for that, thank you." *She turned and headed back towards the house.*

He loped alongside her. "It's just that I'm after a job. My boss let me go, see, and I need some money so I can set up my own business."

"And what's that?"

"I make masks."

She frowned at him.

"For plays and stuff. I was with the troupe here, but they've decided to buy masks now instead of me making them specific, like. I used to help out with the costumes an' all. I'm good with a sewing needle, so..." *He shrugged.* "Got enough cash for a room in that pub back there for a couple of weeks, but I'd need to find something more permanent. The landlord suggested I come over, see if you want anyone."

"I know someone who's renting out a room. Pinstone, the town just over there." *She pointed across the moor at the many houses and buildings. "I can give you her number, if you like?"*

"That'd be great. But can I cut your grass before the snow settles?"

"You'd need to go through a check. This is a children's home."

His eyes lit up. "Is it? I like kids."

She smiled. He seemed amenable enough, and if she didn't have rules to follow and the children to protect, she'd invite him in for a cup of tea and a warm by the fire, but she couldn't.

They'd reached the gates.

"If you could just wait here, I'll write that number down for you and bring it back out." She clomped through the courtyard, getting soaked now, the rain-and-snow mix coming down harder.

In the kitchen, her unconventional family stood in a line at the sink to wash their hands, some of them sucking icing off their fingers.

Fay went to the Welsh dresser and scribbled the number down on a pad, then stepped back outside, heading for the gates.

The man wasn't there.

"Oh. Now where's he gone?"

That was a worry. He wasn't allowed on the grounds, so if he'd come past those gates…

Movement, and she turned to her left. He was on the vegetable patch, pulling out weeds, although he only managed to get the tops and not the roots, stuck as they were beneath the ground. Quite a handy man to have around. Maybe she'd try to sort him employment after all.

She rushed over there. "Excuse me, you can't be here. The children…"

He stood straight and dropped a weed on the mud. "Sorry."

"Look, here's the number. It's a lady called Mrs King. Tell her Fay sent you. And could I have your name and date of birth? I can ask my boss to run a check, and if it comes back clear, you can be the gardener, perhaps do a bit of painting on the outside doorframes once this weather buggers off. And there's always sewing. The kids need hems taking down. Maybe you can help Helen make the new curtains we have planned."

"They grow as quick as them weeds, kids." *He smiled, showing off strange, half-sized teeth.*

Fay shivered but brushed it off. He couldn't help his nose or his teeth, she had to firmly remind herself of that. It wasn't like she was an oil painting, so she shouldn't think snide thoughts.

"I'll pop back then, shall I?" *he asked.*

"Yes, this time next week? I should know something by then."

"Brilliant." He flashed his gnashers again and walked through the open gates, vanishing into the mist that had rolled off the moor and onto the field.

A chill fizzled down her back, and Fay fancied someone had walked over her grave, but that was silly. It was just the rain and snow sneaking beneath her coat collar.

Confession

It's quite fascinating how Yeoman has cowed down in the last six months since I made him aware I know exactly what he gets up to. I feel more of an equal, someone he can't order around anymore, and I'm important instead of the woman who irritates him. I still do that—on purpose—and I think he knows it. It's fun, playing with him. Gives me something to look forward to each day. And then there are the nights. Shame he wasn't happy about me scaring Terry. Not that I give a shit. I'll do what I bloody well like, thank you very much. Just like he does. –
Jane Blessing

Chapter Twenty-Four

Jane had come into work earlier than usual at six a.m. and searched the records. She'd found Oliver's past and itched to tell Yeoman about it. They knew Oliver was a pervert already, but not that he'd worked at Loving Arms from nineteen ninety until he'd got caught with a young girl in Pinstone. He'd been put away for a while for that, served his time, and came out, back into society with the weirdo tag attached to him and people giving him funny looks.

He'd just done a recent stint in Rushford for his part in robbing the electrical shop in town—men with a van and the equipment to remove fridges, freezers, and the odd cooker.

He was released six months ago and lived in Halfway for a while.

But the main thing to take out of this was, he knew Fay Williams. At fifty-seven, to some eyes, he could be classed as old. Yeoman had put in a report that Billy Price had witnessed the man coming and going along Regency—so wouldn't he have recognised him as Oliver, seeing as Billy had been in Loving Arms for years?

The most interesting bit, though, was finding out about the disappearance of the girl in ninety-one yesterday.

A girl. Oliver's favourite gender.

She continued to read the file to see where he fitted in that scenario.

Oliver needed a talking to. She'd have to scare him with her knife later.

Chapter Twenty-Five

At seven a.m., Catherine woke with a start. She sat up and looked around, worried the girl had come back. Worried she really *had* imagined all three sightings of her. It was silly to think a child could just walk in this room, let alone the care home itself. Liz and the other staff would have stopped her as soon as they'd spotted her, asking her name and where her mum was.

Catherine managed a shower and dressed, making her way down to the dining room for breakfast at eight. It'd be the usual menu: eggs on toast, toast and jam, toast and marmalade, toast with bloody everything. She sat by herself at the end of the long table, away from George who had a habit of clacking his teeth while he chomped.

She minded her own business, spreading butter from the little individual plastic pots with the lids you had to peel back, difficult with arthritis, then doing the same with the ones for jam. Rule four: No raspberry jam! The pips got between your teeth or beneath dentures, apparently.

"Fuck's sake," Catherine whispered. Anyone would think they were babies the way they were treated.

She munched her toast, and her mind did that thing where reality faded and she lived in the past for a speck of time which seemed to go on forever, everything around her as it might have been back then, a strange environment, somewhere she'd never been prior to living here.

Children sat around the table, and a younger Fay Williams passed out plates while Helen Donaldson brought in her three-tiered trolley stacked with pots of food. Catherine scanned the faces of the kids, and oh goodness, there sat the girl from her room.

"Stop fidgeting, Ivy," Fay said.

She always had been waspish, right from when Catherine had been in her class at school. *And* she'd had a baby out of wedlock. That just wasn't on in those days, and shame had enveloped Fay, turning her into a sour individual. Add the death of her baby to the mix, and the woman was positively shrivelled in piss and vinegar.

Ivy stared across at Catherine. "Help me…"

Catherine rose to walk around the table, but she caught her thigh on the corner and went tumbling down. She landed on her side, banging her temple on the floor. It hurt, and she reached up to rub it.

"That's what happened to me," Ivy said. "I banged my temple, too."

Catherine struggled to sit up, and pain lanced her hip. She scrunched her eyes closed, and when she opened them again, she was back in the care home dining room, Liz on the floor with her, asking if she was all right.

"Ivy," Catherine said. "It was Ivy."

"Who is?" Liz asked.

"The girl in the nightdress. I remember it now."

And she did. Every horrific moment of that section in her past. The police on the moor. The articles in the paper. Thinking it was her son who'd done that terrible thing.

Catherine cried.

How on earth had she seen a child when she must be in her thirties by now?

It didn't make sense. None of it.

Chapter Twenty-Six

1991

Noah Tate, his name was, the lad who'd come to cut the grass. His background check had gone through fine, and he was allowed on the grounds and in the kitchen and living room for now. Fay was to keep an eye on him, see how he interacted with the children, and if after a few months he was still the nice young man he presented to them at the start, he'd be allowed to live in.

He'd been with them for a while now, beginning in the cold end of winter in February, temperatures not going above freezing between the fifth and the tenth, a dreadful cold spell with awful snowfall that meant the radiators were on day and night. The kids couldn't go outside, the snow too deep to play in, so activities remained indoors.

Oliver had promised to use the shovel to completely clear the courtyard, but the snow had come down so thick and fast, he'd be wasting his time. He'd managed to tunnel a path from the utility door to the gates, though, and he'd kept it free of the white stuff each day. The road to Pinstone was blocked, so no school. Fay and Helen occupied the kids as much as possible, creating a classroom of sorts in the dining room.

Noah had worked through the summer. He'd broadened the vegetable patch and planted things they previously hadn't had: cucumbers, peas, and the lovely soft-leafed lettuces that made for a good salad. New potatoes, too, and they ate them cold with mayonnaise and a dash of garlic salt. Noah had joked it would keep the vampires away, and all the children had bared their pretend fangs.

But that had passed now, and the dreary weather in this late-autumn week meant the children had to play in the courtyard after school in their coats, hoods up, the monotonous, steady rain punctured with teasing snippets of sparse sunshine that gave no heat, just light, but the moor had gone boggy, so no exercising on there with the usual brisk walks.

And it was cold.

And Ivy was still bloody here.

She'd been to Wales and played up, as Fay had known she would, behaving worse than at Loving Arms. At her new home, she'd broken a plate by throwing it, complete with her dinner on top, raging at her foster parents that Helen used to give her iced biscuits, so you'd better give me one right now, you bitch and fucker! The poor mother, distraught, had taken a digestive out of a packet and made icing, but Ivy wanted the homemade shortbreads, and if you don't give it to me, I'm going to bite you in your sleep.

This and so many other things.

Oliver hadn't been his usual self in her absence, morose, dragging his feet, barely a smile, even when something was hysterical. He seemed faraway in his head, absent-minded, eyes glassy, and if Fay asked him a question, he took a moment to register it, blinking in that sluggish-lidded way of his.

The sight of Ivy walking back into the courtyard accompanied by a social worker all but broke the heart Fay had stitched back together since her departure, with threads of love and no room for the awful thoughts she'd had when Ivy had previously lived there. Now, one of those threads had popped free, the fibres filled with hatred and animosity, ready to curl around Ivy's neck and throttle her.

Fay blinked away the image of that thread and stared around the kitchen table. It was the pre-bedtime ritual once again, kids munching on those shortbreads with icing Ivy loved so much, Helen making them more often than usual to "let Ivy know we love her". Tonight they had Horlicks, something the little cow had been given in Wales and decided they should all have it.

She governed things far too much for Fay's liking with her temper tantrums and wheedling, but Oliver was happy again, back to normal. Helen seemed happier with Ivy there, too, and Fay had to question her feelings once again.

Was Ivy really a bad child? Or was Fay only seeing her as Florrie?

Helen ushered the brood to bed tonight, and Fay took on the washing up. She stared out through the gates at the moor, thinking of Noah still living at Mrs King's and how he'd taken to Billy as much as she had. They spent time together, in the same room as everyone else, mind, but separate, in a corner, Billy drawn to him for some reason. Noah laughed a lot, throwing his head back and displaying his weird tiny teeth. Fay was jealous, she couldn't deny it, but if she thought of Billy as her son, she should want the boy to have as many good adult figures in his life as possible, so she pushed that mean emotion down as much as she could and smiled through her envious turmoil, spun into a tornado from observing Noah and Billy.

She'd finished the washing up by the time Helen came back down, and they sat at the table with their own cups of Horlicks and the remaining shortbreads, Oliver joining them, talking about their day.

Such a happy family, albeit with that horrible child a blot on the landscape.

The tidying of the house didn't take long with the three of them doing it, and they spent the rest of the evening in the living room, watching telly.

At ten, Fay declared it a night and made her weary way up to her room on the right-hand landing. Helen's was next to hers, while Oliver was down the end. Maybe Noah could move in now if the authorities allowed it. It would be nice to properly welcome him into the fold.

Fay fell asleep quickly, only to be awakened at two o'clock by one of the children crying, more of a weep, a soft whimper. Helen used cotton wool in her ears so she wouldn't hear it, and it was Fay's job to see to them overnight anyway. She got up, groggy, and wandered down to the left-hand landing, the weeping getting steadier, then a long moan.

Ivy.

She didn't rush in there once she realised it was her, and almost turned back to go to her own room, leaving her to it, but another moan scarpered out beneath the bedroom door, so Fay placed her hand on the knob, poised to go in. She didn't want Billy having disturbed sleep.

"Shh!" someone said. "No one can know. I told you, it's our private time. You're moaning a bit too loud."

What was Oliver doing in there, and what was he talking about?

Angry he'd crossed a line, muscling in on her job, she burst in, ready to send him back to his room—and she'd be having words with him in the morning. He wasn't employed to deal with the children in this way.

Oliver was on the bed, naked, staring at Ivy, entranced, in a daze.

Ivy stood beside it, her white dressing gown with the pink flowers ruched up around her waist, her lower half bare, on wretched, illegal display, still creating creepy moaning sounds with no tears.

Fay shut the door quietly behind her so as not to wake the other children. "What the hell *are you doing, Oliver?"*

He gasped and jumped, snapped out of his fugue, and scrambled off the bed, covering his disgusting erection. "I…I was…I heard her crying."

"So you came in here without any clothes on?" she hissed.

"I wasn't crying, I was moaning like Oliver told me. Get out, you," Ivy said to Fay, cuffing her streaming nose with her wrist.

Stunned, Fay remained silent for a moment. "I beg your pardon, young lady?"

"I said get out. It's cuddle time, and I like it."

"Leave, Oliver." Fay stared at him. "I'm going to have to phone the police."

"No!" Ivy raced towards Fay, hands up, fingers curved into hooks, and launched herself at her.

She leapt and wrapped her legs around Fay's waist, clinging on, trying to bite Fay's cheek, the feral animal. Spittle sprayed out with her snarling, and Fay saw redder than she ever had before. This revolting scene plus Ivy talking to her like that was just not on. She gripped Ivy's arms and peeled the bitch off her, throwing her across the room and loving it. Ivy landed on the floor, and her temple bashed on the radiator knob that controlled the heat.

She slumped, glaring at Fay, crying, her hand over the sore spot. An immediate bruise showed between her splayed fingers. "I hate you, you fucking fat cow."

Florrie, she was Florrie all over again, the baby killer, and Fay couldn't stand it. She advanced on the brat, almost floating to her knees in a dreamlike state, and placed her hands around her neck, squeezing, allowing that loose thread in her heart to direct the pressure, harder, tighter. She vaguely caught Oliver saying, "What are you doing? Fay, stop it, for Christ's sake, stop it!" but ignored him, ignored the desperate clawing of Ivy's brittle fingers that would snap if Fay twisted them backwards.

Oliver pulled Fay, but her hands and arms locked. They grappled for what seemed a long time, and Fay couldn't let go. Ivy's arms dropped to the floor, the child's eyes red, bulbous, glaring at her in accusation: You murdered me!

It penetrated Fay's demented stupor, and she sprang away, letting her go, and scrabbled backwards, pressing herself against the wall.

Oliver crouched beside Ivy and stroked her hair, sobbing. "Oh God, what have you done? Oh God... My precious." And he turned to Fay, venom in his eyes, and whispered, "She was going to be my wife when she grew up, and you killed her."

Fay's heart throbbed, too hard, and her lungs wouldn't allow any air in. "Oh shit... You're vile."

"I'll be ringing the police, not you," he said.

Fay's mettle came back, stiffening her spine. "If you do, I'll tell them what I caught you doing. I'll bloody lock you in here with her and say you *strangled her."*

"No…no." *He curled a lock of Ivy's hair around his finger. "Oh fucking hell, what are we going to do?"*

Fay stood to her full height, pushing her shoulders back. "What else can *we do but take her across the moor?"*

Chapter Twenty-Seven

Early for once, Morgan walked into the incident room, surprised Jane was in already.

"Guess what?" She pounced, standing from her desk and walking towards him.

Fucking hell, first thing of a morning, she wasn't someone he needed in his face. He envied Shaz going to the kitchen to make a coffee. That had been his plan an' all, but clearly, Jane had other ideas. She'd ambush without a thought to him needing a bit more wake-up time.

"I came in to get some things done in peace." Jane clasped her hands up by her chin in one fist. "I couldn't sleep with thinking about Oliver and doing a proper, deep background check on him."

He wasn't going to fuck about playing games with her today. "You've obviously found something, so spit it out."

"He used to work at Loving Arms around the time that Ivy girl went missing. A *girl*, Yeoman."

"Oh." *Shit*.

Jane's face exploded into a smug expression. "Yes, so he could have had something to do with it. Paedo with access to children—not bloody good. Don't you think it's weird he wasn't in any of the papers regarding the child? Fay said something to reporters, as did Helen, so why not him?"

"Maybe because he knew where his perversions were directed, he thought other people might guess what was in his sicko head, so he decided to stay out of the way. Or maybe he wasn't even asked for a snippet."

"*Or* he was involved and didn't want to slip up, which is more likely. I found the police report. He's listed as being there, interviewed. Said he slept through the night, as did Helen. Get this, though. Fay was awake, and so was Billy Price."

Morgan frowned. "Did she state any reason for that?"

Jane pulled a 'I know and you don't' face. "She had trouble sleeping so got up to clean some wellies. *Wellies*? I mean, really?"

"Why would she need to clean them?"

"Exactly. Maybe she was actually out on the moor that night—the wellies had got dirty."

"And Billy?"

"He had a nightmare."

"Par for the course with kids. I should imagine she had a few nights where she didn't get much kip. The sort in Arms would be troubled, have more than a few issues."

"Hmm. She stated she sent Billy back to bed and went up herself an hour later—and *didn't* check any of the other children beforehand."

"Why would you if you think the place is locked up tight?"

"True. But what if she saw someone taking Ivy and just didn't say?"

Morgan considered that. "What, and risk losing her job? Would she even allow someone to just take her? I suppose if she was threatened with a weapon... All right, so why wait all these years for that person to do something about that?"

"Prison, or he could have moved away and the return here set him off." She tapped her cheek with one finger.

Jane was far too close for his liking, so he stepped back.

He stared over at the whiteboard so he didn't have to look at her. "Like I said before, I don't think it's likely the child walked out by herself, even with the stool placed by the door and her supposedly climbing up to unbolt the top. So with this new info coming to light about Fay being awake, maybe she did it and someone found out years later. That sounds more plausible."

She stepped into his line of sight, arms folded. "Something doesn't feel right about it regardless, you said that yourself, which is why you're visiting the copper in that article today, and the reporter. I took the liberty of giving them a ring to make sure they'll be in all day. They will." She reached over to her desk for a Post-it and handed it to him.

"Thanks. Anything else?" He looked at the note. Addresses.

"I suggest another visit to Oliver, see if he recalls anything about Ivy Gibbs."

There she goes again, acting DI. "On my list. I'm nipping to Helen's first thing to see if she can shed any light on it before we tackle him. D'you know, he's my next-door neighbour, and I didn't have a bloody clue. He moved there after the temporary flat in Vicar's."

Her eyes widened, as if she'd thought otherwise and him telling her meant something he might not want to know about. "That wasn't updated in the records. And do you not take any notice of your surroundings or what?" She stared at him. "Not good."

"I haven't been there that long, remember, and I'm at work more often than not. By the time I get home, I take the dog out in the dark, come back, and eat. I leave early every morning. Oliver strikes me as a bloke who likes a lie-in, so there's no chance of me seeing him." *Why am I explaining myself to her?*

"Fair enough, but be more vigilant in future." She leant forward to whisper, "Because anyone could come up to you with a knife." She flounced off to her desk and sat, eyeing him over her monitor.

Was that a threat? Did she intend on scaring *him* with her blade? What would he do if she did, report her?

Bloody nutter.

Shaz came out of the kitchen, a coffee in a to-go cup. "Are we ready for the off then?"

Morgan nodded. "Helen's, the reporter and copper from the nineties, then Oliver's."

"Busy day then." Shaz took a sip. "I'll need this caffeine."

Nigel entered, sloping across to his desk. "Morning. Bloody hell, I'm the last one in." He glanced at his watch. "Nope, not late. What did you all do, shit the bed?"

"Not that I'm aware." Morgan smiled. "You're on the rest of the kids from Loving Arms this morning, aren't you?"

Nigel sat. "Yep, and I did the profile last night." He handed out some A4 paper with the details on it. "Bear that in mind when you're talking to suspects. He's a dangerous fella."

Morgan chuffed out air. "We gathered that. People who cut off tongues and chop fingers tend to be."

"You know what I meant." Nigel booted up his computer. "He's unhinged."

"Right, we're off." Morgan held a hand up to say goodbye and walked out.

He drove them to Regency and parked outside Helen's. It wasn't even nine o'clock yet, but maybe she was up. At the door, he knocked and checked up and down the street. Billy's van was down the way, so he reckoned they may as well go and visit him afterwards, see if he recalled anything about Oliver.

The door opened, and the scent of food wafted out. A stew? Bread? Whatever it was set his stomach rumbling. He hadn't been in the mood for breakfast.

Shaz whispered, "Bloody yum."

"Oh, hello." Helen smiled.

"Excuse the early hour. We just need to have a chat." Morgan gave her a smile back.

"That's handy, I've put the tea on to steep, so you're just in time."

She ushered them to the kitchen, a small galley that ran the width of the house at the back. The narrowness of it gave rise to claustrophobia. The window overlooked a tidy garden, the flowerbeds to the left all mud now, appearing freshly turned over. A veg garden went down the right, and he thought of Olga Scrivens.

"Sit down then." Helen took two more cups and saucers out of a cupboard. "What do you need to know?" She set them on the table and poured. "Just the right colour, look. Lovely."

Morgan sat, and Shaz remained in the doorway, leaning on the jamb.

"Oliver Elford." Morgan watched Helen for signs of distress.

"Oh, such a shame what he turned out to be, if you catch my drift. I never would have known if it hadn't been in the paper. He was such a nice man years ago. Something must have broken in his brain." Helen turned to Shaz. "Milk and sugar, dear?"

"Please." Shaz pushed off the jamb and came farther in.

Helen passed over her drink. "But once I thought about it afterwards, him being around girls at Arms… Dreadful to imagine what could have been going on right under our noses."

"So he didn't display any tendencies while he lived there?" Morgan accepted his tea and sipped.

"God, no. He was just Oliver, you know, Mr Helpful, always there to fix anything, and he was so good with the kids. The only thing that bothered me with him was his need to say some children needed a smack. That wasn't allowed there, so it was frustrating to listen to him keep suggesting it." Helen lowered herself onto a chair. "As you can imagine, with us all living together, we had to get along like a family, and Oliver always fitted right in apart from the smack thing. The revelation of what he did... It shocked me. Part of me didn't believe he was capable."

"Hmm, so you're saying that if he hadn't been caught red-handed, so to speak, you'd say he didn't have it in him?"

"Exactly that. Of course, once we realised what he'd done, Fay and I never spoke to him again. He couldn't stay at Arms, obviously, and besides, he was arrested and kept in Rushford pre-trial. He was away for so long, then when he came out, he called in on us."

"What, at Loving Arms?" Shaz sounded disgusted.

Helen nodded. "Yes, and we had to usher him away, telling him if he came back again, we'd have to phone the police—because of the children, you see. It was such a difficult thing to do, because whenever I see him, even now, I think of him as the Oliver we knew, not the one he'd become."

"When you say 'we'…"

"Me, Fay, and Noah."

Morgan perked up at that. Maybe Jane's probing hadn't discovered him yet. If it had, she'd have said. "Noah?"

"Yes, the gardener. Well, that and helping Oliver inside the house, and me with the sewing. He came to us around...yes, it was the year Ivy Gibbs went missing, so ninety-one. February, because I remember the snow."

Morgan glanced at Shaz. Her lips thinned, and she widened her eyes.

"What's his surname?" Morgan asked Helen.

"Tate. I see him around from time to time, although I don't have a clue where he lives these days. He wasn't there when Ivy disappeared—wasn't living at Arms, I mean, so not present that night, but he worked there on a probation scheme. He rented a room from Mrs King, although she's dead now, so that's no help to you. He moved into Arms after, though. He'd done his trial and proved he wasn't anyone we needed to worry about around the children."

"As far as you know."

"What do you mean?"

"Oliver. You didn't think he got up to anything either."

"Oh, I see what you're saying." Helen lifted her hands to her lips. "Oh dear."

Shaz left the kitchen and closed the door.

Helen stared at it. "Is everything all right?"

"Yes, she'll be phoning in to find an address for Mr Tate. Did he happen to have a key to the place, even before he moved in?"

"God, no. He wasn't allowed to come and go as he pleased. Fay ran a tight ship, and any new person working there had to be supervised by one of us. Same thing happened with me. I didn't live in at first, just worked there during the day. It was a trek over that moor, I can tell you."

"How was Noah's behaviour with the children?"

"Oh, he was great, very funny. Got on with Billy Price the most, though. They bonded, spent a lot of time together. Not alone, I must stress that. They sat with each other at the kitchen table and in the living room. Billy was the most content he'd ever been for a couple of weeks, then his nightmares started, but Noah was able to calm him down the next day, saying there were no such things as monsters."

"Monsters? The sort from under the bed?"

"Yes, the usual child thing. We—me and Fay—discussed it and thought he'd become so settled at Arms, the nightmares were his way of dealing with the fear of having to leave one day. He didn't want to be fostered or adopted, saying he thought all the potential fathers could be the one who'd burst into his house and killed his mother. Of course, that meant no one wanted him. Ivy got fostered then played up so she could come back to Arms, and we had to explain to the others that's not how you behave. Kids learn from each other, don't they."

Shaz came back in and placed her empty cup on the table. "Thanks for that. Um, we should get going."

Morgan finished his drink and stood. "Yes, you've been very helpful, Helen. If we need to ask any more questions, we'll come back."

"Is this all to do with Fay?"

"It is. We have to look into the past to see if anyone there attacked her. Did she get on with Noah?"

"Yes, she got along with everyone, although Ivy prodded her irritation bone from time to time. She was sharp with her now I think about it. She has a way about her where if you don't know her, you'd think she was rude. It's just her personality."

That was interesting, the thing about Ivy. "Well, thanks again, we'll see ourselves out." He paused. "What are you cooking? Smells lovely."

"Oh, that's the soup. For Fay. It's been on overnight. I'm taking it up there shortly. And a loaf, although I don't suppose she can eat that."

"Give her our regards, won't you."

Morgan and Shaz left, and he turned right.

"Where are we going?"

"Billy's."

"Ah, makes sense."

"I wish something bloody did."

"Me, too." Shaz sighed. "The last known address for Noah Tate is Loving Arms. I asked Gray to do a quick check on him, which is why I was so long in the hallway at Helen's. Noah seems to have dropped off the map."

"Fucking hell."

"My reaction exactly."

Chapter Twenty-Eight

Billy sighed at the knock on the door. Sherry had just been giving him an earful about the eggs in the fridge being off, so maybe the distraction of a visitor was welcome really. First thing, she'd muttered something to herself about trying to give him some leeway and stop nagging, but the egg discussion had disproved her claim.

She needed to try harder, and he needed to stop griping back at her. They'd never get to how they used to be if they kept doing that.

Yeoman stood at the door, Tanner by his side.

"Morning, Billy. Can we have a word?" Yeoman's lips stretched into an apologetic smile. "Out here will do."

Ah, that was better. Sherry couldn't earwig then, although he swore the window was open a crack yesterday when Yeoman came. Did she think he was yakking about women to the coppers?

Billy stepped out onto the pavement and closed the door to. "What's up?"

"Do you remember Oliver Elford?"

Billy nodded. "Yeah, he was the odd job man at Arms. Everyone knows him as the paedo weirdo now, though."

"Yeah, we just found that out this morning, that he worked there. What was he like back then?"

"Nice fella as far as I recall. That paedo charge he got stuck with surprised me. I'd never seen him being funny like that with the girls there."

A flash of suppressed memory came. His hands tied. A sock in his mouth.

Morgan frowned. "Well, he was bang to rights on that, so he must have behaved himself while at Arms. Not so much in Pinstone with that girl, though."

"No." It had been difficult to match the paedo side of Oliver to the one Billy knew as a kid. How did you get over a shock like that?

Back in the day, Oliver was fun, did all the washing, and he fixed the house up that time. New taps and pipes, and once Noah came, the pair of them got the place painted up nice. Helen had made new curtains on her sewing machine, Noah helping. Billy's were navy-blue and had red cartoon aeroplanes all over them. As he always kept them open, he never got to see the planes fully, just glimpses of them on the pleats.

"Then you'd know him if you saw him again?" Yeoman asked.

"Yeah. I've spotted him around recently. Didn't speak to him, though."

"So it wasn't him who possibly went to Fay's then?"

"Nah, this one was much older. Like, seventy."

"What about Noah Tate?"

Billy's heart rate scattered. He had mixed feelings about Noah. The man had been kind to him, one of the adults he'd actively sought out, but something in the back of his mind prodded now, that things weren't as wonderful as he remembered, but he couldn't put his finger on it.

"He was nice, too. Did the veg patch and the gardening, helped Oliver."

"We heard you spent a lot of time with him."

An uncomfortable feeling crept up Billy's back. Who'd been gossiping about him? It can't have been Fay because she couldn't talk. Helen? "Yeah. I felt all right with him. He made me laugh."

"So he wasn't someone you'd consider a worry, a bloke to be wary of?"

"Nope." *But I'm not sure now.*

"When was the last time you saw him?"

"Probably last week. He's a regular in The Tractor's."

"What does he look like?"

Billy shrugged. "Brown hair with a bit of grey. Average build. Bit shorter than me. And before you ask, no, he wasn't the old man in the street the other night."

"Do you know where he lives?"

"No clue."

"Would Sherry?"

"Nope."

"Fair enough. Cheers."

Yeoman and Tanner walked off to the car, and Billy remained on the pavement until they'd driven out of Regency. The questions had stirred things up. He'd tried hard to put all that behind him, except for keeping in contact with Fay and the occasional wave to Helen. All this talk of the old man... The monster he'd seen in his room at Arms was old, too, although he had long white hair, the ends touching his shoulders.

He'd come in and told Billy they had to be night-dark friends and their time together was a secret. If Billy ever blabbed, there'd be trouble.

It had started with a slap or two, the monster telling Billy he was a bad, bad boy and needed punishing because he hadn't saved his mother from that gun-toting man. Billy endured it in silence, because he carried guilt from that night anyway, but then things changed, and the monster wanted to do other stuff.

Billy shuddered.

If it wasn't for Fay, Helen, Oliver, and Noah, his life at Arms after the monster first appeared would have been unbearable, although once Ivy went missing, the monster stopped coming. Fay had put a lock on the door to keep him out.

That night, when Billy had gone down into the kitchen and Fay had turned to look at him, at the state he was in, the monster had lurked in the utility room, letting Billy know he was there. Billy had scuttled back to bed, staying awake for ages, thinking the monster would come upstairs and hit him again. Do that other thing again. Until he'd seen the shadowy form of him walking across the moor, away from Loving Arms. Only then had Billy slept.

Sometimes, he thought those times were nightmares.

"Fuck's sake."

Maybe he should finally tell Sherry everything—what he could remember anyway. Talking sometimes nudged the stone statues of memories loose. She was his wife after all, someone who'd always been there for him. They needed a proper chat, to get the recent rumours and his past out on the table, discussing it all and putting it to bed.

Except bed was where the monster liked to be, and the fear of it had stayed with him all these years. Sherry thought he was an insomniac.

If only she knew the half of it.

Chapter Twenty-Nine

1991

Mask held his palm over the boy's mouth while they sat naked on the floor in the corner of Billy's room, deep into the darkest time after midnight. He couldn't allow anyone to hear them or for Billy to call out. He had a good deal at this place and didn't want it spoilt.

Something was going on down the corridor. Ivy often cried at night while Mask was in with Billy, but he always ignored her, thinking she was having a nightmare. Sounded like someone had got up to see to her, though. Fay most likely, but he swore Oliver's tones filtered in.

Was the kid having a bad time getting back to sleep?

Mask put his lips to Billy's ear and said in the voice he reserved just for this child, "Calm down, pet. Won't be long, then I'll go. Just keep quiet for a bit longer." Newcastle, that was where he'd told Billy he was from, in conversation, like, while they were getting friendly at the start, the boy meeting the monster, the monster gaining his trust.

Billy snorted air out of his nose.

Mask wondered how Billy viewed him, what with the rubber on his face, turning him into a wizened old man, long white hair attached, the blunt ends of the strands draping on his bare shoulders. Creepy hair. Nightmare hair. The child had told Mask, as Noah, that a monster came into his room a couple of times a week, breaking his promise to keep it to himself.

"*He doesn't come out from under the bed, though," Billy had said, "but through the doorway."*

Noah hadn't liked it that Billy shared his secret, their *secret. As Mask, he'd told Billy if he opened his mouth, terrible things would happen, and Billy had ignored him, so perhaps it was time to get him to understand that properly now, while they waited for Fay and Oliver to stop talking to each other so harshly in low, grating tones.*

"Have you told anyone about us?" Mask asked.

Billy tried to shake his head, but the hand on his mouth pinned him to Mask's front.

"You're lying. You told Noah, pet. I know everything, see."

Billy made a strangled sound.

"Shh, they mustn't know I'm here." Mask tightened his free arm around Billy's belly and arms, effectively holding him immobile.

They sat like that for some time, then…

A shuffle of footsteps going along the landing. A thud.

"Shit, get back in the room. We need a rug," Fay said.

What were they doing?

Mask reached across to the pile of clothing on the floor, grabbing Billy's sock and stuffing it in the kid's mouth. He hauled them to their feet and sat the boy on the bed, pleased the dressing gown cord was still secure around the lad's wrists.

"Don't touch that sock," he whispered, "otherwise, the monster you told Noah about will have to kill you. If you ever tell anyone again about me, I'll kill you then, too."

Mask was that monster, someone who liked little boys a bit too much, and perhaps Billy had thought he'd seen him in his dreams and it was never real, but it was *real. Bad things did happen in this room, things that shouldn't, but Mask couldn't stop the urges no matter how hard he tried. He'd travelled far and wide with the troupe, meeting boys along the way, kids on the street, playing alone, dragged down allies and into fields for a spot of monster friendship.*

Billy sat rigid, gaze fixed on the door. Was he thinking of freedom, of running?

While Mask dressed, he mused on whether Billy thought he'd wake up soon, this strange recurring nightmare that had a different twist tonight with the goings-on in Ivy's room. Mask couldn't risk staying here, being seen, even though he was a Geordie old man. What could he say if he were caught? That he'd wandered in earlier, found a bedroom, and fell asleep?

No.

Ready for the off, he used the long strands of the dressing gown cord to tie Billy's wrists up against his mouth, ensuring the sock gag remained in place, hoping Billy couldn't utter any sounds apart from grunts. A tight knot at the back of the head had the lad groaning, and tears fell.

"I'll not be back," Mask said.

Not as Newcastle Man anyway. Maybe someone else, a younger fella, another monster for Billy to fear.

That was the beauty of the masks, they gave him anonymity, and each child, if they told on him, would give a description so far removed from Noah, he'd never get caught.

He'd learnt from the most recent kid in another town that being friendly with them as himself brought trouble.

"Go to sleep, Billy." He pushed him backwards onto the mattress. "I'll leave your legs free, but remember what I said."

Mask turned the lamp off and stood by the door, waiting for confirmation that Fay and Oliver were coming. It came with the light thud of their footfalls, and after they'd gone past, he opened the door a crack and peered into the gloom, the night lights in plugs down the landing giving just enough illumination to see what was happening.

Fay and Oliver carried a rolled-up carpet to the top of the stairs. Was it the spare bit from the new one in the living room? Oliver was naked, and Fay had a nightie on. What the hell?

He waited for them to descend and crept out, glancing back at the Billy-shaped shadow on the bed and pointing at him, another warning. It'd be easier to come here once he'd moved in, just a quick run down the landings. For now, he'd keep using the keys he'd got copied for the outer utility room door and the gate padlock. So easy to slip in and out once everyone was asleep, his trot back over the moor into Pinstone unseen, Mrs King sparko from her sleeping tablets, unaware he'd even gone out, let alone returned.

He moved to the top of the stairs, excited by the intrigue, and leant over the banister, the white hair falling forward, swaying. Fay and Oliver had reached the bottom and turned to enter the kitchen, so Mask went down, avoiding the creaky seventh step. He paused at the newel post, peering around it. They were in the utility room beyond the kitchen, whispering loudly.

"We'll put it down then if you can't do it one-handed," Fay snapped.

"It's heavier than I thought it'd be." Oliver grunted.

"Just get that bloody door open, you pervert," Fay said.

For a moment, Mask thought she'd spoken to him.

"Right, now what?" Oliver asked.

"For God's sake, we talked about this." Fay sounded annoyed enough to slap the man. "Just pick it up and get out, will you? Jesus bloody Christ!"

Much fumbling, then they left the house.

Mask slunk along into the kitchen, standing in the doorway and looking out of the window across the courtyard. Fay and Oliver stood at the gates, the carpet on the ground. Both had wellies and jackets on, although a stripe of Oliver's stick-like legs poked from beneath the bottom of his knee-length trench coat. He opened the padlock, swung one gate wide, and they picked their bundle up again, walking through. Fay hooked her heel around the gate and tugged, and the iron clanked upon closing.

Mask contemplated locking the utility door on his way out, but if they wanted to have alfresco sex on a carpet in the cold and wet, they wouldn't appreciate not being able to get back in again. She'd called Oliver a pervert, so that must be what they planned to do. It was a fun scenario while it breezed through his mind, but he ousted it and stepped outside into the cold. He closed the door. Kept to the outskirts of the courtyard on his way to the gate. Once there, he stared through two bars. Fay and Oliver tromped over the expanse of grass to the moor, and rain sluiced down, startling him with its sudden severity.

He listened to it slapping on the courtyard concrete for a moment, Fay and Oliver getting farther away, heading towards Pinstone. They needed to be careful. There was a ditch along there, the ground soft and boggy. They'd fall in if they didn't watch it. He'd almost done that on the way over.

Mask followed, maintaining a decent distance between them, although the darkness bordered on absolute each time a swollen cloud chugged past the moon. Halfway across the moor, they stopped, so Mask hid behind the closest tree and watched them.

They placed the carpet down. Had a rest. A low rumble of thunder rolled, and a streak of lightning forked across the sky, illuminating them for a second.

Then they carried their cargo again.

He tailed them.

The walk took a fair while, the rain coming at him sideways, smacking him hard, pin-sharp jabs to his hands. He recognised the louder gush of water. Ah, the River Idle, deep at this section, skirting the top end of town. It went beneath a bridge over by Drinker's Rest, and he'd often stared out at the water from his room when he'd stayed there, the sun glinting off the ripples, the moon looking down at itself into a mirror, smile reflected back at it.

They disappeared round a bend behind the long hedgerow that broke the moor up from the grassy field closest to Pinstone. He ran over there and stooped, creeping along slowly until they came into view.

They stood beside the river, their burden on the ground, and Fay hunched over, groaning. Her back had a habit of playing her up, and she griped about it from time to time. She unrolled the carpet. The lighter sky from streetlamps over the way gave scant sight but enough for him to know a child's body had been inside the carpet.

Ivy?

Noah's legs wobbled.

Fay and Oliver placed the toes of their boots at the child's side and kicked her. Ivy tumbled into the water. They stared for a long time, then bent their heads to talk, their low murmurs indecipherable.

Mask sidled closer.

"Have you got your story straight in your head now?" Fay asked.

Oliver stifled a sob. "Yes."

"You'll have to find another wife. An older one. Now take the carpet back and leave the gate and door unlocked. I'll stay here for a while to make sure she doesn't float. And I need some time to think."

Oliver rolled the carpet, hefted it up, and walked off.

Mask ducked and pressed himself into the hedge, the prickles jabbing at his back through his coat. He waited until Oliver was but a speck in the distance then stepped out from his hiding place, some of the long hair getting snagged by the branches.

He strode towards Fay, determined to get his own way out of this, and she spun round, gasping, a hand to her chest.

"What are you doing out at this time of the morning, pet?" he asked, in character.

"N-nothing. I'm just... I needed a walk. Couldn't sleep."

"You're in just a coat and boots, and is that your nightie?"

"Please, I just want to be left alone."

He stared at her. "I'm sure you do, but the thing is, I know what you did. You and him. I've been watching ever since you carried that girl from the care home."

She sucked in a sharp breath, and he smiled, cheeks bunching against the underside of the mask.

"We'll go back to Loving Arms," he said. "I want an assurance written on paper."

"W-what assurance?"

He gripped her arm. "You'll see. No need to ask questions, nosy."

He dragged her along, although he didn't need to. She came willingly, maybe resigned to the fact he wasn't going to let her go, and he was stronger than the frail impression his wrinkled face gave, which helped.

He ignored her babbling.

At the gates, he pushed one open and shoved her into the courtyard. "I'll lock it on my way out. I have a key."

Another sharp inhale, and she glanced across at him. "Who are you?"

"You'll see soon enough."

They went inside, and he let her go, unfazed that she might grab the phone and ring the police. After all, a child was missing from this house, probably resting on the riverbed or jostled along it by the strong current, away from Pinstone and into Bawtry a mile or so away, then past that to Stockwith where it joined the Trent.

Fay took her wellies off, ever mindful of getting the floor dirty even in these circumstances with a stranger in the place, and she tutted at Oliver's, mud-caked and wet. She scooped both pairs up and went into the kitchen, leaving Mask in the utility room.

Was she that mired in her own mind, her own thoughts, she failed to care that he was there?

She'd care in a minute. He'd scare her into giving a shit.

"Oh my goodness, what are you doing up, love? And what on earth have you done to yourself?"

Mask spied around the edge of the doorframe, keeping out of sight.

Billy stood there, still tied up, and Fay set about undoing the cord and throwing it to the floor. She took the sock out of his mouth and flung it aside. Billy cried quietly all the while, and she checked his wrists for chafing.

"The m-monster c-came," Billy said.

"Aww, no, there aren't any monsters. How did you get tied up?"

Mask poked his head fully into view and stared at Billy.

The boy's eyes widened. "I-I did it to myself."

"You silly thing. What did you do that for? How?" She paused to kiss his head. *"Listen, we'll talk about this tomorrow. I've got to wash some boots. Go and get your pyjamas on, you'll catch your death — no idea why you'd want to even take them off. Back to sleep now, my love. I'll be up to check on you in a minute."*

Billy padded off, and at the newel, he stopped and looked at Mask, then scuttled up the stairs.

Mask retreated and took his face covering off, stuffing it in his pocket. Then he entered the kitchen.

Fay whipped round, clutching the lapels of her coat, scared, as if she'd forgotten he'd come inside with her. "Oh, Noah, thank God. Did you see the old man leaving?" She stood on tiptoes to stare out of the window, then looked at him.

He smiled, showing his small teeth. "He's not out there, because I am *the old man."*

"You?" She grabbed at the sink unit. "W-what do you want?"

"A written confirmation that you'll do everything you can to allow me to stay here. Then I'll have unlimited access to Billy."

"Access?" Her frown gouged two vertical lines between her eyebrows.

"What, did you really think he tied himself *up?"*
She stared, horrified "It was you?"

Noah laughed. "Now you know my secret." He *paused, glaring at her. "And I know yours, killer."*

Chapter Thirty

Catherine had had such a fright, she'd needed a lie down. She stared at the ceiling, thinking about the strange way she'd seemed to go back in time. Was this what dementia did to you? Did bizarre things happen and you saw people who weren't there?

At first, she'd been convinced the little girl was real, but after the episode in the dining room, it was clear her mind had decided to play games with her. Should she tell Liz she was hallucinating? Maybe the medication had something to do with it. She'd had it changed last week, so it made sense.

She'd speak to Sarah first, see what she said.

"Help me…"

Oh God, the child.

Catherine sat up, but no one stood in her room.

This was getting bloody ridiculous.

She got up and walked towards the en suite.

The shower kicked on, and Catherine jumped. Was there a fault?

She stepped inside the room.

The girl stood beneath the spray, her nightdress sticking to her. "It's raining…see?"

Catherine's heart pulsed too hard and fast, then skipped several beats, and she clutched the doorframe for support. Her head lightened, her chest tightening, and she breathed heavily.

"What do you want?" she whispered.

"It's raining…"

Catherine closed her eyes, unable to look at the grey face, the bloated skin. She opened them again, and the child wasn't there. Reaching inside the cubicle, she switched the shower off, shaking all over, and hobbled out, sitting on her bed.

Her phone rang, the one on her bedside table. Fretful, she answered it, her hand still wet.

"Hi, Cath." Jolly Liz. Grating Liz. "You have a visitor."

"Who is it?"

"Your son."

"Oh." Catherine wondered whether she should see him, tell him once and for all that he wasn't welcome here, that she never wanted to see him again. She'd hinted at it in the past, just never spelled it out for him. "Okay, I'll be down in a moment."

She left her room, legs wobbly, and took the lift downstairs, clutching the handrail for support. In the living room, she stood and scanned all the faces, her gaze finally alighting on him. Her stomach churned, but she pressed on, moving towards him. He sat in one of the spots where people could overhear, so she gestured him into the corner like the stupid imbecile he was. She didn't need people eavesdropping if he talked about his filthiness.

She sat, glad to give her legs a rest, and scrunched her toes in her slippers. "What do you want?"

Oliver plonked down opposite, and a waft of sour-smelling air came up. Turps? "Just wanted to see you."

"Well, I don't want to see you."

"I've changed. I don't do stuff like that anymore. I even went to the police station last night to help them with their enquiries. I gave a statement because I knew someone was going to hurt a lady. I wouldn't do that if I were still bad, would I."

She narrowed her eyes at him. "It's always in you, that badness. Only castration will take those urges away."

"You're wrong. Since I came out, I've—"

"Came out?"

"Yeah, I was back in Rushford again." He dipped his head as if ashamed.

Catherine glanced about to make sure no one heard that. She'd never get over anyone knowing. "Keep your voice down. I have to live with these people." She wished she were having one of her really bad episodes that had her mostly forgetting who he was and what he'd done. "What did you do this time?"

"Robbery."

Her heart lurched. "Oh, for the love of God. I never brought you up to steal."

"I needed the money."

"What you *need* is a job and to keep your hands to yourself—for both reasons."

"Most people won't take someone on who's been in the nick, and they all know what I did, the employers, because they run checks."

"Serves yourself right." She rubbed at a pain in her temple.

Her vision zigzagged. She blinked.

A man sat opposite her, vaguely familiar. She knew him but couldn't place where from. He had light hair and mean features. What was his name again? He was evil, she knew that much.

"What are you doing here?" she asked, adding steel to her tone so he didn't think she was afraid of him.

He frowned. "Told you, I came to see you."

"Like that girl keeps doing. In her nightie. It's white with pink flowers all over it, and there's a pink bow, too." She couldn't grasp why that material was important. She'd heard of it before the girl came, she was sure of it.

"W-what?" The man paled.

"Are you losing your hearing?"

"No, you said a girl in a nightie…"

"She keeps asking me to help her, and just now, she was in my shower, telling me it's raining."

"I have to go."

"And don't come back. Ever. I don't want to see you again." She didn't watch him leave. Stupid chap. He wasn't nice, so Liz shouldn't have allowed him here. What was she thinking?

Liz came over. "Everything all right?"

"Don't let him in again. I've told him not to come."

"Oh, but—"

"He's a pervert!" Catherine shouted and, mortified at her mistake, everyone turning to stare, she rushed as much as she was able, leaving the room and using the lift. She closed her door, checked the shower, then stood at the window.

She stared out. That horrible man walked across the moor.

Whoever he was, she wished he'd fall into a bog and drown.

Confession

Police work was my life. Now, there's nothing much except pottering about in my garden, reading the news, watching telly. Many things from the past still bother me, guilt uppermost because of what I wasn't allowed to do. I should have insisted on being listened to. I'll never forgive myself for not pushing harder about Ivy Gibbs. –
Andrew Yarthing

Chapter Thirty-One

Andrew was on pins and needles. A police officer had rung him earlier, asking if her DI could come round for a chat about Ivy Gibbs. No one had wanted to speak to him about her for years, especially once the case was closed. His colleagues and boss at the time hadn't entertained his theory, that the child had come a cropper *inside* the house, not outside. No evidence, they'd said. No clue she'd been harmed. The stool proved the child had unlocked the door herself.

But her fingerprints weren't even on the bloody handle. No one's were. He'd have to remember to tell the police that. Maybe this DI would listen to him, take it seriously, righting the past because Andrew hadn't been able to.

A knock rapped on the front door, and he went to answer it, his steps slow. A man and woman stood on the step, the bloke holding up his ID.

"Mr Yarthing? DI Morgan Yeoman, and this is DS Sharon Tanner. You're expecting us?"

"Yes, yes, come in." Andrew led them to the living room, a real fire flickering in the grate. He didn't think you could beat that for warmth. "Would you like a cup of tea or coffee?"

The woman's face brightened. "Oh, that would be—"

"No, thank you," Yeoman said. "We're a bit pressed for time today."

Andrew grew saddened at Tanner's downcast expression. He hid his own behind a false smile. He loved having company, a rare occurrence nowadays, and he used to enjoy a cuppa while interviewing people in their homes. Seemed she did, too. "I understand."

Morgan dipped his head. "I'm sure you do."

"Take a seat." Andrew held his arm aloft to indicate the sofa. He'd string his answers out as much as possible so they stayed longer.

They all sat, and a wave of nostalgia swept over him. He'd never wanted detective status, preferring to remain a PC, on the streets with the community, but these two had him hankering after going back to work. He'd retired now but missed the job. Missed feeling vital and an important part of Pinstone, someone people respected and looked up to. Others had given him grief, but that came with the uniform. He'd had his fair share of people spitting on him, lashing out. He didn't miss that part.

"How can I help you?" he asked.

Yeoman cleared his throat. "We've found ourselves looking into a cold case, the one involving Ivy Gibbs going missing in ninety-one. Our records show you as one of the main policemen involved with it, and, of course, you're the spokesperson in the news articles we've read. The reason for this is a woman who ran the children's home has been attacked, and as you know, poking into the past of a victim sometimes brings good results. As the attacker is elderly, we're thinking he's something to do with her from years ago."

He must mean Fay. "Oh, that's appalling. Is she all right?"

"She's minus a tongue and all her fingers."

Andrew knew what that meant. "Ah, shutting her up then."

"We thought the same." Yeoman smiled grimly. "So we'd like your take on things around the time Ivy disappeared. Specifically your instincts regarding Oliver Elford and Noah Tate."

"Ah, nasty business with Elford, but at the time of the Ivy situation, he didn't strike me as anyone of concern. None of them did, actually, yet I still felt it was an inside job."

Yeoman nodded. "I came to the same conclusion. Things just don't add up, do they."

"No, but unfortunately, my superiors didn't agree. They felt the stool being by the exit proved she'd run away—yet her fingerprints weren't on it, and her mittens were in her room, still attached to her coat with those strings kids have on them so they don't get lost. It's plausible she ran off, given that Ivy was a difficult child, and she'd been sent back from a set of foster parents in Wales—a bit of a handful. Rude, swearing a lot. Police in Wales interviewed them, but they weren't involved. Iron-clad alibis. It was the door being locked that bothered me.

This kid, young as she was, maybe in a rage for whatever reason, had the foresight to lock up after she'd walked out? Rubbish."

"Why rubbish?"

"Because the doorknob was wiped clean. No fingerprints in or outside. She wouldn't think to do that."

"Oh. I wasn't aware of that, nor about the mittens. That's suspicious."

"It was, and I'd said as much to the DCI—he's dead now—but for some reason, people seemed to want to sweep the case under the carpet. Like because Ivy was 'one of those kids' in a care home, she didn't matter as much."

"Hmm. So the moor was searched..."

"Yes, we were out there for days, but the weather had been shocking, lots of rain, the ground was boggy, and any footprints we made scouring the area meant we may have trodden on anyone else's." He shook his head at the memory, still so vivid. "It was dark, we had torches, but the situation wasn't ideal for the first search. Door-to-door in Pinstone, every single house, shed, and garage was checked throughout the following week. A massive operation, and it generated quite a buzz, so we had journalists crawling about, some of them on the bloody moor, making things difficult."

He recalled all the people milling around, others wandering close to where they shouldn't be, dipping under the cordon, him shouting at them to "Bloody get back!"

Yeoman appeared to sympathise. "We're off to see one of the reporters after we leave here. Maybe he got the same feeling as you regarding the stool and locked door."

Andrew knew who they were talking about. He huffed. "Didn't seem to at the time. I remember reading the article and getting frustrated at how he'd put things. Like the stool meant everything." He sighed. "What it meant was, someone could have put it there on purpose. Fay was awake that night, you know that, don't you? Washing wellies. Who does that in the early hours?"

"Insomnia? People do strange things when they can't sleep."

"Why did she need to clean wellies, though? There were only three pairs in a row by that exit, all belonging to the employees who lived there. The children all had a pair each in their rooms, and I spoke to those kiddies, and no one had gone out on the moor for a walk to even *get* the boots dirty. One of them said they sometimes went out, see, along the moor to Drinker's Rest for a lemonade and crisps. A treat Fay gave them every so often, apparently."

"Was the river dredged? We haven't got that far into that part of the enquiry yet."

"Ah, that's another thing that annoyed me. Like I'd said, if she *did* wander out, she could have fallen in. There wasn't the budget for the whole section of it to be swept, so they did the part closest to the home, a one hundred metre stretch—the next day, far too late in my opinion. Ridiculous, too, because the current was raging that week, so she'd have gone along with it, nowhere near that stretch. All in all, I had to shut up and move on when they closed the case."

"Why did they take so long to go down the abduction route?"

Frustration bubbled inside him. "That bloody stool again. Honestly, the times I could have screamed. Days had passed before they decided to consider other avenues, and if she *had* been abducted, she'd have been miles away by then."

Yeoman shook his head and looked at his partner. "Sounds like a botched job."

Andrew nodded. "For us, yes, but not for whoever did it. They got off scot-free. My money is on Fay, always was, always will be, although she never behaved oddly enough for me to do anything about it. There was just an air around her, and of course, my boss didn't act on 'airs' or gut instincts. It was the wellie washing that did it. Plus, if it wasn't her, why was she attacked? Maybe one of the kids living there remembered something and decided to mete out justice."

The chat came to an end, and sadly, Andrew showed them out, hopeful something might come of it. Reopened cold cases got solved a lot these days, with fresh eyes and cutting-edge forensics, and Ivy needed finding. He'd kept up with it over the years, periodically checking school records for her being registered, and later, looking for a financial footprint for her as an adult.

Nothing, and once he'd left the job, he'd told himself to put it behind him, but that kind of case never left you, and he'd thought of Ivy every day. She was dead, he knew that. He just didn't know how.

He returned to his living room, cup of tea in hand, mind churning with memories, the emotions he'd felt back then rising to the surface. A little girl, removed from that house by someone who was supposed to care for her.

Andrew had no doubt about that.

Chapter Thirty-Two

1991

Fay hadn't settled after she'd locked the door once Noah had left. He'd seen her and Oliver, knew they'd pushed a dead body into the river, for God's sake. And to think he'd been coming in here to see her beautiful Billy outside the times he was allowed. What should she do about that?

Nothing, she couldn't do a thing. If she did, she risked being found out for murder. What was more important, though, herself or Billy?

Sadly, it was herself. She couldn't face prison, and children were resilient, he'd forget this once he grew up, tuck it away in the back of his mind as just an unfortunate time in his childhood. But to ease her conscience she could get a lock put on his door. She could hang the key around her neck on a string so Noah couldn't copy it like he had with the one in the utility and for the padlock. How had she not noticed they were missing when he'd taken them?

Easy. Sometimes, Noah walked to Pinstone to pick up shopping for the home. He'd have slipped the keys in his pocket, taken them to the little shop that cut copies and mended shoes, then put the originals back.

She'd thought of Ivy, too, and how she'd never taken to her. The child had come to them after a fire in her house, one started by her deliberately, so her mother had said. Lovely. A pyromaniac in the care home. The mother had punched Ivy in the front garden, and she'd fallen, hit her head.

Like she'd done on the radiator knob.

Fay wondered if Ivy had really been speaking to her mum when she'd said she hated her last night. Unconscious at home, she hadn't been able to say those words to her on the garden path. Guilt had wrapped its sinewy arms around Fay at five a.m., whispering to her that Ivy didn't deserve what had happened. She should have been nurtured instead, Fay trying to give her a better life than the one she'd previously led with no food in the cupboard and slaps to her face.

The thing was, Ivy had stolen food from other children's lunchboxes at school, and Fay couldn't abide a thief, no matter that Ivy had done it out of desperation, to feed her growling tummy, to survive despite living an awful life.

Florrie was a thief. She'd stolen Frankie's life. Stolen Fay's and given her a different one where she'd mourned and turned into a bitter cow.

And then there was the river. It had plagued her all night, that splosh of the water as the child had hit it, her sinking into the bristling cold current, her pale hand the last thing Fay had seen, fingers curled towards her palms.

Would she surface today?

Fay got up from her bed, so weary, yet wired at the same time. She showered and dressed, rushing to get down to Oliver's room. They needed to go over their story again and get it completely straight, no gaps in the timeline.

She tapped on his door, and he opened it a crack, peering at her with one eye in the slim space. Bloody man. Who did he think she was, the police?

"Let me in, you prat," *she snarled.*

He stepped back, and she moved inside, shutting the door and leaning on it.

"Right, let's recap." She walked across and sat on his unmade bed.

Oliver tromped over to stare through the window. "No need to go over this again, Fay. I remember what we talked about. I didn't forget. Pointless to come here repeating your bloody self."

Ire rose inside her. "Shut up. I need to repeat it to make sure, even if only for myself. Okay, we're going down to the kitchen and having our usual cup of tea before the children get up. When I ring the bell for them to wake, we act normal when Ivy doesn't show. I'll get cross like I usually would and say I'm going to go up and get her out of bed." She continued going over what they'd discussed while they'd carried the body in the carpet across the moor. "And that's it, have you got that?"

Oliver nodded. "I miss her already."

"Don't be so disgusting. She was a child and didn't deserve having you mauling her."

"She didn't deserve you being nasty, you mean."

Fay stormed out and strode to the stairs, anxious Oliver's mardy attitude meant he'd accidentally on purpose say something he shouldn't to Helen or the police—or, God forbid, Noah.

Noah.

Armed with a new threat, she returned to Oliver's room.

"What do you want now?" he moaned.

"Someone saw us last night." She stared at him smugly, arms crossed.

He paled and gaped. "W-what? Who? It was dark. We were so careful."

"Noah."

"What was he *doing here?"*

"That's none of your concern, but what is, is he followed us across the sodding moor and to the river. He saw us kick her in."

Oliver swayed. "H-how? I didn't spot him when I carried the carpet back. I didn't see no one."

Shit, the carpet. Where had he put it? "Doesn't matter, he knows. We can never tell anyone, do you hear me? He's not going to rat on us, for reasons you don't need to know about, so just act normal with him, as if you're not aware of him watching us. But the carpet. Where is it?"

"In my car boot."

"Right then, you're going to drive off and hide it somewhere, get back before the police come."

He smacked his head with his palms. "Where, though?"

She fancied walloping him one but refrained. "I don't know, do I! Think!"

He stared at the ceiling. "The dump?"

"That'll do. So, the new plan is as follows…"

Once they had it sorted, she left him and went downstairs. Helen already had the tea brewing in the big pot, the radio on low playing a song from the eighties. With cheery greetings given, Fay sat at the table and poured a cup. Helen busied herself with slotting bread in the six-slice toaster. She'd already brought out the various cereals in their transparent tubs with lids, and jugs of milk sat on a tray on the worktop. A large orange juice carton stood beside multi-coloured beakers.

One less would be used today.

"You look tired, love." Helen paused in taking the margarine out of the fridge.

Fay adopted a pained expression. "Bad night. Couldn't sleep. I ended up coming down here. Probably the onset of menopause."

"Oh. The hot sweats, the insomnia. I have that to look forward to."

"Hmm, but not for years yet."

Oliver came in, red-faced and sweating, probably from nerves, and he gave Fay a darting glance. "No brekkie for me until I come back. Got to nip out. I want to get a newspaper. There's meant to be a deal on with a holiday. We could take the children next summer. Three caravans should do it, one of us in each, the kids shared between us."

"Yes, the boys can go in with you." Fay couldn't allow him to have any girls with him. Not after that Ivy business.

"Oh, okay then." Helen smiled. *"Can you pick me up some icing sugar? I've run out—I need it for the biscuits tonight."*

But Ivy wouldn't be eating them.

Oliver nodded and left.

Fay ate some toast and drank her tea, thinking about him at the dump, hoping he didn't see anyone. All too soon, it was time to go to the bottom of the stairs and ring the bell, same as the sort used at playtime in schools. Trepidation filled her at the acting she had to do.

Please let me get it right.

The children came down in their pyjamas and slippers, hair sleep-ruffled, eyes with sleepy dust in the corners. Everyone settled at the kitchen table—they always had breakfast there as well as snacks and the pre-bed drink and biscuit. Lunch and dinner were served in the more formal dining room.

"Where's Ivy?" Helen looked around, finger pointed to count heads.

Fay did a fake count as well. "Tsk. I'll go up and get her."

Fay stormed up there, along the left-hand landing, stomping as she would any other time, for authenticity. Her heart thundered, and flashes of what had happened in Ivy's room zigzagged through her mind. She threw the door open, oddly expecting to see Oliver on the bed and Ivy beside it, time turned back so she could stop the events that had unfurled, but of course, neither of them were there.

She took a deep breath and forced herself into action, haring into all the other rooms, then those on the right-hand landing. Downstairs, she fled through the kitchen, ignoring Helen's worried call of "What's the matter?"

Fay checked all the rooms, then, in fake panic mode, returned to the kitchen. All the children had tucked in, spoons clacking on bowls, so she beckoned for Helen to go with her into the living room. She closed the door.

"Ivy isn't here," she said.

"What?" Helen blinked, her mouth hanging open. "What do you mean, she isn't here?"

"She's not in bed. The covers are ruffled, so she'd been in there at some point, but now she's gone. What are we going to do?"

"You watch the children, I'll go and look outside."

Back in the kitchen, Fay sat with the kids and eyed Billy. Did he remember coming down last night? Did he remember being tied up? God, that was so dreadful for Noah to do that to him. What on earth had the child been going through all this time? Why hadn't Billy said anything to her?

Yes, she'd definitely put a lock on his door, tell the boy it was to keep the monsters out, and if Noah had the cheek to ask why she'd done it, she'd say their boss had suggested it, shifting the blame off herself.

But that didn't keep the other boys safe, did it.

She'd have to lock all the children in.

Helen came back and shook her head.

Fay rose. "I'll just use the phone." She walked out into the hallway and closed the door. Took another deep breath. And told the police Ivy was missing.

Afterwards, while Helen was helping the kids to get dressed, Fay cleaned the doorknob in the utility inside and out, otherwise Helen would get the blame, her prints being the last ones on there. Fay was a bitch, but not that much of one. Helen was too nice to become embroiled in all this.

Then she set a stool by the wellies and hoped Helen wouldn't remember it hadn't been there before. God, this was such an inconvenience.

Chapter Thirty-Three

Florrie smiled. The neighbours had been quiet since Phil had called round to have a word. She peered through the nets in the living room, pleased they were sorting out their shocking front garden. Well, Ray was, bent over chopping unruly leaves off the bush in the middle while Karen stood guard, watching him, some kind of wicked overseer, ready to bark orders at him any moment.

One of their sons came out of the house and got on the bike.

"What are you still doing here?" Karen asked, arms crossed over her belly.

"Overslept." He rode off up Mulberry.

Who didn't realise their child hadn't gone to school?

Karen and Ray were terrible parents. Just like Fay.

Florrie walked into the hallway and shrugged her coat on, sitting on the stairs to pull on her boots, a feat in itself with all her huffing and puffing. While it wasn't raining, she'd nip to Mary Magdalene Cemetery again. The urge to visit baby Frankie was strong. All right, she'd only been there yesterday, but so what?

Brolly in her bag just in case, she stepped outside.

"Happy now, are you?" Karen shouted.

Florrie ignored her and walked down her path, nose in the air, showing Karen what she thought of her.

"We've been told if we don't buck up, we're out for breach of tenancy. So we're bucking up, *okay*?" Karen moved to her gate as Florrie got to hers.

"You do realise who you're renting off, don't you?" Florrie stared at her.

"Well, duh, Phil and Val."

"But you're new around here so might not know *exactly* who he is."

"So?"

"Just watch your back, that's all I'm saying."

Pleased with herself for putting the shits up Karen, Florrie walked along the lane, approaching Wasti's. New posters adorned the windows, lots of red and yellow to catch the eye, offers for all sorts, buy one, get one free. He had a new set of deals every week, but there was no concrete date for them starting. You had to keep your eye on it or lose out. She'd definitely have those pecan pastries, and the Hovis could go in the freezer. The carrot cake looked delicious. It'd sit well on her hips.

She wandered past, her mind full of Fay now the stupid woman had got herself attacked. She had to have done something. No one chopped at things for no reason, did they. Whoever it was must be pretty pissed off to resort to such violence. Florrie understood that. She'd entertained ideas of stabbing Fay herself. Not that she would, mind, but thinking of doing it eased the pressure.

The cobbles leading to the cemetery were thankfully dry, not the treacherous monsters of yesterday. Florrie tromped into the grounds and headed straight for Frankie's grave, the path getting narrower the farther she went. He had a white marble headstone, different to the original, which hadn't fared well in the weather, so Fay must have replaced it. But it looked different again today, something red on it, and that wasn't right. Florrie hadn't brought her flannel and Thermos, seeing as she'd washed it yesterday, but she wished she had.

A word had been painted on it, the brush strokes visible at the tops and bottoms of each letter. Red paint.

Florrie stared at it, her heart thudding. Someone else thought it was Fay's fault, too, Frankie dying. They had to if they'd written that.

KILLER.

She sat on the ground and wept for a long time.

Chapter Thirty-Four

Morgan tapped on Reginald Davies' door.
"Wonder if he'll have anything to add to Andrew Yarthing," Shaz said beside him.

"He's probably in the other camp—that Ivy got out by herself."

"Hmm."

The door opened, and an old man stood there, shoulder-length hair, face ravaged by wrinkles, his grey V-neck jumper pilled and well-worn. Morgan's heart skipped—could he have been the man Billy had seen?

No, too tall, a heavier build.

"Ah, the police?" He slid his silver-framed glasses down his nose and peered over them, his irises a milky grey, the whites tinged yellow. Bad liver?

Morgan showed his ID and introduced them. "We're here to pick your brains about Ivy Gibbs' case."

"Yes, your colleague mentioned that, so I got out my notebook from that year. I've kept them all. A reminder, you know, of my time at the paper. Katie Violet has taken over my job now, and she's good, I'll give her that. Come on in."

Katie Violet. Maybe they should squeeze her in today, too, seeing as she'd been to Helen's. It wouldn't hurt to ask her if she'd gone there to poke her nose in about the attack.

They entered, and Reginald took them to a kitchen at the back with bi-fold doors that overlooked a neat garden.

"Have a sit down, I won't be a minute." Reginald left and came back with a navy-blue notebook, NINETEEN NINETY-ONE on the front in gold letters. "Here we are." He opened it and flicked through. "Yes, this is her."

He turned the book to face them. A photo had been stuck inside, her details below—age, approximate height, her nightie description et cetera. The child had a pinched face, as if she'd been permanently hungry and underfed, unloved.

"Now…" Reginald switched it back to face him and flipped a page. "Ivy was a bit of a naughty girl. Hardly surprising, given who her mother was."

"Was?"

"Died from alcohol poisoning. Not a shock to anyone who knew her. She drank like a fish and barely ate anything except pizza. Ivy had been taken by social services after a fire at the property. The poor girl had tried to make her own dinner, and a tea towel caught alight. Her mother was a dreadful sort, and the neighbours had put in a few complaints over the years that weren't followed up. The girl stole food from lunchboxes at school—one of the teachers told me that."

Morgan's heart panged at that. "Poor thing. During your investigations, did you come up with an inkling as to who might have abducted her?"

"*Was* it an abduction, though? Everyone I spoke to said Ivy was strong-willed, and if she wanted to do something, she'd find a way, hence the stool as an aid in her leaving. Even the social workers prior to her being placed in Loving Arms classed her as 'a difficult one'. The general consensus was that she ran away and came a cropper."

"What did Fay Williams have to say?"

Reginald consulted his notes, moving his fingertip down a page. "I quote, 'Ivy has some hurdles she needs to get over, but once we've given her the appropriate attention, I'm sure she'll become a lovely little girl.' To me, that says she's a brat and it'll be a huge job sorting her out. Note that she spoke in the present tense, which is why I didn't think she had anything to do with it. Most people slip up with that if they've had a hand in a death, but you'd know that anyway."

Morgan didn't disagree. Fay's wording had said it all but without her sounding cruel. However, 'appropriate attention' could mean several things. Love and nurturing, a stricter routine, or a heavy hand?

"So what do you think happened?" he asked.

Reginald pinched his chin. "Small kid doesn't get her own way and plans to run off, maybe to scare them, get the focus on her. She leaves, locks the door. Wanders across the moor, falls in one of those deeper bogs that suck you under, and that's that."

"So didn't the police check the deeper bogs?"

"They poked a few sticks in them to determine if a body was there, but like I said, some suck your right down, covering things over, water on top. They might not have had long enough poles to get down far enough."

Morgan wondered whether Ground Penetrating Radar was used back then like it was today. The incompetence astounded him, and for the DCI and DI to get away with not conducting the search properly…

"What about the people who worked there other than Fay? What did you make of them?"

Reginald lifted his shoulders to his ears then let them drop. "Helen, she was nice, had nothing bad to say about Ivy at all, although she struck me as the sort who'd say the Devil had a good side to him if you only looked for it. Oliver, pre-conviction, was all right as well. Nice enough, if a bit jittery and sweaty, but I put that down to nerves that a kid had gone missing, not anything else, although later down the line, I did wonder. Then there was Noah Tate." He studied his notebook. "Says here: Charming, a gentleman, lovely manners."

Four people who were either innocent or played their parts well.

"Did you notice how they all got along—the adults, I mean."

"Well enough. Fay and Noah seemed to stare at one another a lot, but I just thought they were an item or whatever. You know, eyeing each other up, which, now I'm thinking about it, was a bit inappropriate, considering the circumstances."

So no picking up on facial expressions and guilty behaviour, body language. What sort of sham *was* that investigation? It was clear even the reporter didn't sense anything off, but maybe there hadn't been anything *to* sense.

"The doorknob was cleaned inside and out," Morgan said.

"What?" Reginald's eyes widened. "I didn't hear about that."

"Hmm, which is why PC Yarthing kept pushing for the abduction theory, even after that route had so-called been investigated. What child of that age thinks to clean off her fingerprints?"

"I'd say she wouldn't."

"Exactly. What do you know about the search of her room? Anything?"

"Her bed had been slept in. The rest was tidy. All her clothing was left behind bar the nightie she had on, so she went outside in cold temperatures, without a coat, her wellies, or mittens, so she'd definitely have left fingerprints. This is giving me cause to rethink my initial findings now."

"Nothing but a nightie…" Why hadn't the police flagged that as bloody odd? At the very least she'd been sleepwalking.

"Just that, yes."

"Okay, to wrap this up, did you suspect anyone in particular, even though you believe she'd wandered out by herself?"

"No one stood out as weird. And besides, the general agreement was Ivy running away, and I believed that was the case. Until you mentioned the doorknob. Okay, an older child would have the sense to wipe it, with the nightie perhaps, but a kid her age? No." He rubbed his forehead. "So you've opened up a cold case then? Is that why you're here?"

"No. Fay Williams was attacked, and we're dealing with her past at the moment, trying to see if she had any enemies who might have it in for her now."

"Might just be the people of today, eh? Elderly bashing. I worry a lot about it myself, seeing as I live alone."

"We'd say it was that, too, but things seemed a bit personal." Morgan explained about the tongue and fingers—it'd be in the papers before long anyway. "So as you can imagine, we're going with the theory she was silenced. Can't talk, can't write."

"If it was her who had something to do with Ivy, they'd have sorted her back then, surely."

You'd think so. "The mind is a funny thing, as you probably know from your time talking to people for your stories. Some folks let things fester."

"That's a bloody long fester!"

Morgan's phone rang. "Excuse me. Actually, we'll be on our way. Thank you for speaking with us." Out on the path, leaving Shaz to chat with Reginald in the hallway, Morgan answered. "Yep, Gray?"

"Got one for you. Might well be linked to the attack on Fay Williams."

"What's that then?"

"A Florrie Dorchester has phoned in. Someone's defaced Fay's son's gravestone. Red paint. The word 'killer' in capitals."

"That's interesting. Is Florrie still at the cemetery?"

"Yes. I didn't send uniforms as I wanted to let you know first. Told her to stay put. She said she's been sitting on the ground crying for a while, so if the person who did it was there when she arrived, hiding, I'd say they've scarpered by now."

"Cheers. We'll go there in a minute." He slid his phone away. "Shaz." He got in the car and waited for her.

"What's the rush?" she said, getting in.

He told her about Gray's call. "So is Fay the killer the word refers to?" He drove off towards Mary Magdalene, mind coiled tight with speculation.

"Blimey. Did she kill the baby or Ivy?"

"Or both? God knows, and she can't bloody tell us either."

Shaz cuffed her nose. "We could ask her questions so she can nod or shake her head."

"True."

Morgan tried to match the old lady with murder. He couldn't see it. But she wouldn't have been old when she had a son, and not around Ivy's disappearance either. "If Fay's seventy-five, she'd have been what in ninety-one?"

"Forty-something."

"Right." He pulled into the cemetery and parked. "There's Florrie."

She stood in the distance where two paths cleaved.

Morgan got out. Florrie waddled towards him, arms up, waving like some mad woman who thought they wouldn't see her otherwise. Shaz clambered from the car, and Morgan blipped the locks.

"I waited back there for you." Florrie came to a stop, catching her breath. "But the grave's over in the far corner." She pointed down the right-hand path, where a couple of hundred metres along, more graves stood in regimented lines.

Morgan allowed her to lead the way. "So why would someone think Fay's a killer?"

With Florrie ahead, he couldn't watch her facial expression. *Shit*. He'd muffed up there.

"Oh, it'll be about her baby. It has to be. Otherwise, why paint on his gravestone? Then again, they can hardly paint on hers, more's the pity, because she hasn't got one yet." She walked on, stride determined, arms swinging, her bag bouncing off her rump. "He died when he was three weeks old, you know. She was out that night—dancing, can you believe—living it up after just having him. I thought it was disgusting, to be honest, but our nan encouraged her. I was holding him when he died."

"What was the cause?" Morgan glanced at Shaz: *Did Florrie kill the bloody baby?*

Fay called over her shoulder, "They call it something now, can't remember what."

"SIDS?" Shaz said.

Florrie huffed. "That's it. Anyway, he fell asleep and didn't wake up, although... Doesn't matter." She navigated along the narrowing path, skirting a clump of old flowers.

"What were you going to say?" Morgan asked.

"Just that I don't hold with gripe water, and he had some. I think he was too small for it. Fay's neighbour gave it to her."

"Did you mention that to anyone at the time?"

"No. Funny enough, we were all too busy being distraught." She stopped and gave him a disparaging glare. "Here we are, look."

Morgan stared at the stone. He'd have to get a couple of SOCO down here to handle this—if it was linked to Fay, they might get some answers. "Where were you before coming here, Florrie?"

She laughed, but it didn't sound like she thought he was amusing. "If you think this was me, bugger off. There's no way I'd ruin Frankie's stone. I loved him like my own. That's why I didn't have any kids myself in case the same thing happened to it. My late husband understood and didn't push it. I couldn't have stood another loss, but then he died, then my brother. Someone's got it out for Fay to stoop so low as to do this."

Yep, too right, but who?

Chapter Thirty-Five

1965

Despite hardly anyone talking to Fay at the party, she'd had a good time. She'd danced, had some sherry, and now weaved through the streets towards Nan's. She was staying there overnight as Nan had said it wasn't advisable for Fay to look after such a small baby while under the influence.

She walked down Nan's road, singing From Me to You. *A lot of the men had the same hairstyles as The Beatles now, while the women had the Dusty Springfield look with all the eye makeup to match. And there was Fay, Miss Plain, no one anyone would want to be seen dead with.*

Frankie's dad and his fumbling attempts down the alley after another such party should have told her he wasn't really interested in anything but sex. His second and last approach had been marginally better, this time in the back of his car, but still, he'd hardly treated her as if she mattered. In the pub after, he'd passed her a glass of Mother's Ruin, saying, "Get that down you." And wasn't that a bit of irony four weeks later when she hadn't got her monthlies.

Mother's Ruin, Fay being such to her mum.

A Morris Minor was parked outside Nan's, the kind no one wanted to see.

A police car.

Stomach rolling over, she hurried her steps, anxious, and rushed up the garden path. She knocked, and Florrie opened the door, her face blotchy, eyes red. Had something happened to Nan? Did she have a fall? A heart attack?

A policeman appeared at the end of the hall, filling the kitchen doorway, the top of his head nigh on touching the lintel. God, had there been a break-in? Was Frankie all right? And Fay was still outside on the step, as if she didn't belong here and wasn't welcome inside.

The copper came over.

"This the mother?" he asked Florrie.

She nodded.

"Ah, come in then." He guided Fay by the elbow to the kitchen.

Nan sat at the table where she'd been when Fay had left, clutching Frankie to her and rocking. She spotted Fay and bawled, a terrible sound coming out of her gaping mouth. Another man stood nearby, and it took a moment for Fay to register him in his brown tweed suit and white shirt, black tie knotted loosely, as if he'd been in a rush to put it on and come to Nan's.

Doctor Hemmel. What was he doing here?

Fay looked at Frankie, who seemed too pale, his lips a strange purple-blue.

"Frankie?" she whispered, rooted to the spot. His mouth didn't make that sucking movement like it usually did while he slept. She glanced about at everyone in turn, then back to Frankie. "W-what's going on?"

"I'm afraid he's gone." Dr Hemmel moved to stand by her.

"Who's gone?"

"Your son. He passed in his sleep. Not uncommon for babies."

"Passed?" What the hell was he talking about? Passed what?

Her legs wobbled, and a massive wave of heat flashed through her, growing in intensity the farther it spread. She shook with it, this unseen abductor of her body, and shifted her gaze from her little boy to Florrie.

"I'm so sorry," her cousin said. "I was holding him, and he just went to sleep and wouldn't wake up. I gave him to Nan, and she...she smacked his back to shock him into breathing. It didn't work, God, it didn't work." She wailed, clutching at her hair.

"You...you killed him...?" Fay's eyes burned.

"Now, now," the doctor said. "There'll be none of that. I've given the cause of death, so me and the police will be going shortly after the body has been taken."

"Taken?" She shook her head. "No, you can't take him. You can't just walk out of here with my baby. He's mine, and I love him."

*"He's **dead**, my dear." Doctor Hammel took her hand and squeezed it. "Nothing can be done now. He's not coming back."*

Fay screamed. For what seemed like eons.

It was so incredibly painful, thinking about that. Fay hated her memories, the way they came alive, reliving themselves, a film in her head. She couldn't bear this any longer, the torture, day in, day out, relentless. And that Noah, coming here in his stupid masks and putting on silly voices to trick her had stirred other memories, too, of her wickedness with Ivy.

Perhaps that was what she deserved, Frankie's death. Some higher power had foreseen how she'd kill Ivy and took her son away from her as an early punishment. Noah had babbled about dreams and how they'd told him to come and see her, to remind her to keep quiet, but that was stupid. She'd already *remained* quiet.

And she'd be quiet forever in a minute.

She stared at the knife Louise had left on the tea tray, along with an apple, saying she'd eat it when she came back. That was a bit insensitive, but maybe she'd forgotten Fay's tongue had been cut out and she couldn't eat.

Fay used to cut the peel off of apples and pears in one long, curly strip. It reminded her of Billy and how he'd been amazed at the feat when a little boy.

"How did you do *that*?" he'd asked, eyes wide.

"Magic."

There'd been some fun times at Loving Arms, challenging as well, but mainly good, and she felt she'd done her penance in the years she'd worked there after Ivy, never being mean to a child again, always ensuring Noah couldn't get to the boys or Oliver to the girls. She was the kids' fierce protector, something she should have been for Ivy, too, and in failing that girl, in keeping Noah's secret as well as hers and Oliver's, she'd failed the other children. Unable to fully relax around them, she hadn't given them as much of her as she should have. Kind but aloof. Hugging them but with stiff arms.

All too late now, to fix what she'd broken. Those children were adults, living their own lives.

Hopefully, they remembered her fondly despite her prickliness.

Louise was hanging the washing out—she'd said that while it was cold, the rain had stopped, and there was an ideal wind. Fay was safe to do what she wanted. If she hurried, it would be too late, and Louise wouldn't be able to help her.

Fay shuffled upstairs, thinking of Gary Flint from Mulberry Lane and how he'd hung himself from the banisters in Halfway House, unable to continue on. Word had it he'd helped kill little

Jacob Everson, and Gary couldn't stand to face a prison sentence for murdering a minor.

Fay knew that feeling.

But what Gary had done gave her an idea, one she'd been thinking about on and off since Noah had revealed who he was behind that mask. She should have clocked it, really. He'd had a mask on *that* night, too.

In her bedroom, she took her frameless mirror off the wall by gripping it with her wrists and placed it on one side of the bed, folding the quilt over it using what remained of her hands. She sat on the mirror and smiled at the sound of a delicious crack. Quilt flung off, she stared at the three jagged pieces. One had a decent point, so she picked it up, again with her wrists, and admired the large piece, catching a glimpse of herself, an old woman she no longer recognised. She saw Nan, not Fay.

She walked over to her bedside table and knelt, using her teeth to grip the knob of the drawer and open it. Picking up the mirror shard using her wrists, she put it in the drawer so the flat edge rested on the bottom, the point poking upwards, about ten inches above the cabinet top. Drawer closed, Fay studied the thing that would take her away from all this, to Frankie, and a better place.

She could say sorry to Ivy for letting her down, too.

Fay took a deep breath and fell forward, the bite of the mirror on her throat, the heat of gushing blood no less than she deserved.

Chapter Thirty-Six

Helen was glad the wind had dropped a bit, although it was still pretty blowy. The soup was done—potato and chicken, another favourite from Loving Arms. She'd poured it into a Thermos so it kept warm, and in her other hand she had a home-baked loaf in case Louise wanted soup, too.

Was that insensitive? Should she go back and leave the bread at home? Fay might be upset at not being able to eat it.

God, this was all so difficult.

She made the decision to carry on, and Louise could hide the bread if she thought that was best.

At Fay's door, she knocked with her elbow, creating a bit of a racket, but that couldn't be helped. It took a while for Louise to come and open up.

"Oh, I just about heard that. I've been hanging some washing out, then did a bit of weeding while I was at it. Come in."

Helen stepped inside and whispered, "Do you want to put this bread in the kitchen? Or will Fay be able to manage it if it's soaked in the soup?" She held up the Thermos.

"She might well do. That was very thoughtful of you. I pureed the stew and dumplings yesterday, and she enjoyed that. So did I, but I ate mine out of the way. Didn't want to rub it in that I could eat solids, like."

"No, that wouldn't be nice."

Louise took the soup and bread, walking off to the kitchen, and Helen pushed open the living room door, smiling ready to greet her friend.

Fay wasn't there, so she wandered off to find Louise in the kitchen.

"Aww, has she fallen asleep?" Louise asked while wrapping the loaf in a tea towel.

"She's not in there."

Louise put the bread on the side. "Maybe she went up for a nap. I'll go and have a look."

She crept upstairs, and Helen waited in the hallway, gazing up.

A scream came, frightening Helen silly, and she struggled up the steps, each stair a trial to climb. Breathless at the top, her skin going hot then cold, she hobbled to Fay's open bedroom door and walked in, turning to face the window on the right.

Red had splashed one side of the bed and the carpet, the wall beside the headboard, and Helen blinked, trying to take it in. Louise stood beside Fay, who knelt in front of a bedside cabinet, her wrist in Louise's hand. She must be taking her pulse.

"W-what's wrong?" Helen's voice had gone all croaky.

Louise looked over at her, tears streaming. "I-I think she's killed herself."

Helen fainted.

Chapter Thirty-Seven

In the early afternoon, Mask stood at Helen's front door as the thirty-year-old reporter, confident she'd spill some beans to a man. Him coming here as Katie Violet had been a softener, to get her to relax, and now, here he was, Aiden Zone, Katie's trusted colleague.

She took ages to open the bloody door, and he was conscious of being spotted by this interfering lot peering through their nets. News of Fay must have spread, so people were being hyper vigilant or just extra nosy. Sometimes, he forgot he had a mask on and felt exposed, vulnerable, his real self. He had to give himself a stern reminder that no one knew who he was.

A police car being up at Fay's didn't help his anxiety either.

"Hello?" Helen peered at him, a frown wiggling her forehead. She looked tired. And had she been crying? Maybe Fay's attack had only just set in today.

"Ah, hello. I'm Aiden Zone from *The Pinstone Star*. Katie may have mentioned me?"

"No…" She bit her bottom lip. "Now isn't a good time."

"Oh, anything I can do to help?"

She appeared indecisive, the cogs in her brain all but visible, clicking and turning while she decided whether to relent and allow him inside. "Well, it would be good to talk."

He held his arms out to the sides, palms up, giving her a massive smile. "I'm your man. I like a good chat, and I'm a great listener."

Her shoulders sagged. "Oh, go on then."

She took him into her little kitchen and prepared tea in a pot, just like she had at Arms. It was a smaller version of the huge steel one there, and he had to admit, it did make a good cuppa. He busied himself taking his notepad out from his suit jacket pocket, and a pen, and waited patiently for her to pour. She took longer than she had when in her thirties.

Time was a cruel master.

She sat and pushed the cup over to him. The noise of it scraping set his nerves alight.

"Can you pass something on to Katie for me?" she asked. "I don't think it should be published in the paper, though, as it's dreadful, but if you can just let her know…"

"What's that then, Miss Donaldson?"

"Please, call me Helen."

She always was a nice woman. He'd loved her cooking, her baking, and the way she'd used food as a tether to bind everyone together.

"Okay, Helen. Fire away."

"Fay's dead."

He had to stop himself from laughing. "Oh dear, well, that's very unfortunate. How did that happen? I heard about the attack from Katie, of course, but dead…?"

Helen nodded and stirred her tea absently. "Yes, she k-killed herself." A pause. "Using a shard of a mirror."

'Mirror' had gone up at the end in her distress. What an ingenious way to top oneself. The question was, how had she managed *that*?

He had to know all the details. "Um, forgive me for sounding cruel, but she had no fingers. How did she…?"

"The police said she broke the mirror then somehow put it in a drawer so it poked upwards. She…she leant forward, and…and it stabbed her in the neck. There was…there was so much blood." She shuddered and closed her eyes. "I went to take her some soup and bread, you see. Saw her like that."

So the bitch hadn't been able to stand herself after all. She'd carried what she'd done on her shoulders for years, then he'd shown up, reminded her, and she'd decided to end it all. Was that because she couldn't talk anymore, didn't have fingers? Or was it because of his threat that he'd expose her, regardless of her countering it by telling the police what he'd done with Billy?

He'd carried it on *his* shoulders for years, too, prepared to zip his lips.

Until the dreams.

"I'm so sorry for your loss," he said, hoping he sounded genuine but feeling he'd failed. "Katie told me you and Fay were good friends."

"Yes, she could be a bit abrasive at times but, you know, she was good deep down."

I doubt that very much. People who kill little girls aren't nice.

It could be argued that people who messed with little boys weren't either, but he wouldn't go into that.

He had two cups of tea, getting Helen to reminisce about her time at Arms, and it seemed she didn't know anything about the real issue there. So Fay had kept her mouth shut, even with her closest friend.

So why had the dreams told him otherwise? Was it Oliver he needed to go after instead?

"What about the night Ivy Gibbs went missing? What can you tell me about that?"

"Oh, that was just dreadful. I slept with cotton wool in my ears in those days. Always had trouble sleeping if I heard anything, see. That night I went right through, although…" She scrunched her eyebrows. "Yes, I do remember waking up momentarily now."

I knew it! She does know something.

"Did you get up then?" he asked.

"Yes, to use the toilet. I still had the cotton wool in, but I heard something. That was it, people going downstairs. But ignore me, that's been explained by Fay. She'd had a bad night so got up to clean the wellies, and Billy woke with a nightmare, so it must have been one of those two I heard."

"Do you ever wonder whether it could have been someone taking Ivy?"

Her eyes grew wide. "Oh, do you think? I hadn't thought it might be that. How dreadful. Should I tell the police?"

"Too much time has passed, to be honest. They won't be interested now." He paused for the finale. "And what about Billy Price? You said he had a nightmare. Did he ever say why?"

"Monsters," she said. "He saw monsters. Maybe I'll go down and ask him about that, see if he still has night terrors. He'll need a mother figure now Fay's gone. Oh God, I wonder if he even knows?"

Mask couldn't have that. If she spoke to Billy…

The dreams were right after all. Helen had to go.

He got to work, doing to her what he'd done to Fay, using extra-strong black bags to cover his suit jacket this time and putting her yellow Marigolds on, uber fetching. As an extra precaution, he placed her meat cleaver down after lopping off her fingers and tongue and drove a large knife from her pine display block into her chest.

He stared at her until she stopped twitching and breathing.

Mask hadn't expected to do this today, but never mind. One less visit to her as the old man, which was just as well, considering Fay was dead and the police would continue sniffing around.

He took the black bags off and scrunched them into balls, disposing of them in her washing machine, set to wash with bleach. The coppers would know what he'd done, but that just added to the amusement, thinking of them trying to work out what on earth he was playing at.

Face mask washed with her dishcloth, he peeled the gloves off so the blood was on the inside. Those he'd be taking with him. DNA on them wasn't something he wanted to leave behind. He stuffed them in his pocket along with her tongue and fingers in a Ziploc bag and left the house. A glance up the road to check for anyone outside Fay's, then he was off, past Billy's place at the end and along the way towards home.

He entered Griffin's, greeted with that bloody dog barking, and it was no good, he'd have to let it out. The walker wasn't due until for a while, and Rochester would hopefully be long gone by then.

In the copper's garden, he used a large stone from the rockery to smash the window in the door. He paused to wait for someone to come and investigate the noise. No one was bothered, obviously. A quick reach inside the hole with his sleeve over his hand, a twist of the key, and he let the animal outside. It whimpered from standing on a piece of glass, so Mask called the daft thing over and pulled it out of his paw.

"Bugger off now, there's a good boy." He closed the door so Rochester couldn't get back in.

The silly thing bounded around the garden, a loony, and Mask walked out, propping the gate open. He strode down the street and turned the corner and, beneath a tree with low-hanging branches, he took the mask off and rolled it into a sausage. Returned to Griffin. Scanned the street. No one seemed to be around, so he went home, pleased with his morning's work. Now, as he didn't have to go to Helen's again, he'd made some space to create the Beauty and Beast masks.

Everything happened for a reason.

Chapter Thirty-Eight

Morgan and Shaz knocked at Helen's, having given her some time to come to terms with Fay being dead. The call from Gray about it had been a bombshell. Louise, the carer, had called it in, and uniforms had come out. Morgan had wanted to go there to make sure it definitely wasn't murder, but all the clues pointed to Fay doing it herself.

It was a shame they had to push Helen to switch gears, going from her friend's death to the nineties, Oliver Elford, and Noah Tate, but needs must.

"She might not remember much, you know," Shaz said.

"Who forgets a kid going missing?" He sighed. "While I don't think for one second Oliver did that to Fay, we still need to ask questions. If her attack and suicide is linked to Loving Arms, despite it being a long time ago, we need to discuss it with Helen."

He knocked again. Shaz nosed through the living room window.

"Must have been a shock for her to find Fay like that," she said. "I mean, imagine taking some soup and bread round for your mate and coming face to face with all that blood."

"I know. The poor cow was distraught when we arrived, wasn't she." He scrubbed at his chin.

"I nearly cried when you told Billy."

"Don't. Sad as fuck." He knocked again. "Look, she's probably out or having a lie down—"

"Hello? Excuse me?" a woman called.

Morgan turned to his right.

A lady next door stood on her step, arms crossed, about forty, her blonde hair in a messy bun. "She's not long had a visitor, and now *you're* here, I'm a bit concerned. What with Fay being attacked and everything…"

"Who was it?" Morgan asked.

"Some fella. About thirty. In a grey suit. Blond. He left about twenty minutes ago."

Not an old man then. "Did you hear anything through the wall?"

"Hmm, might have been her chair falling over maybe? The one in the kitchen. It's wooden."

Morgan glanced along the row. Only one ginnel halfway down, which probably led to the back gardens. "Okay, thanks."

She went inside, and Morgan tapped Shaz's arm to get her to follow him. They used the ginnel, and he counted along to get the right back garden. He needn't have bothered, a number plaque was screwed to the tall gate, so he opened it and walked up the path between the rectangles of grass either side. At the kitchen window, he peered in.

"Oh fuck. Call for assistance, will you?" He gestured for Shaz to look inside.

"Bloody Nora."

Morgan covered his hand with his jacket sleeve and turned the handle. The door opened, thank God, and he assessed the scene. Helen, on the floor with no fingers, claret everywhere. Her face turned to him, covered in red, mouth open to reveal a tunnel filled with blood. He couldn't see if she had a tongue. A knife stuck out of her chest in the heart area, and it was more than clear she was a goner. Black washing tumbled around in the machine behind her head.

A wooden chair had indeed fallen over. Tea things sat on the table, two saucers but only one with a cup on it, the tea still inside. Where was the other cup? He bent over to check beneath the table. Nothing. It wasn't in the sink either.

He went outside and took a deep breath.

"The team is on the way," Shaz said.

"Cheers. I'd walk through to open the front door, but there's so much blood in such a tight space, I don't want to step in it and fuck the scene up."

"Lock this door from the outside, and we'll wait out the front."

He managed it with a bit of difficulty, his hands covered by his jacket sleeve again, and they walked around to the street, remaining by the ginnel entrance so no one could go down there.

"It's definitely Loving Arms related," Shaz said quietly.

"Got to be, with Fay *and* Helen."

"When I looked through the window, I spotted they used one of her knives. There's one missing from her block on the worktop. Why kill her and not Fay?"

"Maybe he chopped her tongue out and fingers off, then decided it was more hassle to let her live—us snooping around, more likely to find him—and stabbed her as well."

"According to the neighbour, though, Helen's visitor was about thirty."

"Two mates working together? Father and son team? The dad did Fay, got tired because he's old, so the son took over? Probably a load of rubbish, but it's out there, something to consider."

"Two different people at any rate."

"Cameron's here."

Morgan waited for everyone to climb out of the van. The SOCO team grabbed protectives while Cameron approached, a grim smile in place.

"Helen Donaldson, stabbed, no fingers, probably no tongue," Morgan said. "I've got the key as I locked up—had to go in round the back. I stood just inside the door and touched nothing. Next-door neighbour said a man in his thirties left just before we arrived. He killed her recently—the scent is fresh in there." He handed the key over into Cameron's gloved hand. "I haven't touched the key with my skin. We're on course to find out who did this, so we'll leave you to it because time is running out. If we get to our next stop and the resident isn't there, maybe we'll catch him coming home. He was on foot—not that I believe Oliver Elford can pass as a slim thirty-year-old."

"Right. Will you be nipping back?"

"Yep, after." Morgan walked off and waved over some uniforms in patrol cars. Once they all got out, he said, "I want a log at the ginnel entrance and one on the back door, because people might come and go from their rear gardens, and we need a record of that. House-to-house, please. We've got to nip off but will be back to help out."

Morgan and Shaz dived in his car, and he drove them to Griffin's Holt. It was odd, as if he were going home, and he parked outside his house, frowning at the side gate being open and flapping in the breeze. He'd sort it after.

Shaz knocked on Oliver's door, and he appeared within seconds, holding it open as if he didn't have anything to hide.

"Aww, what now?" He closed his eyes momentarily.

"Where have you been all morning?" Morgan asked.

"Went to see my mum, then came back here."

"Can anyone verify that?"

"You can check at the care home. Her nurse is called Liz. She saw me. Cobbs Moor Residential."

"We need to come in, have a bit of a chat."

Oliver stepped back. "I could say this is harassment."

"You could, but no one will give a toss." Morgan walked inside. The place had a sterile feel, and it smelt of paint. The stuff used on the gravestone?

Shaz came in. "Like painting, do you?"

Oliver nodded. "I do as it happens. Not long lived here, so I've been scraping gaudy paper off the walls then plastering them."

So *that* was what the noise had been the past few nights. "What colours have you got?"

"Eh?" Oliver stared, expression blank.

"Of paint." Shaz tapped her foot.

"Oh, just white for the walls and a light-grey for the skirting boards and doorframes. Don't touch the kitchen one, only just finished glossing it." Oliver had a splotch of paint on the top curve of his left ear.

If he'd gone out *after* seeing his mother and painting here, there'd be some at Helen's. Transfer.

"Look, what do you want?" Oliver picked up a small can of paint off the floor, the brush balanced on top. He started on the living room doorframe, a strange humming coming out of the weird bastard.

Morgan watched the brush going up and down and thought of Billy saying Loving Arms had been done up by Oliver. May as well stick the boot right in... "We're here about Ivy Gibbs."

The brush stopped for two seconds, then Oliver resumed, but the tell was enough.

He knew something.

"I didn't kill her."

Morgan raised his eyebrows. "No one's saying you did. We still don't know if she's even dead. Yes, it's likely, given the weather at the time, the bogs on the moor, but if she was abducted and sold, she'd have a new name anyway. Why was your first thought death?"

"Like you said, the weather. She put the stool by the wellies. She went out on her own. She closed the door and locked it. She got lost on the moor or fell in the river."

He'd said it as bullet points, something he'd drummed into his head. She, she, she.

"How was Fay's behaviour with her? How did she act?" Shaz asked.

Oliver lost his perfect motion with the brush for a moment. "Why is this being dragged up again? It was years ago."

"Because someone from her past might not be happy with her." Morgan opened the front door a bit to let out the paint fumes.

Shaz stood in the gap in case Oliver bolted.

"What, from all the way back then?" Oliver dipped the brush in the paint. "There must be elephants around here."

What the fuck was he on about? "Come again?"

"Elephants, they never forget. Maybe someone's struggling with forgetting and paid her a visit. Not me, I didn't go and cut Fay up."

"But someone did. Know who that's likely to be?"

"No!" Oliver shouted, giving Morgan a manic stare. "I don't want anything to do with that lot at Arms. They ignored me after I did what I did with the girl from Pinstone—they said they were my family, then they turned their backs on me. I was on my own. My sister cut me off, and my mother, well, she's told me this morning she doesn't want to see me ever again. I bought her a nice tartan blanket just before I went in the nick the last time an' all. It cost me fifteen quid. Shows you how ungrateful she is."

Is he fucking serious?

"The care home is the same house as Loving Arms. How do you feel when you go back there?" Shaz asked.

"They've put up wallpaper, new stuff, and there's all that lino everywhere, nothing like it used to be. They've ruined it by taking up the carpets. They were durable, would have lasted another ten years at least, but they said the pile was too thick for the wheelchairs. I laid those carpets myself. All that hard work for nothing."

"A bit obsessive over the carpet, aren't you?" Shaz stared at him.

"I've got memories attached to it."

"And what are those?" She folded her arms.

"Just reminds me of happier days, when I was busy doing Arms up, that's all. The kids were so excited about it. They all got new curtains, made by Helen, Noah helped—she was good with that sewing machine of hers. One night, after I'd glossed all the banisters and rails while the kids were asleep, I went down into the kitchen to make a cuppa, and she'd baked me an apple pie. Left me a note saying I should enjoy it for all the effort I'd been putting in. Helen was nice like that."

"Helen is dead, as is Fay," Morgan said.

Oliver dropped the brush. It landed on his boot, paint smearing the black leather. Shaz stooped to pick it up.

"W-what? How?" Oliver's eyes watered, and he glanced from Morgan to Shaz.

"Helen had her fingers cut off, maybe even her tongue cut out, just like Fay." Shaz sounded positively sinister. "Then they stabbed her in the heart, and that's just nasty, because it sounds like her heart was the best bit of her. She was kind, didn't deserve that. Fay killed herself. Know of anyone who'd want to hurt Helen?"

"Oh, fucking hell…" Oliver staggered off down the hall, into the kitchen.

Shaz followed, careful not to let her arms touch the frames, and Morgan brought up the rear. Oliver had placed the can on the worktop and hung his head over the sink. Shaz put the brush on a piece of kitchen towel.

Oliver sucked in deep breaths. "Not Helen, she's nothing to do with anything."

"What do you mean by that?" Morgan gripped the back of Oliver's top and hauled him upright, swinging him round to face him. "What aren't you telling us?"

"Nothing, I meant…I meant that she wouldn't be involved in anything bad to have warranted her being killed."

"You sound suss as fuck." Morgan shoved him towards the worktop. "If you know something…"

"I don't know anything." Oliver held his hands up, eyes bugging.

"What, about Fay and Helen being sliced?"

Oliver nodded. "Yes, that. I know nothing about that."

"Seems to me, people who worked at Loving Arms are being targeted now," Shaz said.

"They are." Morgan paused. "You might be next. Then Noah Tate."

"Oh fuck…"

"Yeah, oh fuck." Morgan stepped away from him. "If I find out you're lying to me…"

"I don't know who did that to them, I swear."

"If you have a change of heart, my number's the first one you ring, got it?" Morgan jabbed a finger in the air towards Oliver. "Me, no one else. If you suddenly remember something and it's nighttime, knock on my door, *neighbour*."

"I will, I promise."

"That's if the killer doesn't get to you first." Shaz smiled sweetly.

Morgan walked out, inhaling a big gulp of air. Oliver knew something, although whether that had anything to do with now or the past, Morgan wasn't sure. He'd have another go at him later—on his own after work.

He stomped up his own path and went into the garden, locking the gate instead of just using the latch. The wind wouldn't be able to open it then. He walked through into the back, expecting Rochester to jump up at the door glass and greet him, but the dog wasn't there. A ruddy great hole in the glass was. Inside, some blood on the tiles in the shape of a paw pad along with broken glass. Someone must have broken in.

Morgan went inside, searching the house.

No dog.

He ran back out the front and met Shaz on the pavement. "Rochester's gone. Someone's smashed the back door."

"Helloooooooooooo!" a female shouted.

Morgan stared across the road. A grey-haired woman of about sixty stood on the grass verge, Rochester by her side, and he had a blue collar and lead on.

"He's been legging it up and down the road, having a right old time of it," she said. "I took him into my house."

Morgan crossed to collect the dog, relieved he was all right. "Thank you very much. I'm sorry to have caused you any problems."

"Lovely animal, so affectionate. I've cleaned his paw—there was a cut on it. He gets along lovely with my animals—I have a rottie and a cat. The only problem I have is his barking. Funny how he doesn't do it when he's with someone."

"Yeah, he's been used to...used to my late wife being at home all day."

"Oh, I'm sorry you lost her."

I'm not. "Thank you."

"I see you have a dog walker taking him out. I could do that, you know. Keep him at my place, too, until you get home. I'd walk him with my Tyson."

Morgan couldn't believe the generosity. "Oh, um..."

"It'll save people getting pissed off with the barking. My name's Trudy. I'll take him into mine now, shall I?"

"If you can, just until I get the glass fixed in the back door. Someone broke in."

"I saw a young man of about thirty at yours. Blond. Grey suit."

Fuck. "What time was that? Did he have blood on him?"

"Ooer, can't say I noticed that, no. And it wasn't that long ago, actually. He walked off down there and disappeared around the corner. Forgot to say, I'm at number ten. You can do one of those checks on me, if you like. I'll wait. No criminal record." She smiled. "Trudy Baker."

Shaz ran off round the corner.

Morgan addressed Trudy. "I'll need you to give a statement about the man."

"Of course. Look, let me get your dog settled in while you go about your business. What's his name?"

"Rochester."

She patted the mutt's head. "Oh, get you, posh as anything." She laughed and went to her house, Rochester wagging his tail beside her, looking up at her while listening to whatever she said to him.

Some people just had a knack with dogs.

Shaz returned, shaking her head. "I've called for patrol to come and see if they spot him."

"Cheers." He explained what Trudy had said, then rang a glazier to come and sort the window. He wasn't going to fuck about getting uniforms poking throughout his house, but he did need them for door-to-door. He organised for someone to collect a swab of that blood in case it wasn't Rochester's.

So, they had a man in a grey suit. The same as the one at Helen's? Same age and hair colour.

What the *fuck* was going on, and why had he been to Morgan's?

Unless he thought it was Oliver's…

Balls. He spoke to Oliver again, impressing upon him the importance of being vigilant. "If he's coming for you, too, you need to be alert."

"Why would he want to chop me up?" Oliver's hands shook.

"You tell me."

Chapter Thirty-Nine

Morgan drove them to Helen's. Trudy had left Rochester in her house and promised to stay at Morgan's until the glazier had finished and the swab was taken. Morgan had got Gray to run a check on her, and as she'd said, no criminal record, and if the dog trusted her, then he would, too.

He parked and took protectives out of the boot. They signed the log at the ginnel entrance then walked single file along it, making their way to Helen's via the back. Suited up and the second log signed, Morgan entered the kitchen, Shaz behind. They stayed near the door. The room was full of SOCO, evidence markers, and steps to avoid treading in the blood.

"Ah, hello." Cameron turned from the body and tugged his face mask down. "Lisa's been and gone. Time of death was close to when you'd called it in. The stab wound to the heart did it, obviously. Curious, though… There was washing in the machine, and when it finished, I took the items out as they may have been put in there by the killer—you know, wanting to clean whatever it was."

"And?"

"Black bags."

"What?"

"Yep, he washed bin bags. One has a large hole in the top, like for a neck. Same with the other two, but they'd been tied at the bottom with a smaller hole left open. Perhaps sleeves?"

"So he wore them while killing her?"

"Yes. An empty packet beneath the sink for Marigolds, size medium. Yellow. Did he take them out to wear those, too? Must have left with them, as there aren't any here. We've checked the bin, nothing in there."

"Any white or grey paint transfer?" It wasn't Oliver, Morgan had phoned the care home to see if he'd gone there, but he had to check regardless.

"Not that we've seen so far. Can't find the missing cup either, so perhaps they stayed for some tea and took it with them. Fingerprints, saliva... The tongue and fingers are absent."

"So if they had a cuppa, she'd have either known them or trusted whoever they were to let them in."

"Yes, no signs of a struggle at the front door, although that chair toppled over indicates all wasn't well."

"I think the body bloody shows that," Shaz said.

Cameron laughed, the wrinkles at the sides of his eyes crinkling. "Just a bit. Any news on Oliver?"

Morgan shook his head. "It wasn't him, I don't think, but someone was at my house after Helen's death—same description as the fella who was here. Smashed my back door and let the dog out. Nothing stolen as far as I could see."

"So the killer knows who you are? As in, that you're dealing with the case?"

"Seems like it. Maybe releasing the dog was their warning. You know, don't pursue me or the dog gets it."

Cameron chuckled. "Don't disregard that. You know how nutty some of them are."

"Or he could have thought Oliver lived there, got the door numbers mixed up. Anyway, it's fine, I've got a new dog sitter. A Trudy Baker."

Cameron beamed a smile. "Oh, my mum's friend. Nice, she is. Got a rottie, that the one?"

"It is."

"Small world, eh?" Cameron lifted his mask into place. "Your pooch won't want to come home, so watch it if you're the jealous sort."

"I could tell she's good with animals."

"Spoilt rotten, her dog. Tyson. Built like a brick shithouse, same as his namesake. Anyway, fuck all you can do here, so you may as well get on. I'll send the pictures along later. To Nigel or Jane?"

"Nigel, please." Morgan's phone rang. "Speaking of Nigel… See you soon, mate." He walked out and answered the call in the garden. "Yep?"

"Just giving you an update. Jane wants to speak after me."

"Joy."

Nigel laughed. "Right, all the kids who were at Loving Arms have been spoken to over the phone. All checks have been made on them. Not one criminal among them, clean records, so however Fay brought them up, and the fosters and adopters afterwards, they did a bloody good job, considering some of the childhood stories they told me before they were taken into care. It'd send anyone loopy."

"Shame."

"It is. Anyway, unless any of them are lying, we're barking up the wrong bloody tree. All of them who lived there when Ivy Gibbs went missing were in bed, although a few of them said she was a little cow, always playing up and getting Fay annoyed. Interesting, yes?"

"Very, but it doesn't do us much good, because Fay killed herself."

"Fuck me."

"Yeah, sorry I didn't ring to tell you. It's been a bit manic. Stick speakerphone on so I can update you both on everything at the same time."

"Rightio."

"Hello, Yeoman," Jane said.

"Hello. Here's where we stand." He gave them the rundown on what had happened today. "So we're looking for a nutter who thinks Fay is a killer—*if* it's the same person who defaced the gravestone."

"What on earth has she been up to, to have someone do this?" Jane mused.

"Getting herself in a heap of shit by the look of it," Nigel said. "So, what do you want us to do next?"

Morgan pinched the bridge of his nose to get his brain into gear. "Keep poking into her past, especially the Ivy Gibbs year and Fay's time at Loving Arms. There's *got* to be something there. The care home is the one solid thing that ties Fay and Helen together."

"There's something else," Nigel said, "totally unrelated."

"What's that?"

"Martin Olbey has been apprehended in Shadwell. I let the woman there know that once she's dealt with him at her end, we'll also be needing a word. She'll give you a ring tomorrow to arrange things. It's Fran."

Morgan's guts rolled over. If Olbey mentioned Lydia in his interview, the shit could hit the fan. He knew she had something to do with that lad's death. Morgan would have to play it carefully so he didn't step in any crap and walk around with the stench on him. "Fine. Thanks. Jane, what did you want to talk about?"

"Noah Tate. I've got a bit more info on him. He worked for a troupe of actors, travelling the country prior to staying on in Pinstone after being *let go*."

Morgan's mind was too full to play guessing games with her. "Elaborate."

"His employment was terminated, because the company owner later found out that while they were in Smaltern, playing at the theatre there for the summer holidaymakers, there were rumours that someone fitting Noah's description was sexually inappropriate with a minor—a boy. Now, the company owner is dead, but his daughter is a similar age to Noah, and she remembers it well. Noah denied anything had happened, but he was let go anyway, and no one told the police, not even the boy's parents."

"So we have someone who could possibly have been a pervert, working then living with young kids."

"Dodgy, right? However, you said today's murder was carried out by a man in his thirties—if that's even the one who did it. Fay's attack was an old man. Noah is fifty-two. He's in between those ages. Oliver is fifty-seven."

"Got anything else on Noah?"

"As you know, no present address, his financials are in the wind somewhere and have been for years. No record of his death, so unless that was accidental and he's on the moor or in the river, or any number of other places in other towns, we're not going to find his body now."

Nigel chipped in. "Maybe he changed his name."

"We'll never know," Jane said. "Deed Poll are funny about realising those details."

Morgan blew out air. "So we have a bloke who could or couldn't have been a perv. His name disappeared years ago and no one reported him missing, so we assume he hasn't got anyone who gives a shit, and if he *is* around here as we've been told, we have no bloody clue what name he uses now or where he is." He paused to think. "So unless he can change his appearance to look thirty *and* old, or unless Billy and Helen's neighbour, and Trudy Baker need glasses and they're seeing someone younger when they're not, we're shit out of luck."

"Want me to have a chat with Oliver?" Jane asked. "I could probably get more out of him than you."

"No!" That came out a bit too forcefully. "No." Gentler. "He's hiding something, but I'm going round his place to speak to him later, after work."

"On your own," Jane stated.

"Yes, on my own."

"Right…"

"What's going on?" Nigel said.

Bollocks. Morgan had forgotten he was still on the call. "Nothing. Jane's just worried I'll rough him up."

Nigel laughed. "Wouldn't be the first time you did something like that."

"Don't know what you're talking about." Morgan hoped Nigel left it there. "Okay, I'm off. The day has been long, so leave on time, please, get some rest. There's nothing we can do now until tomorrow. Me and Shaz will be in The Tractor's if you fancy meeting up. I want to speak to Terry about this Noah. Apparently, he's a regular there. See you later." He put his phone away.

Shaz came out into the garden. "Did I hear you saying we're going for a drink?"

"It's four o'clock, so fuck it. We'll be there on police business to start with anyway."

"So I heard."

"Listening to other people's phone conversations is almost as bad as eating those Scampi Fries of yours. Revolting."

"Yeah, well, Nigel and Jane were in on it, so why not me?"

"Because you know everything already."

She let her mouth drop. "No, I don't."

"Yes, you do."

She poked his chest. "Sounded to me like they had something to say."

"Ah, yeah, I'll fill you in when we're in the car." Morgan signed the log. "We'll check with uniforms first, see if any other neighbours spotted the bloke at Helen's."

"Shouldn't we be going round to tell Florrie about Fay?"

"Shit, it slipped my mind. Okay, Florrie's first, then the pub."

Some days, it was never-ending.

Chapter Forty

1965

Florrie couldn't stand it. Fay had accused her of killing Frankie, and in front of Doctor Hammel and the policeman, too. But it wasn't Florrie, she'd just rocked him to sleep like she'd said. The thing was, she didn't know what had happened after, because she'd gone to sleep an' all.

Had she accidentally smothered him?

No, she'd asked Nan that, and she'd said Florrie had sat there the whole time in the armchair while Nan listened to the wireless, keeping an eye out.

When Florrie woke and shifted Frankie from one arm to the other, he'd been limper than usual, heavier. She'd lifted him to check his breathing, spotted his lips, then glanced at Nan who'd shot up and taken over.

The next few minutes were a blur, with Nan shouting for Florrie to run down to Mrs Armitage. She had a phone, and Florrie was to ring Doctor Hammel and explain Frankie wasn't breathing. Mrs Armitage had been in a dither hearing the news but allowed the call just the same, then followed Florrie back to Nan's and went inside.

Nan sat in a chair in the kitchen, rocking Frankie and sobbing.

"Maybe it was the milk," Mrs Armitage said. "He's been fine up until now on his mother's tit."

Florrie glimpsed the bottle of gripe water then, and, as she had when Fay had put it on the table, she experienced a sense of dread. Maybe babies as little as Frankie shouldn't have that. What if it had poisoned him or something? Florrie didn't know, she was too young, not well-versed in babies, but nevertheless, she ushered Mrs Armitage out onto the street then returned to the kitchen.

"Did he have some of this?" Florrie asked. She held the bottle up.

Nan managed to stop sobbing and stare at her. "H-he cried, remember, like he was in pain."

"Could this have done it?" She waved it about.

"I doubt it." Nan frowned. "But it didn't smell the same as usual, I know that. I just thought it was a newfangled one."

"What?" Florrie's heart pounded. "What if…? What if it isn't gripe water? What if Fay gave it to us so it'd look like we killed him?"

"Get rid of it." Nan suddenly sobered from her crying fit. "Put it in the outhouse for now, and don't mention a word about it to anyone. Fay'll be in no fit state to ask where it is if she's not behind this, and I can't see she is. Why go through getting rid of the baby after *you've had it when the damage to your reputation has already been done?"*

"But her neighbour. Shouldn't we ask her where she got it from? Her baby might die an' all if there's some bad gripe water going about."

"Leave it." Nan stared down at the baby. "We've got a mess to get through yet, and adding to it isn't going to help matters by bringing some woman into it."

Florrie couldn't argue with Nan when the old girl was in this sort of mood, so she left via the back door and stepped into the outhouse. She wedged the bottle behind the toilet and took a moment to let the tears fall. They turned into a torrent, and she didn't stop bawling until the faint sound of the front door knocking pulled her out of it. She hurried inside, double vision for a moment from the tears, and opened the door, only to find a policeman standing beside Doctor Hemmel.

What was a copper doing here?

"Ah, Florrie." Doctor Hammel brushed past her. "The police are here to check it isn't a suspicious death."

The word 'suspicious' almost had her blurting out about the bottle.

She stared at them walking down the hallway. Did they know about the gripe water? How could they? No, she was just being silly. Paranoid.

She sucked in a big breath and closed the door.

How on earth were they going to tell Fay her son was dead?

Florrie wiped the tears from her face. Yes, she could remember the past well enough, and that stroll down Memory Lane proved it.

With the policeman and Doctor Hemmel gone, Frankie taken away, Nan had spent the rest of the night into the early hours consoling

Fay, who'd railed and screamed between crying. Sometimes, she sat there with just tears, no sound at all, and others she let out disturbing howls that hurt Florrie's heart.

Eventually, Fay went to bed, still in her party dress, and Nan stood by the table staring at the bottle she'd used to feed Frankie, and his little shawl draped over the chair, his crocheted blue hat, so tiny.

"Get the gripe water." Nan rubbed circles on her temples.

Florrie had obeyed, and Nan poured the lot down the sink then rinsed the bottle out with soda crystals in water.

"Don't forget," Nan had warned, "not a word about this."

The past was such a bind, wasn't it, keeping you pinned in its spiteful talons, never letting go. Nan and Florrie had gone round to Fay's mum's to break the news, even though it might not be welcome, seeing as how she'd cut Fay out of her life.

"Good," Beryl had said with a brisk nod as if it made what she'd said okay. "She's better off without that thing."

'That thing'? Frankie was a baby not a thing.

Florrie shook that memory off, got up, and bustled out to the shed at the bottom of her garden. She had some of Beryl's stuff in there, packed up in a box, and she really ought to give it to Fay. She hadn't wanted to before, but maybe now Fay was older, she'd have forgiven her mother for turfing her out.

Time healed most wounds, didn't it?

But not baby Frankie dying. Never that. And never Fay's accusation either.

She found the box and carried it indoors, placing it on the table. The tape closing the top had got damp over the many years the things had been in storage, the edges peeling upwards, so she'd strip it off and transfer everything to one of her plastic containers she used in the spare room for her sewing bits.

Florrie opened the box, and the scent of age puffed up. She peered inside. A musical jewellery case sat on top, the fuzz of grey-green mould obscuring the intricate carving in the mahogany wood. She put some Marigolds on and lifted it out, thinking to give it a good clean prior to passing it on to Fay—or getting someone else to take it round there at any rate. Fay wouldn't appreciate Florrie on her doorstep.

A further dig produced some china figurines, the newspaper wrapped around them from the late eighties, yellow and brittle. One was of a horse and dray cart, the leather bridle wrecked by damp.

And at the bottom, beneath numerous other knickknacks, a leather-bound book, the cover burgundy, the word DIARY on it in silver. Florrie shouldn't, it was private no matter that Beryl was dead, but a little look wouldn't hurt, would it?

She turned the pages, mildew on their edges, and marvelled at how small the writing was. The entire book spanned from the forties to eighty-nine, the dates showing Beryl only wrote in it for high days and holidays, special moments she perhaps wanted to keep in written memory.

One such date had Florrie gasping, and she couldn't *not* read it.

The day of Frankie's death.

IT IS OVER

Some will say I've done a wicked thing, but it's for the best. My mum once told me that her mother had said: 'A child conceived on the wrong side of the blanket is the Devil's spawn, not fit to breathe air into its lungs at birth.'

Perhaps she's right, as I've killed my grandson. I am the Devil's spawn, one of those children created before marriage, a sin child, implanted via debauchery. And I lived my childhood and early adult life being talked about: 'That girl over there? Her mother and father weren't married when…'

Folks like to point fingers, and while I'd told Fay she could no longer live under my roof, those fingers of shame also pointed at us once she'd announced to everyone she was pregnant and keeping it. She could have gone to Mrs Poggitt down Mulberry Lane to have the thing removed. Her gin and knitting needles had helped many a silly girl out, but oh no, Fay insisted she'd be a single mother, and I couldn't bear it.

Someone had told me what he was like, the thing, a boy with dark hair and a robust set of lungs on him, and I'd thought that was a shame—he was healthy, unlikely to slip away quietly, living, breathing, perhaps coming down my street when he's older and asking me if I'm his nanny.

No, I could never be a nanny to an illegitimate brat.

Of course, my mother, a woman of sin herself, helped Fay, getting her installed in that hovel of a house before the birth, which just so happens to be next door to my friend's daughter who's also had a baby, although she got married first, God love her. Mrs Poggitt had been helpful in finding me something to kill the thing, clear liquid, no scent, no bitter taste. She'll keep her mouth shut because I paid her well.

My daughter's neighbour was under instruction to pass it off as gripe water to give to Fay, and she did, although things went wrong after that. I never would have thought Fay would desert the thing so soon after having him, foisting him off on my mother and dear, sweet Florrie, the girl who should have been mine. Fay has always been wilful, so eager to break the rules, whereas Florrie obeys and is a good girl, if a little caustic sometimes. Like me.

The child died in Florrie's arms instead of Fay's, and I shall forever detest myself for that. I should have ensured the neighbour pushed Fay to give him the stuff sooner, right then and there, saying it aided sleep and would give Fay a rest. She always did like her bed, although I heard the thing was conceived down an alley.

Foul.

But it is done, no more Devil in our midst, and now I shall go to church and tell the good Lord what I've done. He will understand. I've given Florrie a lifetime of terrible memories, the poor love blaming herself as well as Fay accusing her. I've heard all about it.

Still, that's the end of it now. I can only wish Florrie learns to understand it wasn't her fault, despite everyone blaming her with their spiteful words and nasty looks, and all because Fay set the rumour going.

If she doesn't behave, I'll give her *the liquid next. God will understand that, too.*

Florrie hiccoughed a sob and dropped the diary back in the box. It was Auntie Beryl all along? How many years had Florrie suffered with those rumours? How many years had Fay continued to breathe life into them, never letting the past die down? Even now, going to Wasti's and blathering on at him about the fact they no longer spoke.

Still, Fay being a bitch or not, she had a right to know what had happened.

And Florrie wanted an apology.

She picked the diary up and slid it in her bag. Coat and shoes on, she marched to the front door, gearing herself up for what was to come. She opened the door, and Yeoman and that woman copper stood there. What did they bloody want *now*?

"We need to come in," he said. "No arguing about it, Florrie."

She let them inside but didn't take them to the living room. She still hadn't hoovered, for Pete's sake. "What is it?"

"Shall we sit down?" he asked.

"No. Here is fine. Spit it out."

He glanced at his colleague, who shrugged.

"Well, come on then," Florrie barked.

"It's Fay," he said.

"What about her?"

"I'm sorry to have to tell you she's dead."

Well, that was just a big bag of bollocks, wasn't it. Florrie would never get her sorry now. Why was life so unfair to her?

"That old man come back and do it, did he?" The diary seemed to burn her side through the bag.

"No, she took her own life, although a small team of SOCO are there to make doubly sure of that."

"Well, isn't that just wonderful." She hustled past them and opened the front door. "Cheerio. I expect you've got work to get back to in finding the man who chopped her about." She needed them to go. Away from her.

Both walked out and turned to stare at her as if she'd lost her mind, and she slammed the door on the buggers. Angry beyond measure with Fay, who couldn't even stay alive long enough to say sorry, Florrie stalked into the kitchen and flung the diary in the box. If Fay couldn't apologise and let everyone know Florrie wasn't a child killer, she'd do it herself.

Yes, she'd ring that Katie Violet woman at the paper. That'd set things straight.

Chapter Forty-One

While eating pickled onions out of the jar, Mask had been spying on the glazier going into Yeoman's, and Trudy Baker, who seemed to have wrangled it so the copper's dog went to her house. Thank heavens for blessed silence, the bloody animal not barking anymore, so letting him out *had* been a good idea.

Problem solved.

He'd managed to get the first part of the Belle and Beast masks done, and they were drying, ready for the next stage. What a productive day so far. He'd got up at the crack of dawn—amazing what an extra couple of hours did.

Yeoman had been to Oliver's, probably to warn him he might be the third victim if they'd already found Helen. Two people being dead from Loving Arms was a bit of an alarm bell, wasn't it. Maybe they knew Mask had worked there, too, but they wouldn't find him if they searched using his birth name.

He'd given Noah Tate up years ago, although people still called him that.

Oliver must be thick if he didn't recognise him. Mask didn't think he'd changed that much, but maybe the years had gone some way to altering him enough that Oliver wasn't quite sure who he was. Or he'd blocked him out. Or he didn't care that Noah lived opposite, their lives together forgotten.

His next project, Florrie, had a shock coming to her when she spotted that gravestone. A nice touch, he reckoned, although to make sure she saw it sooner rather than later, he'd snapped a Polaroid of it in the early hours and planned to take it with him in a minute.

With the lady mask on, plus a navy trouser suit and the court shoes, he left the house carrying a briefcase and a large umbrella, unconcerned that two men in white protective suits had just arrived at Yeoman's.

He strode along the top of the comb towards Mulberry Lane, amused at a bloke driving past and tooting his horn. Little did he know that what lurked behind the mask was a man, not a woman, and beneath his tight knickers, meat and two veg.

He could just do with a steak, chips, and peas now, with peppercorn sauce. He could go and have that at The Tractor's once he'd visited Florrie. It'd be amusing to have people look at him, not knowing who he was.

Striding down the lane, he paused at Florrie's gate and stared at the botch job someone had done in her neighbour's garden. A bit of a sight. He checked the house out to see if anyone was watching, and yes, a woman stood behind the window, giving him a nasty glare. He waved and opened Florrie's gate, clip-clopping up her path and knocking on the door.

She opened it, large as life, a scowl in place. "Yeah?"

He held up his fake credentials. "Katie Violet, crime reporter for *The Pinstone Star*."

"Bloody hell, that was quick, love. Come in."

He didn't know what the fuck she was talking about. "Quick?"

"Yeah, I only rang to arrange a visit half an hour ago."

"Oh, right, yes, I had an earlier slot." Now, this was a problem. "What time did I originally say I'd be here? Sorry, I'm away with the fairies."

"Half five. Are you coming in then or what?"

That gave him enough time to say what he had to before the real Katie arrived. He wished he could be a fly on the wall for that, watching the confusion, but he'd be tucking into his steak by then, out of the way.

"Yes, I'm coming in."

He followed her into a lounge that had hoover stripes on the carpet. She must have tidied for Katie's visit. What did she want to talk to her about? He breathed through his mouth to save having to smell the strong scent of Mr Sheen. He'd recognise that original scent anywhere.

"Want a cuppa?" Florrie asked.

"No, thank you. I can't stay long." He sat and placed the briefcase on his lap, unclicking the clasps.

"Suit yourself." She swiped up a book off the arm of a chair. "Here it is. I've folded down the corner of the page you need."

He should chop her fingers off just for that. Who folded down page corners?

Book in hand, he flipped to the correct place and read. My, my... Fay's mother had killed the baby, not Florrie or Fay. How he wished he'd had this information a long time ago. He could have tormented Fay with it, got her crying whenever he felt like it. Life was cruel sometimes, taking away those sorts of pleasurable opportunities.

"Oh, well, this is just dreadful," he said.

"So you'll print it in your paper? I want everyone to know it wasn't me. I've been carrying this label round with me since the sixties, and it isn't fair. Fay's bloody dead, so she can't say sorry to me, which would have been nice and the least she could do, so I need someone on my side."

He held back a smile at Fay being dead. No time to rejoice with Florrie. He had to find out what she'd mentioned when she'd arranged the interview. "Can you recap what you told me on the phone?"

Florrie rolled her eyes. "Away with the fairies? More like you're not all there. Blimey. I phoned to say I wanted my name cleared, especially because of the gravestone business."

So she knows what I've done to it... "Ah, yes. I went there and took a photo of it. Do you want that in the paper as well?"

"I'm not sure. Pictures speak a thousand words, don't they, so if people see 'killer' on that stone, that's what'll stick in the readers' heads. I thought we could maybe have one of me in my armchair, looking sad and whatnot."

"I'd have to send a photographer round for that, okay?"

"Yes, that's fine."

"So, from what I can gather, going by gossip and previous newspaper articles—I like to do my research, you see—there was bad blood between you and Fay because she thought you'd killed her baby. Obviously, you didn't, as we have the proof right here." *Although you could have written the diary yourself, you stupid cow.* "I've already spoken to Fay, as have my colleagues, and Helen, about Loving Arms. We wanted to do a piece on how carers have an impact on children—for the good, you understand. Is there anything you can add to that? As in, the Ivy Gibbs issue?"

Florrie's cheeks reddened. "Because of what happened to Frankie, I always thought Fay did it, got rid of the girl."

"Do you think Fay killed him then?"

She waffled a story about Fay going out dancing, blah blah blah, and mentioned gripe water. Florrie had thought it was Fay's fault because she'd provided the water, so if she could give Nan something for the baby, why not kill another child?

"I see," he said. "So did you have any contact with her around the time Ivy went missing?"

Florrie laughed. "I haven't spoken to her since the early seventies. Washed my hands of her."

"And she hasn't contacted you?"

"No, but she apparently harped on about us not speaking to whoever would listen."

That was true, he'd heard her himself.

"The one I didn't like from Loving Arms is that weird fella, the chap who always smells of pickled onions." She sniffed. "I can smell them now, can you?" She shrugged. "Must be my imagination."

His heart seemed to clutch at itself. "Which man is that?"

"One of the blokes who worked there. Can't remember his name for the life of me. See, now we know Auntie Beryl killed Frankie, not Fay, and we also know what Oliver Elford is like, we can assume *he* did something to Ivy. Probably got help from Pickled Onion Man. Shifty-looking bastard, he is."

He wanted to stab her eyes out. "I think I know who you mean, and no, he's not the type. Probably best for you not to cast aspersions, especially as you've done it for years about Fay and have now found naughty Auntie Beryl to be the killer."

"True."

"Okay, I'm going to go now, I have what I need for the article."

"Don't you need a copy of the diary page?"

"Yes, that would be a good idea. Do you have a scanner?"

"No."

"Not much good to me then. It doesn't matter, I'll remember it."

"Don't know how when you couldn't remember what we talked about on the phone."

"Okay, well, I'll be off then." He could have taken a photo of it with his mobile, but he didn't really want the fucking thing. He snapped the clasps back into the locks on the briefcase, not needing to produce the Polaroid now Florrie already knew about the gravestone. Shame, he'd wanted to frighten her silly with it and watch her flail.

She showed him out, and he walked down the path, pondering whether to leave her be, certain she didn't know anything about him for sure, just that he was supposedly shifty-looking so therefore must have helped harm Ivy.

Gate open, he strode up the lane, smirking at Katie Violet going past in her flashy green car. He dipped into the pub and almost walked out again, forgetting he had a mask on.

Yeoman and Tanner were in there along with two other people who also had the air of pig about them. A spare table stood beside them, so he sat and browsed the menu while eavesdropping.

"Terry says he usually sits in that corner over there," Tanner said.

"Who, Noah?" the other woman asked.

Mask's heart leapt.

They were onto him.

He'd have to put his contingency plan into place. Make his face disappear, yet he'd remain in Pinstone, still live in his place. He'd shave his hair, slap on a beard and moustache until a proper one grew, and whenever he left the house, he'd use contacts and some of those fake veneers he'd bought online. Speak differently.

People round here were so dim, they'd think he was someone else, and he could finally use his new name publicly instead of them knowing him as Noah Tate or Pickled Onion Man.

Plans were important. Now more than ever.

Chapter Forty-Two

Sherry didn't know how to take Billy in this mood. Sombre, watery eyes, not knowing where to look, as if guilt swam in his veins. It stood to reason he'd be upset about Fay. To lose two mothers in a lifetime must be awful, both tragic events, too, a shooting and a suicide brought on by a savage attack.

Sherry had never had a mum as such, shunted from foster home to foster home, returning to Loving Arms twice when no one else was available to take her. That was where she'd met him. It was ninety-three, their first encounter, two years after the Ivy business, and she'd stayed for seven months.

She hadn't liked Fay.

The woman had been too abrupt to anyone other than Billy. It was hard to describe, because she was nice at the same time. She did all the right things, looked after them all, just with a sharp edge to her. Billy would never hear a bad word said against her, of course, but he'd been treated differently, so he wouldn't. If all you had was pleasantness off her, you wouldn't see her as anything but kindly.

Billy was the only human being to ever want Sherry around for an extended period. The rumours had dug into her psyche, pushing her to believe she'd lose him, too, just like all those people who'd pretended they'd wanted to be her parents. Maybe she'd helped the loss of a good life along by acting out so she got their abandonment of her over and done with quickly, ripping off the plaster, when in reality, she was peeling it away bit by bit, giving herself prolonged pain with the move to several different homes.

"We need to talk," he said, hands dangling between his open legs, his arse perched on the edge of the sofa, as if he wanted to bolt rather than chat. "I've started remembering things."

She sat forward in his favourite chair, threading her fingers together. Sherry knew all too well what it was like to hide things from yourself, only for them to pop out later when you least expected it. "What things?"

"That's just it, I don't really know. I do, but it's only me putting two and two together. I might have come up with ten…"

She frowned. "What have you been adding up?"

"Something about Noah."

Ah, another one at Arms who'd doted on Billy. Noah's little teeth had always given her the creeps, still did whenever she saw him in The Tractor's. The man had an air about him that raised an internal alarm, and she'd steered clear of him at Arms. He'd seemed jealous of her when it became clear she and Billy were getting close.

During her second stint there, age fifteen, they'd grown even closer. They'd written to each other, like old-fashioned pen pals after she'd left the first time, although Billy said he hadn't got some of the letters. Sherry had always wondered whether Fay had intercepted them, or maybe Noah.

She'd always been a suspicious sort. And no wonder, given the life she'd led, where trust wasn't a major thing for some people but everything to her. Without it, you had nothing. If you couldn't trust someone, any relationship you had with them broke down eventually.

She didn't want that to happen to her and Billy.

"What about Noah?" she asked.

"I've got something telling me he was the monster, but I can't see how that's true. The monster was old."

"Monster?" Confused, she bit her lip. He'd never mentioned a monster before.

"This is why I said we need to talk. There are things you don't know about me. Things I never mentioned. I had nightmares where a monster came in—that's what I saw him as anyway—but they became more than dreams. They ended up being real."

Dread seeped into her gut. What was he really saying? "What happened?"

He rubbed his eyes, his bottom lip wobbling. Then he stared at the floor rather than at her.

Maybe he thought he'd see blame in her eyes over whatever he was going to say. "Okay, look, this is really hard for me."

"It's just me, Billy. You know I'll never tell anyone."

"But still…"

"Just pretend you're talking to yourself. Always works for me."

He nodded as though convincing himself that would be okay. "Right. This bloke used to come in." He shivered. "Fucking hell, I can see him as if he's here. An old fella with long white hair. He…touched me and stuff."

Shock barrelled through Sherry, and she wanted to rush over and hug Billy, but knowing him like she did, he wouldn't want any fuss until he'd told her everything. And besides, when he needed to get things off his chest, he was best left alone to push through it, no cuddles or her stroking his hand.

"Stuff?" she prompted.

"Yeah, you know, abuse."

Fucking hell, you poor man. "And you think it was Noah?"

"Yeah."

"But Noah wasn't old back then."

"I know, and that's why it's so confusing. The monster shoved a sock in my mouth on the night

Ivy went missing and tied me up with my dressing gown cord."

"*What?*" Her heart seemed to roll over. "You seriously forgot this? For all this time?"

"Yeah, I did."

"Why did he do that to you?"

"To shut me up. He was in my room. We were…naked. You know, because…" He sighed. "I heard Fay and Oliver next door in Ivy's. Sounded like she was having a bad dream, crying and stuff, then there was a thud. This is what I mean about remembering things. With Yeoman asking about Arms, Fay being attacked then killing herself…" He looked at Sherry and blinked. "What if something happened in that room? To Ivy? Why am I only just remembering it now?"

"You know why. Trauma."

Billy had been through therapy a couple of years ago when memories of his mum's murder had resurfaced, too vivid for him to cope with on his own. He'd decided it was best to get some things out in the open with a stranger who might be able to fix him, but him and Sherry had never let on to anyone else. People thought you were mental, didn't they, if you told them "I'm seeing a therapist." They gave you funny looks, like you were someone to avoid, and that was just arseholey, but the folks round here… Not many of them would understand. You pulled your bootstraps up and marched on, not telling all to some bloke sitting in a squeaking leather chair, his hands steepled, his expression full of pity.

Billy was too ashamed to admit it to others.

"You blocked it out," she said. "Like you did with your mum. It was too much. Too big. And now, because of what happened to Fay…"

"Yeah."

"So why do you think it was Noah? How could it be if the monster, the man who came into your room, was old? Noah didn't have long hair back then, let alone dyeing it white."

Billy let out a long breath. Finally stared at her. "It was the pickled onion smell."

Chapter Forty-Three

1991

The police had interviewed everyone—staff, children, even the bloody postman—their questions invasive, or perhaps they were normal in these circumstances and Fay's guilty conscience meant she saw things differently, picked things apart that didn't need picking. The veil of culpability and the fear of getting caught wrapped itself around her, claws digging in, promising to never let go. She rose in the mornings full of trepidation and went to sleep the same way.

Murder didn't gel with you if you weren't the type to enjoy it.

But I had enjoyed it…

The press had come, many of them had, with their cameras and microphones, their voice recorders thrust at her when she left the home for trips into Pinstone. Fay only allowed one to enter the house once the police had finished searching it. Reginald Davies, the crime reporter. He was nice, pleasant, and seemed to work along the lines that Ivy had left of her own accord and got lost on the moor, falling into a deep bog.

A relief, then, that Fay had pulled the wool over his eyes. The police's eyes, too.

Until they'd announced the abduction theory half an hour ago.

Terror like no other seared her soul, and she couldn't even speak to Oliver about what they should do next, seeing as Noah watched them all the time in his creepy way, stubby teeth on show, bared as if to tell her he'd bite if she uttered a word about their secrets.

The children were at school, and Fay, Helen, Oliver, and Noah sat around the kitchen table in a rare moment without the police or Reginald present. There was always someone else here, asking questions, checking rooms, especially Ivy's, which remained empty, of course. Now it had been cleared for use, she'd send Oliver up at some point to clean it ready for the next person.

"Abduction..." Helen shivered.

"How can it be a sodding abduction if there's no sign of anyone breaking in?" Fay snapped. "The door was locked when we went to bed."

"Maybe it was that man." Noah widened his eyes at her, too obvious that he was warning her to agree. "The one who delivered the carpets. He could have swiped a key."

While Fay wanted to latch on to that as a good angle to point the police towards, it wouldn't work. There were only two keys to the utility door—three if you included the one Noah had copied. One in the actual door, another in a safe in her bedroom, along with the spare for the front door. There were four of those—one each for Fay, Helen, and Oliver, the other put away, although Noah would soon get the fourth as the letter announcing he could move in had come earlier this morning.

She hadn't told him yet.

The night they'd kicked Ivy into the river, Fay had dropped the utility key on the mat inside. Helen must have found it when she'd gone out to look for Ivy that morning, yet she'd never said anything about it being on the mat. The police hadn't asked about a second key either.

Fay wasn't going to remind them of it, but still, the investigation had holes even she could spot. It was obvious Ivy hadn't left of her own accord. She wasn't old enough to think of wiping the doorknob.

"No," Helen said. "The key was on the mat that morning, so how did Ivy lock up from outside? Would the carpet man have been able to take the key, copy it, and bring it back before any of us noticed?"

Noah smirked at Fay.

"I don't know." Fay sighed. "Noah, perhaps you can tell the police about the carpet man, seeing as you thought of it. They're still out on the moor. You can grab hold of one out there."

"But they'll say what Helen said. Ask questions about the key."

Fay laughed bitterly. "Well, they haven't thought to ask yet, have they, so I'd say they're not bothered. We're telling the truth when we say we have one key in circulation for that door." She stared at him to get her true meaning across: *Don't mention your spare to anyone.* "And it was on the mat, inside, like Helen just said. It must have fallen out of the lock."

"It wouldn't be the carpet man anyway." Helen wrung her hands. "I've known him years. You can tell a pervert a mile off, and he isn't one of them."

Noah smirked again. Oliver coughed as if he might choke on the tea he'd just sipped.

We didn't spot it with these two.

Of course, Fay couldn't say that, not now they'd gone this far into their skein of lies. The only innocent one around this table was Helen, and hopefully, she'd remain oblivious as to what had really happened.

Someone knocked on the front door, and Fay jumped. Helen let out a little squeal, and Oliver's face reddened. Only Noah remained passive, unfazed. What sort of monster was he to be able to—

Monster.

Poor Billy.

"I'll get it." *Fay rose on shaky legs and walked out into the foyer. She took a deep breath and peered through the spyhole. Christ. What did he want now? Door open, she smiled to hide her annoyance and fear.*

PC Yarthing dipped his head. "Sorry to bother you yet again, but I've got a query about the utility room key."

She might have known he'd twig eventually. Her heart sank, and her stomach clenched, bile lurching into her throat. It burned, and she swallowed it down. "Oh right, come in then. Would you like some tea? We've got a pot brewed. We were just having our break anyway."

"That'd be very nice. Damn cold out there." *He stepped inside and rubbed his gloved hands.*

Fay closed the door and wished he was on the other side of it. "So you're still looking on the moor then, even though it's now an abduction? I saw some officers there not long ago."

"Well, yes. She could have been abducted but dumped there, see. It's a big area, as you know."

"Yes, it is." *She walked into the kitchen and collected a cup and saucer for him, not putting the two together while she carried them in case they rattled.* "Sit down, will you?"

Yarthing chose a seat between Oliver and Noah. Did he do that on purpose? Fay couldn't stand much more of this. She worried about every little thing.

She placed the cup and saucer down and poured his tea, watching Oliver's and Noah's reactions to the copper wedged there. Oliver appeared jittery, guilty as sin, or maybe that was because she knew he was. She'd have to find a private moment to speak to him about the way he was acting, away from Noah's probing eyes. Noah was as laid-back as ever, a good actor. Watching those in the troupe had paid dividends. He knew how to behave, to hide his dark side.

Yarthing had had tea here before, so she knew how he took it. A splash of milk and three spoonfuls of sugar.

"There you go." *She sat and folded her hands in her lap under the table so he couldn't see them if they shook. It would only set his police radar off if he spotted it.*

Yarthing took a sip. "That's lovely. Thanks. Now then, like I said, I'm here to ask about the key. It's been bothering me."

"What has?" Fay frowned for effect.

"Well, by rights, it should be missing. Ivy or her kidnapper would have taken it with them." He glanced around at everyone.

"How do you mean?" Noah asked.

"Think about it. If Ivy left of her own accord and locked the door on the outside…" Yarthing raised his eyebrows. "How did you, Helen, open it the morning of her disappearance to go and look for her if there was only one key?"

Helen gulped. "It was on the mat."

"But how is that possible if Ivy or the abductor had it? Is there a spare she could have got hold of?"

"They're in Fay's safe, and you looked in that." Helen sounded exasperated.

"I didn't, one of my colleagues did."

Pedantic bastard.

Helen became flustered. "I didn't mean you, as in, you, I meant the police in general. The spare key is in that safe, and only Fay knows the combination."

"Right."

"Not that I'm saying Fay would have…" Helen propped her head in her hands. "Oh God."

Fay patted her shoulder. The poor woman was digging herself into a hole. "It's all right, we know what you meant."

Noah poured another cup for himself, hand steady. "Maybe the stool is a ruse. The abductor put it there to throw us all off. We thought she went out the utility way, but she could have been taken through the front, put in a car, and he drove off with her."

Yarthing traced the lip of his cup with a fingertip. "The utility doorknob had been wiped clean, so, Helen, did you have gloves on when you opened the door?"

"No," *she said.* "At least, I don't think so. Maybe I had my Marigolds on."

"That would have left an impression. They have raised circles on them. The knob had nothing, so it was cleaned **after** you touched it."

A prickly silence encompassed them all.

"It must be like Noah said." *Helen tugged at her earlobe.* "They took her out the front way."

Yarthing sniffed in air. "But it doesn't explain who wiped the handle. Did any of you do it?"

Everyone mumbled that they hadn't.

Yarworth went on. "And with regards to going out the front way, even that doesn't make sense. How did they get in? No sign of forced entry at all, anywhere. Let's say we're thinking it's the front. The only fingerprints on that door should belong to everyone in this house—the employees, the children."

"We have people coming from the social," Fay said, "so there must be other prints on both doors."

"Nah." Noah shook his head. "You always open the door for them and close it behind them. They don't even get a chance to use the knocker or the bell because you watch for them coming up the road and get there in time."

"Why do you do that, Fay?" Yarthing asked.

All heads turned to her. She didn't like being under the spotlight and could stab Noah for putting her there. "I don't know. They say what time they're due, and I just wait, that's all."

"It'll be the carpet man." Noah leant back.

Yarthing took his notepad and pen out. "Carpet man?"

"I've already said it wouldn't be him," Helen cut in.

"Let me be the judge of that." Yarthing put pen to paper. "Name, please, Noah."

"Ken something."

"Hinds," Helen said.

"I shall be having a word with him then." Yarthing put his things away and sipped his tea. "Another thing."

Fay's guts rolled over.

"You were up that night, washing wellies." Yarthing smiled at Fay. *"Why? The children's were all clean and in their rooms. They said no one had gone out on the moor that week because of the weather, so no chance to get them muddy. Wouldn't you have cleaned the adult ones when the children's were done back when they* were *dirty?"*

"Mine were clean," Helen piped up.

Fucking shut your silly mouth.

"I'd been out to the vegetable patch earlier in the day," Fay said.

Helen nodded. *"Yes, for the winter cabbages. I wanted to make soup."*

Fay silently thanked her. *"I took mine off and got mud on Oliver's when I placed them beside his, so I washed those as well. It was just something to do while I couldn't sleep. Like I'd scrub the skirting boards or windowsills. A time-filler."*

Yarthing pursed his lips. *"Did you notice the key on the mat at the time you picked the boots up?"*

"I didn't."

"Right. And Billy. He had a nightmare. Now, I've asked him if he heard anyone coming in or walking about, and he says only you were up, Fay, although he said he heard a thud in Ivy's room previous to him coming down to the kitchen."

Fay hadn't known that. Helen had sat with Billy when Yarthing had interviewed him. Why hadn't the silly cow said?

"Did you not hear the thud while in here?" Yarthing looked at the ceiling. "Because the left-hand wing is over this room."

"Ivy's is farther along," Fay said. "And no, I didn't hear a thud. Maybe the water was running at the time, in the sink."

"Hmm." Yarthing drank the rest of his tea.

Everyone else just sat there. Fay didn't dare cast her gaze about in case he watched who she stared at. Much as she didn't want to admit it, she'd have stared at Noah for help.

"So much just doesn't add up." Yarthing stood. "Thanks for the tea. I'll go and see Mr Hinds now."

Fay jumped up to let him out and closed the front door on him, scared out of her mind. They'd know Ken Hinds hadn't done it once they spoke to him. He didn't have a bad bone in his body. The question about the wellies had thrown her—no one else had queried that, they'd just accepted it as something she'd done. Was Yarthing one of those jobsworth people who poked into every little thing?

She returned to the table. "Well, isn't he a nosy beak." She attempted a laugh, but it came out as a strangled sound.

"He has to be." Helen served herself another cuppa. "And I'm glad he is. This is a child missing here, not something trivial."

Fay wanted to hurt Helen, throw that bloody cup of tea in her stupid face.

Oliver shook, rubbing his arms, once again looking guilty.

Noah's lips stretched into a smug grin. "The plot thickens. Bit unfortunate, isn't it, Fay?"

"What do you mean by that?" Helen asked, clearly bewildered.

"Nowt." He flashed his tiny teeth. "Nowt at all."

Helen was suspicious, Fay was sure of it. They all seemed terse with one another this past week, their previous harmony obliterated by the actions of that fucking horrible girl who'd pushed Fay into strangling her. If Oliver hadn't been such a pervert, they wouldn't be sitting here now, around the table together yet miles apart, fissures in their relationships forming.

They all gawped at one another.

"Right." Fay slapped the table. "The day still needs to be lived. We're all innocent, and that's what we need to remember. Whatever Yarthing suggested, it's nothing to do with us. So, I've got rugs to beat because the hoover isn't much cop. Oliver, can you help me take them out the back to hang them on the line? You can beat them with me. Noah, I'd like you *to give the room next to Oliver's a good clean. It'll be yours come tomorrow."*

"*Oh, he's approved to move in?*" *Helen smiled wide.*

"*Yes, he is."*

Noah grinned.

Pleased with herself for securing some time alone with Oliver, she walked off to collect the rug in the living room. She'd be having words with him. Words regarding a new plan.

They had to get rid of Noah somehow. Preferably for good.

Chapter Forty-Four

"I'm seeing ghosts." Catherine blushed. It sounded so silly now she'd said it out loud, but that was the conclusion she'd arrived at.

"Ghosts?" Sarah frowned, pausing with her cup halfway to her mouth.

"Hmm." Catherine picked up her tea from the coffee table in their private corner spot in the main living room. "That's who the little girl is. Ivy Gibbs, that one who went missing years ago."

Sarah's eyebrows shot up. "How do you know it's her?"

"It's the nightie." Catherine sipped, some tea dribbling down her chin. She hated it that her mouth didn't work like it used to. And she hated doing old lady things when she didn't feel old inside.

Sarah wiped the drip away with a tissue. "When did you last see her?"

Catherine shuddered at the memory. "She was in my shower, telling me it was raining. And that's significant. I've been thinking about it ever since. Why she said that, why she's chosen me to show herself to. It rained all the time during that week she was missing, you know. I remember it well. The police were out there, searching, thinking she'd fallen into a bog or the river. Then they said she'd been abducted, and PC Yarthing mentioned something about a key to me, which escapes me now. He was down all the streets, you know, in his spare time, going door to door, desperate to find the kiddie. But as there were no signs of forced entry here, they let the abduction idea drop and went back to the theory that the girl walked out by herself. Still, that key... Now what was it he'd said?"

Catherine pinched her chin. Her mind had gone blank.

Sarah placed her empty cup down. "Do you think *he* had something to do with it?"

"That's what I meant about why Ivy chose me. She's trying to tell me he did it. He was here, you know."

"Who, *Oliver*? I told him not to bother you after he'd brought that bloody tartan blanket."

"Well, he *did* bother me. A lot. He said he just wanted to see me. Then a man was here, I can't think what he's called, and I told him to leave, never come back, because he's evil."

"Who could that have been?"

"I don't know."

"Hang on, I'll go and ask Liz."

Sarah got up and walked from the room. Catherine glanced around. George, the one with the noisy eating habit, stared at her with those creepy, glassy eyes of his.

"What are you gawping at?" she sniped.

He continued staring as if she hadn't spoken.

Sarah came back. "It was Oliver, Mum. No one else visited you."

Catherine frowned. It didn't make sense. "It must have been my..." She clasped her throat.

"That terrible thing I have. It messes with my mind."

"Don't you worry about it. I've let her know you saw Ivy, okay? She's going to look into your medication. Said something about a recent change that might bring on those sorts of sightings."

"I thought the same. I think she comes to see me as well because I'm in her old bedroom, she told me. Should we tell the police?"

"Um, probably not a good idea to mention you seeing Ivy to anyone else but me or Liz, all right?"

Catherine nodded. "He keeps staring at me." She pointed at George.

"That's just his way, Mum. He zones out."

"But I don't like it."

"Shall we go for a walk down the drive and back?"

Catherine shook her head. "No. Too cold. And I'm tired."

She rested her head back and closed her eyes, hoping, if she fell asleep, she wouldn't wake up ever again.

Sarah wouldn't have to come here and put up with this rubbish then.

Chapter Forty-Five

Everyone had paid for their own food and waited for it at the table. It was Morgan's round, so he stood at the bar while Heidi pulled a pint of lager for Nigel.

"What do you know about the fella who always sits over in that corner?" he asked.

"He stinks." Heidi placed the pint on a Guinness bar towel. "Of pickled onions."

"Nice. Anything else?"

"Small teeth. Like, they're half the size of normal ones. That's what stands out about him the most. They're the first thing you see."

"How does he strike you?"

"A bit weird." She poured Morgan's orange juice from a small Britvic bottle. "Doesn't say much—doesn't even ask for his tipple because me and Terry know what it is."

That reminded Morgan of Li Wei in the Chinese.

Heidi bit the inside of her cheek. "What else… He stares a lot, especially at the door, as if he's waiting for someone. No one ever comes in and sits with him, though, so him doing that is well odd. Florrie reckons he's a right weirdo."

Morgan chuckled. "She'd think a saint was a weirdo."

Heidi sorted Cokes for Shaz and Jane. "She's all right once you get used to her. Wins at bingo nearly every week. I'd say it was rigged if it wasn't me pulling out the numbers."

"Any idea where the fella lives?"

Heidi shook her head. "Couldn't tell you."

He paid, thanked her, and took the drinks over to their table. A brunette woman sat at the next one and watched him while cutting a slab of steak. He wished he'd had that now instead of pie and chips.

Morgan sat and smiled at Shaz and Nigel in a debate about Walkers versus Golden Wonder and how the flavours weren't the same.

"Walkers all the way for me. At least their cheese and onion actually taste of onion," Shaz said.

"Nope, it's the other way around," Nigel insisted. "Golden Wonder have got it right."

Jane tapped Morgan's foot under the table. She leant closer to talk quietly. "How the hell are we going to find this Noah if no one seems to know where he lives?"

"Old-fashioned police work. I'll ask Heidi to give me a ring next time he's in. I don't trust Terry to do it. He'd rather we weren't in here asking questions. I'll come down and have a word when Noah turns up, ask why his name disappeared from any searches." He sensed the stare of the steak woman. What was her problem? A quick glare back didn't have her lowering her gaze, though. Morgan planted his elbow on the table and covered half his face with his hand, facing Jane more.

"Someone's got an admirer." Jane smiled.

"Fucking creepy cow," he mumbled.

"Me or her?"

"Both, if I'm honest."

"Ever the charmer." She rolled her eyes.

"What's your take on all this?" He sipped some juice.

"The obvious one. Fay pissed someone off, and they came after her. Same for Helen."

"What about the other strangers in the street that Billy mentioned? A woman and a younger man—could the younger man be the bloke in the grey suit?"

"They could have just been passing through."

"Are we chasing our own tails by digging into Arms?"

"Nope. As you constantly say: All leads must be followed. What do Fay and Helen have in common? The care home."

He wondered why he was even discussing this with Jane. He didn't usually seek her out. Maybe because Shaz and Nigel were busy yakking, he needed to sound off to someone. Anyone.

"Soreen malt loaf, no other kind," Nigel said.

"Tesco do a nice one." Shaz sipped her Coke.

"Nope, not the same as Soreen."

"Get a life, you two." Jane tskd. "You'll be talking about the merits of butter next."

"Lurpak." Morgan scratched his head. "Had it in a sandwich Phil made me."

"So that's what it was," Shaz said. "In that case, I agree."

Jane's mouth dropped open. "You had sandwiches from Phil bloody Flint?"

Morgan nodded. "Amazing what people will do for you."

"Did you threaten him to make your lunch?" Jane asked.

"Nope."

Their dinner arrived, cutting the convo off, and everyone tucked in. Steak Woman got up and walked past, nudging Morgan's elbow so his hand whacked the side of his plate and half his chips jumped off onto the table.

"Err, excuse me?" Morgan looked up at her.

"Sorry. *Butter*fingers."

Had she been listening to their conversation?

"I do apologise." She clutched a briefcase and smiled at Shaz, lips closed.

"Do you come here often?" Morgan asked.

Steak Woman tittered. "That's original."

He took his ID out and flashed it to her. "*Do you come here often?*"

Her eyes widened at his harsh tone. "No. Why?"

"Because I wanted to pick your brains about something. There's a man who usually sits in the corner over there." He jerked his head that way. "Small teeth, creepy-looking. Ever seen him?"

She sighed, and her breath wafted over him. Christ, she must have had strong onions in her side salad with that steak.

"No, can't say I have. Sorry!" She walked to the door, glancing at him over her shoulder on her way out.

Shaz and Nigel roared with laughter.

"She thought you were coming on to her." Shaz speared a chip. "Good grief, that was funny."

Morgan didn't think so. It'd irritated him. "Whatever." He stared at the chips on the table. Steak Woman's behaviour was still bothering him, but he didn't know why.

The rest of the meal passed without incident, and Shaz got up to buy the next round.

"Not for me, thanks." Jane stood. "Places to be."

Morgan glared at her.

She patted him on the shoulder. "Calm down, Yeoman."

He watched her trounce out, pleased she didn't have all black on. Then again, she could go home and change. She'd mentioned going to see Oliver, and he'd shot her down, but… Shit, she'd better not disobey him.

"What did she mean, 'calm down'?" Shaz asked.

Morgan shrugged. "Fuck knows. She's a rare one. Who can tell what goes through her mind?"

He craned his neck to see through the window. Jane drove off and turned left, in the direction of her home. He relaxed a bit but declined another drink. He needed to get home an' all. "Come on, Shaz, I need to pick Rochester up from Trudy's. Unless you get a taxi."

She glanced at Nigel, who nodded.

"I'm here for a few more." She took a step towards the bar. "I'm having wine if we're making a night of it, Nige."

"Mine's a G and T then," he said. "I'll be pissing all evening if I have more lager."

Morgan nipped to the bar and asked Heidi to ring him if Noah Tate came in, said his goodbyes, and left the pub, bumping into Florrie who was on her way to the door, thundering towards him.

"Ah, just the man I need to see." She thumped his arm. "Someone's been round my house pretending to be a bleedin' reporter. I came here for a nip of sherry to calm my nerves, wondering what to do about it, but seeing as you're here…"

"How do you know they were pretending?"

"Because the *real* Katie Violet just left my place. She arrived after the other one left. She's going to tell my story of how I didn't kill our Frankie."

"Right… So who knew you were having Katie round in order to impersonate her?"

She gawped at him. "I don't bloody know, do I!"

She stormed inside, leaving Morgan pondering on what to do about that snippet. Florrie was elderly, the same as Fay, but he wouldn't class Helen as such, yet she *was* in the higher age bracket. Was Florrie next on this killer's list?

He got his phone out and accessed Google. Put in 'Katie Violet' and the name of the newspaper. Links came up. He clicked IMAGES, and various versions of her face filled the screen. Thin. High cheekbones. A platinum-blonde pixie cut, although in some older ones she had long brown hair.

Back in the pub, he approached the bar. Shaz and Nigel had abandoned the table and stood talking.

"Oh, did you change your mind?" Shaz asked.

Morgan showed her his screen. "Is that who you saw at Helen's? Katie Violet?"

"God, no. Katie was in here earlier. The woman who thought you were chatting her up."

"*What?*" Morgan rushed outside and glanced up and down the lane. No one around. He got in his car and drove down each street in search of her, but she'd either driven off herself or disappeared on foot.

He phoned Amanda Cartwright on the front desk and asked her to find Katie's address. It was time to go and see her. Let her know someone was going around making out they were her.

Why the hell would they want to do that?

To get inside the homes, that's why.

Were they dealing with a group of people here? Two men and a woman?

That was all they bloody well needed, a trio of killers.

Chapter Forty-Six

Jane had left the pub and nipped home to change. She'd given Yeoman a little warning of what she was about to do, so he had no excuse if he tried to make out he didn't know. Couple that with her asking him earlier if she should go and talk to Oliver, it should be enough to apprise him of her destination. She doubted he'd join her, but it'd be fun if he did.

She crouched in Oliver's back garden, behind a green wheelie bin, getting ready to tap it, create enough noise so he'd come out to investigate. She had a clear view into his house—no curtains or a blind hung at the kitchen window or over the glass in the back door. He used sandpaper around a block to rub the larder door. A can of gloss sat on the worktop, so his decorating still hadn't been finished.

The window was open, and the scent of paint filtered out.

What a busy bee he was.

The doorbell *ding-donged*, and Oliver paused.

"Fucking Yeoman again, I bet," he muttered. "Why can't he just leave me alone?"

Jane stifled a laugh.

He walked down the hallway, and she waited in the darkness, straining her ears. Front door open, she stared through at a woman on the doorstep, mid-forties perhaps, strawberry-blonde hair, dark eyes. Jeans, black puffa jacket, beige boots with brown fur around the tops. Uggs or knockoffs.

"What are you doing here?" Oliver asked. "Thought you didn't want to know me."

"I don't. Let me in." She stared at him like he resembled a piece of shit and she struggled to be anywhere near him.

He stepped back and watched her walk into the kitchen, his face a picture of disbelief. Door shut, he followed her, his expression one of wariness. He placed his sander on the worktop next to the paint. Some dust fell off it and landed, reminding Jane of icing sugar it was that fine.

"You went to see Mum," the woman said, hands on hips, fingers biting into her coat.

I recognise her from somewhere.

Hmm, Yeoman had rung and said Oliver had an alibi for when Helen had been killed. Jane had checked the timing. His walk back over the moor meant he couldn't possibly have got to her house at the time the man was seen by the neighbour.

"Yeah, so? Sarah, you're not my bloody keeper. You're younger than me for a start. Just because you're some fancy solicitor, doesn't mean you can boss me about. You're such a self-righteous cow." He shoved his hands in his pockets.

Court, that's where I know her from.

"Whatever you think of me, Oliver, I have our mother's best interests at heart, which is why

I'm here, otherwise, I wouldn't be speaking to you now. Why do you insist on going there when she doesn't want you to? You know she's not comfortable after you got caught being a nonce."

Oliver shrugged. "I wanted to see the old place again, that's all."

"So you didn't go to see Mum at all then really. You upset her for nothing?" Sarah shook her head, disgust clear on her face. "You're something else, you are. An absolute arsehole. You go there to 'see the old place', knowing it'll get her distressed, but that's okay, because what Oliver wants, Oliver takes."

"I know what you're really saying."

"Do you? What's that then? Or are you going to deny what you really are?"

"No, I've admitted what I did. That girl. She was going to be my wife and—"

"She was a *minor*."

"I know. I was going to wait until she grew up, honest I was, so I just asked her to moan for me—"

"*Moan* for you? Fucking hell."

"Yeah, then Fay—"

"Wait, Fay Williams?"

Oliver's cheeks flushed, and he closed his eyes for a moment. "Forget I said anything."

"No. Anything you know about Fay that might help the police find out who attacked her…" She prodded him in the chest and recoiled as if he'd burnt her. "You have to tell someone."

"No, I can't."

"Why not? It's your moral duty—not that you have any morals, but now's a good time to develop some."

"I promised not to say. I didn't mean to blurt that, it's just everything is so stressful at the minute. And I wasn't on about *that* girl anyway. I didn't mean Ivy. I was talking about the one I got put away for."

"Do you know something about Ivy Gibbs?"

"No."

"What you said implies you do."

"I *wasn't on about her*, I already *said* that." He raked a hand through his hair, flustered.

Jane's interest piqued.

"So what does Fay have to do with the Pinstone girl?" Sarah asked.

"Nothing."

"Why mention her then?"

"I don't know, I just… Oh, get out. Go on, bog off. You say Mum doesn't want to see me, well, I don't want to see you."

"I'll leave, gladly, but I'll give you a little warning. You've got until the morning, and if you don't contact the police by then and tell them what Fay has to do with whichever girl you meant, I'll be phoning them, got it?"

Oliver nodded, staring at the floor.

Sarah moved into the hallway. "And don't go and see Mum again—ever, okay? She doesn't want you there. I don't want you there. You know how dementia works, and it's only going to get worse, which means she'll go through more distress. I won't have you upsetting her, you selfish bastard."

She stalked out. Oliver stayed in place, and once the door had slammed, he burst out crying, grabbing at his head then slapping it.

"Fucking hell, Noah's going to come for me now..."

Jane's heart rate scattered. *Noah...* Was *he* the killer? It had sounded as if Oliver knew something about Ivy. He'd royally fucked up by letting that slip out, his sister pouncing on it at the same time Jane had.

This bastard needed a shove in the right direction.

She tapped the bin, a constant knocking beat. He frowned, lowered his hands, and stared outside. Cocked his head.

Come on out, you little bastard…

She carried on tapping, changing the tempo, and he walked to the back door and peered through the glass. If Derek Denham wasn't dead, she'd bet he'd have thought it was him lurking in the dark. Or maybe he thought it was Noah.

He opened the door. "Who's out there?"

Like anyone would ever say, "Me, Oliver. Just nipped round for a cuppa."

She scraped the side of the wheelie bin with her blade, and it created an eerie noise, a loud scuffing. Oliver stepped outside and crept over to investigate, his face in shadow with the light from inside the house behind him. She dragged the knife down again then paused, ready to spring out at him. He bent over to check behind the bin, and she launched herself into him, shoving him over onto the grass, facedown, and landing on his back.

"Don't make a fucking sound," she said, voice disguised. She gripped his hair, yanked his head up, and held the blunt side of the knife to his throat, just enough so he'd get the gist of what was there. "Now then, I just heard a very interesting conversation between you and your sister. What's that about Fay and Noah?"

"W-who are y-you?"

"Doesn't matter who I am, fuckface. What matters is you do the right thing. Got your phone on you?"

"Y-yeah, in my p-pocket."

"Which one?"

"Left. My t-trousers."

She fumbled for it. "Ring Detective Yeoman." She shoved the phone in his hand. "If the number isn't programmed in, I'll tell you what it is. You were meant to let him know if anyone came round. Even go to his house to tell him, but you didn't, did you." In truth, she hadn't given him the chance, but ho hum.

"It's…it's in my phone." He managed to select the contact list despite his hand shaking. "What am I telling him?"

"That you know something about Fay and why she was attacked. Helen, too. Tell him it's to do with Ivy Gibbs, and Noah will come for you if he finds out you told your sister his name." She paused. "You may as well, because Sarah's going to do it in the morning anyway. If I were her, I wouldn't have given you a few hours. She's generous." She pressed the knife a tiny bit harder.

"Ow."

"Call his number. Put it on speaker. Say what I said."

He obeyed. The ringing seemed to fill the garden, too loud in the quiet. If Morgan had come home since she'd arrived here, he wouldn't be long in bolting to the front door. She'd have to escape from the back garden and leg it to her car hidden in Vicar's Gate once he'd gone inside.

"DI Yeoman." He sounded as though he was in the car. Traffic noise and the *tick-tick-tick* of the indicator seeped from the phone.

"It's me," Oliver gasped out.

"Who?"

"Oliver Elford." He panted.

"What's the matter?"

"I've got to tell you something." He paused to catch his breath. "About Fay. And Noah."

"Hang on, I'm on the estate. Nearly at yours. You at home?"

"Yes, but I need to tell you now, before I lose my bottle."

"Right."

"Fay killed Ivy Gibbs. I was there when she did it. She strangled her. In Ivy's bedroom. Ivy had woken up, and I'd gone in to see if she was all right. Fay barged in, took over, and Ivy went all mad, like she was maybe still asleep even though she was awake? Sleepwalking? Anyway, Ivy ran at Fay, clawing at her hair, and Fay threw her. Ivy banged her head on the radiator knob, then Fay got on the floor and throttled her. I couldn't stop her. I asked her to stop, but she wouldn't. It was like she was in a trance. She made me roll her in a piece of carpet and carry her to the river. She forced me to help her. Then the next day, she sent me to the dump to get rid of the carpet."

"I'm one street away, Oliver. Just sit tight."

"I don't know what to do. Noah knows as well—he was the monster, Billy's monster."

"Monster?"

"He saw us kicking Ivy into the river."

"Kicking?"

"Yeah, and that's the real reason Fay had to clean the wellies in case they had some of Ivy's skin cells on them or whatever."

The rumble of an engine chuntered close by.

"Cut the call," Jane whispered in Oliver's ear.

He jabbed at the screen.

She got off him and hauled him to his feet, his back still to her. "You mention me, and I'll fucking kill you, understand?" A rush went through her, the thrill of being in charge.

"Right…okay…"

"I'll be watching you to make sure you don't." She steered him towards the door. "Now fuck off." A big shove sent him flying inside, and he landed on hands and knees.

Jane moved to the corner of the house closest to the garden gate, still at a good enough vantage point to see inside.

The doorbell. The scrabble of Oliver getting up. Him moaning, crying, saying, "Fucking hell, fucking hell." Footsteps. Muffled voices. Yeoman and Oliver coming into the kitchen.

"Now then." Yeoman gave Oliver the death glare, one that had been sent Jane's way one time too many. "What the bloody hell else have you been keeping a secret all these years?"

Jane opened the gate—she'd left it ajar earlier—and sneaked through. In the front garden, she pulled her hood lower and pelted down the path and onto the street. Speeding along the bottom of the comb, she made it to Vicar's in record time, out of breath but pleased with the scare she'd given Oliver. Adrenaline pounded through her, and she laughed.

In her car, she turned the engine over and drove away slowly, not wishing to draw attention to herself. She needed to get home and change her clothes in case Morgan asked her to come back to work.

All in all, a productive evening so far.

Chapter Forty-Seven

Mask had heard all the conversation in the pub between Yeoman and that woman at his table. They were after him, and unless he wanted to get caught, he'd definitely have to sort his hair, beard, and teeth. Noah needed to disappear completely now, his face hidden from those with a view to dobbing him in. He'd bet Heidi had been asked to keep an eye out for him—at least that was what he guessed Yeoman had spoken to her about on his second visit to the bar.

He'd still sit in his usual corner in The Tractor's, though.

He'd have to switch beers. Ale was a Noah drink.

Lager then. That'd do.

He'd hidden down the side of the pub in the darkness for a while after he'd left, paranoid that if he walked home, Yeoman might follow him, what with the chips-on-the-table incident. The copper *had* come out, and Florrie had stomped along in her bargy way and spoken to him.

He'd almost laughed at the indignation in her voice, but no doubt Yeoman would go and see the real Katie Violet, poking his nose in where it wasn't wanted, doing the maths and realising Mask had visited Fay, Helen, and Florrie as the reporter.

Yeoman had gone back into the pub, and Mask grabbed a passing taxi, going straight home, his disguise covered in the darkness as he approached his front door. Inside, he'd peeled Katie's face and hair off, wincing at the tug where the glue had set a bit too hard around his mouth, then washed his face. Two minutes later, he'd slung macaroni cheese in the microwave.

He'd eaten it at the front window, straight from the plastic tray, staring across at Oliver's, thinking to put a man mask on and go over there, scare the silly bastard, but a woman turned up in a flash car and knocked on Oliver's door.

Who was she? Too difficult to tell with the limited light, the streetlamp doing sod all except give her an orange glow. She'd gone inside, leaving a few minutes later.

With a can of peaches in syrup for his pudding, he'd stood at the window again and witnessed something interesting. Yeoman arrived and entered Oliver's, keeping the dog with Trudy instead of relieving her of the hairy burden.

Someone had crept out from Oliver's back garden, dressed all in black, hood up so he couldn't see the face, but going by the way they moved, the body shape, it was a woman. Or maybe it was one of those minor girls Oliver liked so much, escaping because the big bad policeman had arrived. She ran out of the street, head bent.

What on earth was going on?

The front door opposite opened, and Yeoman came back out. He ran across to Trudy's, then returned without the dog to Oliver, who stood on his doorstep, the light from inside his house rendering him a podgy silhouette. He closed the door and got into Yeoman's car.

Mask's chest hurt. Was Oliver going down to the station to tell the police all about what he'd done with Fay? Was he going to grass Noah up? Or was it to do with the woman's visit, the one in the car, and the slender one running away?

I should have sorted Oliver first.

He left the living room and went upstairs to select a mask. God, he still had to do the next stage of the Belle and Beast ones—time had got away from him. He spread the glue on and attached his new face. A man. Old. Long white hair and immense eyebrows.

A bit like the monster.

Chapter Forty-Eight

1991

Finally, the police left the area, and PC Yarthing stopped coming round. Weeks had passed since Ivy's death, and the investigation had been scaled back.

Fay wouldn't rest until it had closed.

Now, she had the job of smoothing over their relationships. Everyone was on edge and had been since that first morning, Helen waffling on about them being splintered or something, poking one another with jagged edges. Fay ignored her outbursts and focused on being normal—or as normal as she could be with her dented nerves and constantly waiting for a knock at the door, PC Yarthing saying, "Oh, and another thing…"

Who knew killing then disposing of a body could be so stressful?

Once again, they all sat at the kitchen table for their mid-morning break.

"I think we should have a little party," Fay suggested.

Helen stared, aghast. "What? That's disrespectful to Ivy."

"No, it isn't. The children need something to look forward to, and a party will make them all feel happier. Don't forget, it isn't just us who've been through trauma, they have as well."

Helen looked suitably chastised.

"Good idea." Noah nodded. "Billy will like that. Make sure we have pickled onions on cocktail sticks, and cheese and pineapple. Sausage rolls. You know, a proper buffet."

"And iced shortbreads in memory of Ivy," Oliver said.

"That's a lovely idea." Helen got up and took a pad and pen out of a drawer. *"I'll make a list now, shall I?"*

With Helen busy, Oliver staring into space, and Noah picking at a hangnail, Fay thought about her conversation with Oliver when they'd been outside beating the rugs. She'd warned him to stop acting so guilty—Helen and PC Yarthing would pick up on it, maybe they already had. He'd mumbled, so low she'd had to ask him to speak up over the slapping of the rugs.

"I can't stop thinking about what happened," he'd said.

"I can't either, but we have to put it behind us. Pretend we didn't do anything."

"Noah keeps looking at me funny, like he's going to tell on us any minute."

"I know, but ignore him. He's getting off on it. Just...just pack it in behaving like you've killed her. That was me, remember. Okay, it was because of you I did it—if you hadn't been in her room, I never would have gone in there—but you're just an accessory."

"If Noah didn't know..."

She'd stopped whacking the rug and gripped his shoulder. *"But he does, so deal with it. We stick to our story, and eventually, all this will go away."*

"Yarthing won't let it go."

"He will. There will be other crimes he has to deal with."

Now, Fay sighed, staring through the kitchen window. Yarthing was back. He was at the gates, measuring the width between the iron poles. Checking whether a little girl really could get between them.

She nudged Oliver. He looked out, pushed his chair back, and ran from the room.

"What the fuck's up with him?" Noah asked.

Helen glanced up from her pad. "Should I go and see if he's okay?"

"No, he's just upset." Fay nodded at the window. "Yarthing is measuring the gate."

Noah stood. "For Pete's sake, can he not just leave it?"

"Obviously not," Fay said.

"He's on Ivy's side, as we all should be." Helen got up and went to the window. "Even I can tell you she was thin enough to get through the gap, but I suppose he can't imagine it, as he hasn't seen how skinny she was."

Fay's heart played up, beating in an uneven rhythm. Yarthing walked away, to the right, as if heading for the front door. She wished she could ignore it if he knocked or rang the bell, but she couldn't.

An engine coughed to life—how had she not heard him drawing up in his car in the first place?—but he was leaving, and that was all that mattered.

She exhaled in relief.

How much more of this could she take? How long before Oliver lost the plot? Or Helen caught on that something was wrong? Or Noah's smirks and strange looks got noticed by her?

Fay wished Ivy had never been born, then none of this would be happening.

Chapter Forty-Nine

It had taken a lot out of Billy to continue the conversation about monsters. While he remembered those times, he couldn't quite recall the true sharpness of them, the memories faded, fuzzy, with the potential to smudge into something other than what had happened if he let them. His therapist had said: "We remember what we last remembered, layer upon layer of memories, so we never get a true representation of the actual event, except maybe for that first time of going back over it."

Billy didn't agree with that. When he thought about it, the memory was exactly the same as all the others, although yeah, like he'd just thought, there was that potential to make it into something else, something he could handle better. Less alarming. Less abusive.

Still, he'd told Sherry everything as best he could, and she'd sat there listening, leaving him be until he'd finished, knowing he wouldn't want her mollycoddling him. But in the end, he'd wanted a cuddle, her words whispered into his hair that they'd get through this together and she was sorry for believing the rumours.

"Tell me why you listened to them," he said, safe in her arms on the sofa.

She stroked his cheek. "You know me. If I see I'm going to get hurt, I push it along so I'm hurt quicker. Get it over and done with. Except you're still here, and I don't understand that."

"I'm here because I married you, because I promised to love you forever, not withhold that love just because you turned bitchy on me."

She laughed—thank God. Any other reaction would mean she was on the verge of imploding. He couldn't handle that, wrung out as he was.

"I didn't do anything with the pipe lady." He closed his eyes.

"I know. I just… It's complicated. *I'm* complicated."

"Same, but we'll be complicated together. Fuck whoever says shit. We've been through some tough times as kids, and it followed us, buggering us up, but they can all go and do one. The rumours will die down eventually, and if they don't, I'll set Phil on them."

"Doubt he'd do that, not now he has Val."

"No, but he'll know a man who can."

Someone knocked on the front door. Billy opened his eyes. What shitstorm was going to hit them next? It was getting on a bit, closing in on nine. Had to be urgent if they'd called round now.

He stood and rubbed his palms down his face. "I'll get rid of them. I'm not in the mood for company tonight. We should have a glass of wine then go to bed. Don't know about you, but I'm shattered."

"Me an' all. I'll open a bottle, get the glasses."

Sherry walked into the kitchen, and Billy went into the hallway, telling himself he didn't even have to open the door if he didn't want to. There was no law saying you had to, was there, but nevertheless, he did.

He sucked in a breath and gripped the edge of the door with one hand, his other splayed on the wall to help him keep his balance. What the fuck was *he* doing here?

"Hello, pet."

Billy stared at him, that voice swirling around in his head. His heart rate picked up, and a lump formed in his throat, choking him.

The monster had come back, and he was smiling.

With Noah's teeth.

Chapter Fifty

Interview Room One had grey walls decorated with scuffs and a wide band around the middle in royal blue. That colour covered the floor, lino, with scrape marks from chairs constantly being pulled out and pushed back in.

Morgan had phoned Jane and asked her to come and sit in on the interview with him. Shaz and Nigel were probably three sheets to the wind at the moment, so it was pointless contacting them.

Morgan and Jane sat opposite Oliver and his solicitor at a Formica-topped table, cups of tea for them, water for Morgan. The solicitor, a middle-aged blonde woman called Evelyn Gasborg, who had a face like a slapped arse and bird's nest hair, had spoken with Oliver for around an hour previously, then announced her client was ready to talk.

A uniform stood at the rear beside the door.

Morgan set the recording up and said the usual, introducing those present and the reason for them all being there. Oliver had already been cautioned. Morgan had scribbled a hasty few lines of questions he wanted to cover but anticipated them being forgotten once the chatting got underway. If Oliver had a lot to say, the conversation would go down many routes.

"When you phoned me this evening," Morgan began, "you told me things that implicated you in a crime and were possibly the reason for the attack on Fay Williams and the murder of Helen Donaldson. I would like you to answer questions regarding that. Firstly, why do you believe that happened to the two women I mentioned?"

Oliver fidgeted. "Because of Ivy Gibbs."

"Please clarify, for the tape, who that is."

"She's the girl who went missing from Loving Arms children's home in ninety-one. She was eight and was going to be my wife."

Jane clenched her fist on the table. Morgan swallowed. Evelyn shook her head, her cheeks turning a fetching shade of pink.

"What do you mean, your wife?" Morgan asked.

Oliver hugged himself and rubbed his fleshy arms. "When she grew up, like." He went on to explain what had gone on in Ivy's bedroom during his visits—apparently, she just moaned a lot and nothing else happened. "We couldn't do anything proper until she grew up."

"Performing a lewd act with your penis in front of a minor, whether you touched her with it or not, is illegal," Morgan said. "Did you ever do that?"

"No, and I don't go after girls anymore."

"What *do* you do? It isn't something that just goes away, Oliver. Multiple studies have shown that."

Oliver shrugged. "I just think about it. I don't touch, though, not that."

"Okay, back to that night, please."

"Like I said on the phone, I went into Ivy's room…" He continued until he'd reached the part where he'd placed the rolled-up carpet in his car boot then entered the property via the utility door.

"So Fay told you what to say and do throughout?"

"Yeah."

"Convenient of you to say that. We have a woman who is dead and can't corroborate or deny what you've said."

"It *was* her. She didn't tell me to put the carpet in the boot, though. I did that all by myself. I put it in the dump the next morning so the police wouldn't see it—discussed it with Fay first. I also went to the shop to get a newspaper and buy Helen some stuff. Icing sugar, I think. Then I had an alibi for being out, in case my car got spotted, see."

"If you were only in Ivy's room to calm her after she'd woken up, why couldn't you just tell the police that Fay forced you to help her dispose of the body?"

"Because of the moaning."

"Moaning?"

"Yeah. She knew Ivy did that for me."

Morgan's guts churned. "Did she ever do more than moaning?"

"N-no."

"Given what you did with another girl years later, I'm struggling to believe you." Morgan stared at him. "You said you don't touch, but you touched *her*. It's important for us to know what Fay had on you—you're expecting us to believe it was just the threat of you aiding and abetting a murderer…"

"She thought me and Ivy were being rude." He drew a circle on the table with a fingertip. His skin must be sweaty; it created a squeaking noise.

"Right. Tell us what the plan was after the investigation into Ivy's disappearance died down."

"We weren't to talk about it. We had to pretend it didn't happen. And we stuck to our jobs, and Fay tried to be nicer to the kids—she was always nasty to Ivy, picking on her—but the only one who got her kindest side was Billy Price. Noah got attached to Billy, too, and after Ivy…after she was gone, Fay got me to put a lock on Billy's door, and all the other kids', said something about stopping Noah going in their rooms. She said, 'He's a bloody raging pervert an' all.' I took it to mean Noah had a thing for Billy, that he did rude stuff with him."

"Like you did with Ivy?"

"Yeah."

Did Oliver realise what he'd just admitted?

Evelyn leant across and whispered something to him, and he paled.

"Shit," he whispered.

Morgan resisted punching his lights out. "So you *did* touch her."

"I'm sorry…"

Morgan would pursue that angle during another interview. He couldn't stomach it tonight. "Tell us about Noah. When he started working there, things like that."

"It was when we had all that snow in ninety-one, the beginning of the year. Might have been February, but don't quote me on that. He'd been in a troupe, travelling the country. A mask maker, that was what he was. Kept boasting about how he could make one so no one would ever know it was a mask. Like it was the same as skin."

Jane kicked Morgan's foot and wrote on her pad, holding it beneath the lip of the table: *Did Noah do this and he's been wearing masks all along? Is he Katie Violet, the old man, and the thirtysomething bloke?*

Morgan stopped himself from drumming his fingertips on the table and looked at Oliver. "Did he ever wear any of the masks in your presence?"

"Nah, but he told me he was Billy's monster—later down the line. Before Noah moved in, he'd nicked the utility key and got it copied. He used to come and go at night when we were all asleep, walk in and sneak to Billy's room. Another time, he told me he was in Billy's when Fay was killing Ivy. He saw me with no clothes on at the top of the stairs with Fay—we had Ivy in the carpet by then."

"No clothes on?" Jane sounded brittle and on the edge of striking the man.

Morgan knew that feeling, he'd just bloody well had the urge himself. Mind, since he'd laid Lydia to rest, he'd reined in his compulsion to lump people—he'd always known his unethical behaviour had stemmed from an unhappy marriage, plus something in his past, and now schooled himself not to follow the instinct of gripping someone up if they pissed him off.

It was proving difficult at the minute.

"I repeat," Jane said. "You had no clothes on?"

Oliver got flustered. "Y-yeah. I sleep naked, see, and with Ivy waking up, I just rushed down there to her."

Morgan regained control. "Did you cross the *moor* naked?"

"Of course not. I put wellies on and my mac."

Jane snorted. "A mac. Typical pervert attire. How was Fay dressed?"

"Oh, she had a nightie on, wellies, and her coat."

"So what was Noah doing at this point?"

"He used to tell me snippets over the years, just randomly come out with it, like: 'And I followed you out of the house and across the moor, hiding behind a tree when you stopped for a break.' Then he'd just shut up and not saying anything else for months."

This Noah was a control freak, wanting to scare Oliver over an extended period—most likely to remind him to remain silent.

"After, Fay used to get up at random times of the night and check on the kids. She said it was so me and Noah would never know if she'd walk into the rooms and catch us with them—she was paranoid we'd copied the bedroom keys. She was always tired because of it, sometimes had a kip in the living room during the day when the children were at school, but she said she had to keep them all safe. I don't understand why the girls needed to be safe, because I didn't do anything horrible to them."

"That's your perception of it," Morgan said. "Touching is horrible when a minor is involved."

"No, it's beautiful."

Morgan glanced at Evelyn to see what she made of this. She appeared to want to be sick.

"Okay. Let's go in another direction. How do you know Noah is Billy's monster? I take it that's a nonce way of saying you're their abuser."

"Noah said that's what he was." He recited his memories of that conversation.

They painted a vivid picture in Morgan's mind, and it appeared Evelyn struggled with this. Jane just filled herself up with rage. It nigh on crackled off her.

Morgan would have to get Billy in. With Noah still alive, despite the abuse Billy had suffered being historic, charges could be pressed. Then there was phoning all the kids, now adults, from Loving Arms to check whether they'd suffered abuse.

"Right." Morgan cleared his throat. "Are we to assume Helen Donaldson was also involved?"

"What, with Ivy?" Oliver shook his head. "No, she didn't have nothing to do with it. Maybe Noah thought she knew, and that's why he killed her. I mean, it has to be him, doesn't it?"

Morgan ignored that. "Why did you suddenly choose to open your mouth about this after all these years? You weren't even prepared to do so when myself and DS Tanner came to your house to inform you of Fay's and Helen's deaths. What changed?"

Oliver looked at Jane who stared back at him, her face blank.

He focused on the tabletop. "Because I'll be going down for my part in what that Derek Denham bloke got me roped into, so I may as well go down for this an' all. I'll be safer in Rushford."

So will little girls with you locked up.

"Are you sure that's the only reason?"

Oliver made eye contact with Jane again.

Fuck, is this what I think it is?

"Yeah, that's the only reason." Oliver coughed. "Can I have a wee?"

"Interview suspended at…"

Morgan and Jane exited, leaving the uniform to escort Oliver to the toilet. Morgan indicated for Jane to go into the empty break room, and he closed the door behind them.

"Tell me you didn't go to Oliver's house," he said.

"I'm not going to lie…" She smiled. "It worked, didn't it?"

Morgan slapped his forehead and paced. "What did you do?"

"Hung out in the back garden—don't worry, he didn't see my face at any time. His sister came round, had a word about him visiting their mother, saying he shouldn't go anymore. I waited for her to leave then made a noise so he'd come out. I jumped him, pushing him to the ground. Sat on his back. That's it."

"Your knife?"

"At his throat."

"Christ."

"Not the sharp edge, Jesus. I made him phone you. Said I'd kill him if he told anyone I was there, not that I would, obviously. That's a crime." She laughed at herself.

"So is threatening someone at knifepoint."

"Says the man whose go-to was to get arsey and shove people about. Just because you've stopped being so aggressive, doesn't mean it erases what you did in the past." She rammed her hands on her hips. "Look, I needed a bit of a thrill, all right? It got us results. If he's to be believed, Noah is going around killing people from Loving Arms. That bit about masks…"

"I think he's been wearing them to visit the ladies. It's probably the strangers Billy mentioned going up and down Regency." He paused to think. "Did you change your voice when you dealt with Oliver?"

"Of course I did!"

"Then why was she staring at you in the interview room?"

"I wondered that. Maybe he recognised my lush figure."

"Behave."

Jane laughed again. "Shall we leave him to stew overnight? He's said most of what we needed him to say. I'm tired. Adrenaline rushes take it out of me."

"You're unbelievable. Yes, we'll call it a night." He told her about going to see Katie Violet earlier, who'd said she hadn't visited anyone but Florrie to discuss Frankie's death.

"Great way to get inside their houses. Those masks he makes must be pretty good. Ah, actually, I'm going to do that tonight."

Morgan frowned, dreading what she was going to say next. "What…"

"An online search. If Noah's so good at making masks, maybe he still does and they're available for sale."

Morgan shook his head. He wouldn't put it past her to buy one.

Chapter Fifty-One

Billy had watched the clock since the monster pushed him into the living room, waving a meat cleaver about. An hour and a half had passed, each minute, each second excruciatingly slow. Noah had grabbed Billy's hair and pressed the edge of the cleaver blade to his throat, instructing Sherry to back the fuck off.

Their phones sat on the coffee table.

A bottle of wine and two glasses stood next to them, their evening changing in an instant from a drink before bed to…this.

"Sherry, if you attempt to pick one of those phones up, I'll chop his fucking neck to bits. Now, put your hands behind your back and walk in reverse to me." Noah had kept the blade at Billy's neck and fumbled for something, then he'd clicked cuffs around Sherry's wrists. "Go and sit your arse down."

She had, not moving from then to now, although her eyes said: *I want to get up and hurt him.*

Billy had replied silently: *Do as he says.*

"And if you kick back at me, Billy, or raise your hands to try to hurt me, I'll move this cleaver away from your neck and throw it at your wife. It'll bury itself in her forehead. How does that sound?"

Noah's little story about the past had been the entertainment after that. He recalled it differently to Billy, but then again, of course he would. Another snippet from the therapist: "We may all see and live an event, but none of us will view it in the same way. There are different angles, different roles played, different perspectives. Never tell someone things didn't happen that way, because for them, it did."

Billy didn't agree with that either. He understood the premise of what was said, but if someone put a sock into Billy's mouth and tied him up with a dressing gown cord, then that was what they'd fucking done.

Sherry cried at some parts of the telling, undoubtedly knowing it was lies, Noah fabricating things to salve his conscience perhaps, or to make himself look better. But nothing he said could make *any* of it better. He'd abused a young boy, one who'd lived through a traumatic event previously: "Mummy, Mummy, wake up…" The blood, so much of it, splattered everywhere. Him being taken to Loving Arms after the police and social workers had asked him to talk until his voice cracked and his throat dried out. Life gaining a sense of normality until the monster had come.

It was strange to hear that monster talking like Noah. The Newcastle accent hadn't lasted long, Noah maybe abandoning it in an attempt to show Billy he hadn't known the true identity of the monster until now, and that had almost been true had Billy not remembered the smell of pickled onions.

Billy's legs ached from standing in one place for so long.

"I cared for your husband, Sherry." Noah breathed heavily. "I loved him like my brother."

Billy opened his mouth to speak.

"Shut up right now, Billy." Noah twisted Billy's hair in his fist. "Don't you dare say we weren't like brothers."

Brothers don't put masks on and come into your bedroom to frighten you. Brothers don't pretend they speak differently. Brothers don't stuff socks in your mouth and do disgusting things to you. Did they?

"And I let him live his life when he aged out of Arms," Noah continued. "I left him alone and found a new brother. Three more since then. Have you ever told anyone about the monster?"

"No," Billy said.

"Not even Sherry?"

"Who is the monster?" Sherry frowned, playing the part of a confused person so well. "What are you on about?"

"Shut up," Noah shouted. "I wasn't talking to you. Now then, everyone who was there when Ivy disappeared needs to have no tongue and fingers. The dreams told me, and I have to do what they say."

The dreams?

"So I'm going to take Billy upstairs and sort him out. You"—he pointed with his free hand at

Sherry—"stay there and don't move. If you do, I'll slit his throat."

Billy stared at her: *Run as soon as we've gone. Get out.*

She stared back: *But what if he does what he said?*

Billy: *It doesn't matter. Go.*

Her eyes filled with tears, and Billy had to look away. He couldn't stand seeing the suffering in them, how she clenched her hands, those cuffs biting into her soft skin.

He allowed Noah to turn him and push him towards the door, the blade still in place. Up the stairs, that blade lower now, at his stomach. Into the spare bedroom at the back. He flicked the light on.

"Now then." Noah shoved Billy sideways onto the bed. "The monster wants the fingers first, but get that sock of yours off and stuff it in your mouth. Like old times, eh?"

Billy did as he'd been told. If Noah hacked at his fingers, Billy might not be able to hold the scream back, and Sherry wouldn't leave the house, she'd come up here and try to help. She might do that anyway and get hurt, killed.

Fuck.

Billy had to keep him talking. It was the only way his wife could find freedom.

Chapter Fifty-Two

Halfway House didn't feel the same anymore. Emma had been pondering the idea of asking for a grant to get it done up, make it look different so there were less reminders. She'd already requested double glazing for the foyer window — no way was she risking anyone smashing a single pane again. Someone had come and boarded it up for now, and as that wasn't as safe as she'd like, she jumped at every little sound.

Earlier this evening, she'd sat in the main living room with the remaining lads after a day of scrubbing all the blood away. The residents had pitched in and helped, and the place stank of bleach, although she knew that blood was still there, hiding beneath the falsehood of the floor and walls appearing clean.

They talked their feelings through, and Emma apologised for it being her ex-husband who'd killed Ryan and scared everyone silly. Various murmurs of it not being her fault had followed, and a bond of sorts formed, all of them in this shared experience, struggling to come to terms with it.

She was in her flat now, the place locked up for the night, and her work mobile rang, startling her. She picked it up. Lenny's name flashed up on the screen, so she answered it.

"Everything okay?" she asked.

"Can you come to my room and look at this? Shit's going on opposite."

"Oh God…"

"Someone's arguing, I think."

"Okay, two secs."

She unlocked her flat door and the one in the kitchen, then rushed upstairs to Lenny's room.

His door stood open, and he was at the window, looking across the road. This room had been Gary Flint's previously, and she shivered at the memory of him killing himself.

She approached the window and stared out. The house opposite was in darkness, but the one behind, Billy's, had the kitchen and back bedroom lights on. Silhouettes. A head and shoulders, as if someone was sitting, and another, darting about, agitated, and was that a knife being waved around?

She selected Yeoman's number and phoned him.

"Hi, Emma, what can I do for you?" he asked.

"I think something's going on at Billy's. They might have a knife."

"Can you see who it is?"

"No, they're just dark shapes."

"Okay, I'm on my way."

Emma didn't know whether to stay and watch or close Lenny's curtains.

Could she stand to see someone stabbed?

Chapter Fifty-Three

Sherry stood at the bottom of the stairs. She dithered, thinking she should go up there and help, take the baseball bat propped behind the sofa, but Billy had—

No. She'd do what he wanted.

She turned and ran to the front door, trying to be quiet, her breathing ragged and her chest sore from panic. She opened it, glanced upstairs to make sure Noah wasn't at the top, then ran out into Regency, the cold air a double slap to her cheeks. Sherry headed straight to the only place where the resident would know what to do and hammered on their door with the heels of her hands, the metal of the cuffs digging into her wrists, conscious Noah might hear it and know exactly what she'd done.

And kill Billy.

"Fuck, fuck, come on…" She pushed the bell instead, dancing from foot to foot, contemplating knocking on someone else's as well.

Phil opened up and stared at her bound wrists. "Sex game gone wrong, has it, love?" He smiled. "Lose they key, did you? I've got a spare you can have. Hang on." He turned to go and get it.

She reached out and grabbed his top. "It's Billy…"

"I should bloody well hope so, seeing as he's your husband."

"No, it's Billy. He needs help. Someone's at ours with a bloody machete thing."

"What?"

Phil brushed past her and darted along the street and into Sherry's house. She dashed after him, Val's "What the bloody hell is going on?"

trying to follow but fading as Sherry entered the hallway.

"Get the fuck away from him," Phil shouted.

A quick bolt up the stairs for Sherry.

The sounds of a struggle.

An "Ow, fuck!"

Sherry turned right on the landing. Stared into the spare bedroom.

A man on the floor clutched the top of his arm, scarlet flowing between his fingers. Two others stood there staring down at him. One with the machete, blood on the blade. One drawing his leg back and kicking the prone fucker in the gut.

Billy, it wasn't Billy who was hurt. It was *him*, Noah, his creepy white hair splayed on the carpet, and he groaned from the kick, easing his legs up in pain.

"Who the fuck is that?" Phil pointed down at Noah. "Why is an old man in here with this?" He held up the cleaver. "Have you got some dodgy racket or other going on that you haven't told me about?"

"He's not that old," Billy mumbled. "And it's complicated."

Phil touched Billy's shoulder. "Is it the pipe woman's bloke?"

"Fuck off." Billy sounded weary. "I didn't do anything with the pissing pipe woman, all right?"

A muscle spasmed in Phil's forearm where he clutched the weapon tight. "Does he need sorting?"

"I-I don't know." Billy stepped back and pressed himself against the wall. "I fucking want him dead, but—" He gazed across at Sherry.

She shook her head.

A car engine. The screech of tyres.

Sherry stared down the stairs at the front door.

A man burst inside.

She turned to face the bedroom again. "No sorting. Not now anyway."

"Why the fuck not?" Phil said. "He was just about to chop Billy's fingers off when I came in."

Sherry sighed with relief, the decision taken out of their hands. "Because Yeoman's here."

Phil groaned. "Bollocks."

Chapter Fifty-Four

Morgan stood in Billy's spare bedroom and looked around at those present. Billy. Phil. Some old boy on the floor. Sherry on the landing, whittling her fingers, cuffs around her wrists. He'd called for backup on the way here and hoped they arrived *after* he'd found out what the hell had happened, just in case he needed to sort someone the wrong way.

"What's been going on? I had a report of someone waving a knife around in here." He settled his gaze on Phil and narrowed his eyes. "Was it you?"

"Was it fuck." Phil held both hands up, the steel cleaver glinting in the light. "He was going to chop Billy's fingers off, the old fucking bastard."

What? Morgan stared at the man who bled from his arm. He'd need a doctor to look at that.

"Would have been his tongue next," the fella said.

Morgan pushed him onto his front and, despite the wound, wrenched his arms behind his back and held his wrists together, fishing a cable tie out of his pocket. He secured the wrists and hauled him standing, shoving him against the wall.

"Got a mask on by any chance?" He applied pressure to the bloke's shoulder so his arm hurt more.

"Ow. Shit. What if I have?"

"He must do," Sherry said. "Because that face isn't Noah's, yet it *is* him."

Morgan's guts twisted. Fuck, he had their man. "Smile."

Noah stared instead, lips closed.

Morgan kneed him in the nuts. Noah bent over, growling, and Morgan gripped the long white hair and yanked his head up. Noah must be grimacing beneath the rubber or whatever it was, revealing his stumpy teeth.

"Right, it *is* you." Morgan nodded. "I take it this'll sting a bit."

He undid a button of Noah's shirt and checked where the mask edge was near the collarbones. Pinching it with finger and thumb, he peeled it upwards. The damn thing stuck at the mouth, so he tugged hard. It broke free of the skin, and he took it off his head.

"Is this Noah Tate?" he asked Billy. "The monster?"

Billy winced, his cheeks blazing bright red, and nodded.

"Noah Tate, I am arresting you on suspicion of murder, grievous bodily harm with intent, sexual abuse involving a minor, and entering homes under false pretences. You do not have to say anything, but it may harm your defence if you do not mention when questioned something you later rely on in court. Anything you do say may be given in evidence."

Noah spat at him.

"I am also arresting you for assaulting a police officer."

"Noah doesn't exist," Noah said.

"What?" Morgan was seriously losing the will here.

"I changed my name years ago." He laughed maniacally, his eyes watering.

"To what?"

"Mask Maker."

Morgan paused to take that in. "Your actual name is *Mask Maker*?"

"Give yourself a gold star, pig."

Morgan resisted the urge to nut him one. "Mask Maker, I am arresting you…"

In the same interview room as he'd spoken to Oliver, Jane once again by his side, a male solicitor present, Morgan stared across at Mask. Fucking stupid calling him that, but a search by Amanda on the front desk had proved that was Noah's name now. He'd changed it after leaving Arms in twenty-eleven, not telling anyone he came across, existing as Noah but not, all his bills and whatnot in the name of Mask.

Jane had found his business online—Mask Maker's Magical Masks. He'd been running it from home for years now. A warrant had been requested to search his house, where he ran his business from, and officers were there now, looking for evidence.

Mask's arm had been stitched up, and he had a bandage on it.

Morgan didn't have proof of what he was about to ask, but he'd ask it anyway. "Mask, I'd like to know why you went to visit Fay Williams and Helen Donaldson with different masks on, and why you also had a mask on and entered Florrie Dorchester's home masquerading as Katie Violet, *The Pinstone Star's* crime reporter."

"I had dreams."

"We all have dreams, but sometimes we can't do whatever we want in order to see them come to fruition."

"Not those dreams, you thick cu—"

"I'd advise you not to go down the name-calling route."

"Whatever. Like I said, I had dreams, and they told me I had to shut them all up."

"Who?"

"Fay, Helen, Oliver, Billy, maybe Florrie if Fay told her what had happened. The kids."

"Shut them up about what?"

"The monster."

"Who is the monster?" Of course, Morgan knew, but he had to get Mask to say it.

"The person I become when I'm with little boys."

Jane sniffed in a sharp breath.

"And who do you become?" Morgan didn't want to hear the answer, but they needed it for the tape.

"Their brother."

Two perverts denying their true purpose in the space of a few hours was too much in one hit.

"Tell us what your plan was regarding those at Arms," Jane butted in.

Mask gave her a filthy look. "I went round there as Katie Violet, Aiden Zone, and Lionel Jebs."

"Which mask went with which name?" Jane asked.

"Katie is the woman with long brunette hair. Listen to how she speaks: Good morning. I'm from *The Pinstone Star*, and we're doing a feature on all those who cared for children at Loving Arms." His female voice was high-pitched and false. "Aiden is the thirtysomething man. Well, hello there! I'm Mr Zone! And Lionel is the old one: Happy afternoon to you, I'm—"

"We get the picture." Jane slapped her pad down. "What about the one you were tonight at Billy's?"

"That's the original monster. He comes from Newcastle, pet."

A shiver crawled up Morgan's spine. "So...you got into their homes as Katie first?"

"Yeah, then I told them other people would come, Aiden and Lionel. They fell for it. Stupid bitches."

"What do you know about Ivy Gibbs?" Morgan held his breath.

"In for a penny... Fay killed her, then she got Oliver to help carry the kid to the river. I watched them kick her body in." He chuckled. "You know, if they'd just asked me, I'd have hacked the girl up for them. I'd got a dab hand at using the axe to chop the wood for Arms. We had a proper fireplace in the kitchen."

A knock at the door, and Morgan got up to answer it. Amanda stood in the corridor and gestured for him to join her.

"DI Morgan Yeoman has answered the door to Sergeant Amanda Cartwright and is leaving the room," Jane said for the tape.

Morgan stepped out and closed the door. "What have you got?"

"Did you know he's your neighbour?" she said.

"What? No!"

"Yes, lives opposite. I took the liberty of asking Oliver if he was aware of that when we booked him in, and he paled quite a bit and said no. I could almost see his thoughts. You know, asking himself how he didn't know Mask was there."

"Surely he'd have recognised him."

"Maybe time changed him."

"Maybe."

"Right. The initial report from his house is a picture found of the gravestone with 'killer' in red paint, and a load of pieces of paper with his plans on it in a briefcase. Plus, under his kitchen sink, a pot of red gloss and a brush. Several masks with necks and hair attached, two currently being made. They apparently resemble Beauty and the Beast. Unhappy customer there, as he won't be finishing them, will he."

"No. Anything else?"

She consulted the file she held. "A white shirt, bow tie, and tuxedo all showed blood beneath the tester lamp—Billy had mentioned those if you remember. The shirt had been washed, but it didn't get rid of it all. A couple of meat cleavers—can't see any blood, but we both know some may be on them. A cupboard of jars containing pickled onions—we're talking one whole cupboard full of them. Another cupboard has what appears to be tongues in clingfilm, the tops of the wrapping secured, airtight, by a sealing device. There are fingers hanging from his living room lampshade with cotton. Oh, and a cup on top of his telly with a finger and teeth poking out of some soil in it. Yellow Marigolds in his bin."

Morgan shook his head to settle the information. "Um…"

"Yeah. Nutjob. Here's the list." She nodded at the door. "He needs a comfort break soon. As you know, he went from speaking to his solicitor and straight into the interview."

"I've taken about as much as I can at the moment anyway. I'll just present him with this lot then call it a night." He glanced at his watch. Half twelve. "Or early morning."

"Welcome to my world." She smiled and walked off.

Morgan went back into the interview.

Jane turned to see who it was. "DI Morgan Yeoman has entered the room."

Morgan sat, and she showed him her pad beneath the table: *I didn't ask any questions. We sat in silence apart from 'Mask' humming some song or other.*

Morgan responded by taking the list out of the file and placing it over Jane's note. While she read it, he got on with asking questions again.

"Mask, can you explain why there's a can of red paint and a brush under the kitchen sink?"

Mask came to life, laughing, throwing his head back. He didn't shut up for one and a half long-arsed minutes. How Morgan waited patiently he didn't know.

"The gravestone." Mask wiped tears from his cheeks. "I did it so when Fay eventually got herself to the cemetery, she'd see it and shit herself. She'd know exactly what I meant—not that she'd killed her precious Frankie, but Ivy. Just another warning. As if the fingers and tongue weren't enough. She killed herself, though. Shame she won't get to see it."

"What about all the plans found in your briefcase?"

"What about them? They are what they are. Plans. Are you deliberately acting stupid?"

"We found meat cleavers."

Mask rolled his eyes. "Yes, I used them to chop off their fingers. The end of the handle was superb for bashing out Fay's front teeth."

His nonchalance was pressing Morgan's last nerve button. If the cameras weren't on and the solicitor wasn't sitting there... "Why do you have a full cupboard of pickled onions?"

"Why not? It isn't relevant to this anyway."

"Your lampshade. In the living room. Fingers are attached to it with cotton."

"Fay's and Helen's. Oh, and get it right. That's not cotton. I took some of their hair. It's just as strong as cotton, maybe even stronger."

"Did you cut the hair?"

"No, just a yank was enough. Some also have roots on." Mask grinned, his horrible little teeth so strange in his large gums. "You're going to ask about the cup, aren't you."

"I was, yes."

"Helen's cup and finger, Fay's teeth. The soil is half from the moor, half from the cemetery, the latter taken from a fresh grave, no idea whose it was."

This man was sick, and Morgan couldn't stand it anymore. Tomorrow was another day, asking Mask and Oliver more questions. He'd probably get Shaz and Nigel to interview Mask—out of the two, he preferred Oliver.

"Shame you won't get to finish the Beauty and the Beast masks." Morgan sat back and folded his arms.

Mask smiled again. "Shame you'll never know where John, David, Harry, and Kevin are."

Morgan resisted sitting bolt upright and instead eased forward, his heart pounding. "Who are they?"

"The four boys who met the monster after Billy." He paused and stared right into Morgan's eyes. "They were going to tell, so I shut them up. Their fingers and tongues… Well, I suspect your officers will find them in my house eventually. Now, it's late. I've cooperated. I'd like to go to bed on my thin mattress in my cell."

Morgan wouldn't have that same luxury. He'd be looking into missing persons, specifically lads, to see if any names matched up. He needed to organise house-to-house enquiries for tomorrow as well, in Griffin, to see if anyone noticed the comings and goings in Mask's house.

Good job Trudy said she'd keep Rochester overnight.

He sighed.

"Interview suspended at…"

Chapter Fifty-Five

Oliver sat on the bed in his holding cell, shaking. How had he not known Noah lived opposite? All right, Oliver hadn't been in Griffin's that long, but surely he'd have seen him, wouldn't he?

Actually, now he thought about it, there were a few people in and out of Noah's place at all hours. A young woman and man, and the old fella, and then the other bloke who must be in his fifties. Was *that* Noah? Then again, Oliver might not recognise him anymore. He'd been in Rushford for a long time to do with the Pinstone girl—they called it rape, he called it love—and he didn't look like his old self when they'd lived at Arms, so it stood to reason Noah might not either. Weight had piled on, jowls sagged, distorting young features into an old person even he didn't recognise when he stared at himself in the mirror.

The flap on the door slid across, and Yeoman's face appeared. "I hear you didn't know Noah was in Griffin's."

"I didn't, but then you had no idea you lived next door to me."

"Fair enough, can't argue with that. We'll talk tomorrow, all right?"

Oliver nodded. "I need a wee."

"Your toilet's right there."

The flap snapped shut.

He didn't reckon he'd have any chance of having a wife now. Years in prison loomed ahead of him, and he'd be *really* old by the time he got out.

If he ever did.

Chapter Fifty-Six

At seven a.m., Florrie trotted up to Wasti's, excitement flickering in her belly. Her article was out, two days after Katie Violet had been round, and she was eager to see her name cleared of any wrongdoing regarding baby Frankie.

The latest BOGOF offers were now on, so she shoved inside the shop, intent on snagging the pecan pastries for her breakfast, the Hovis for lunch, and the carrot cake for after her bangers and mash at dinnertime. She'd have mushy peas and gravy, too.

Basket hanging in the crook of her arm, she waved a hello to Wasti and divebombed the BOGOF shelf. She also bought some Ritz—she'd forgotten to before, and she still had some Brie left. Today was a feast day, a celebration. She threw a Cadbury's hot chocolate jar into her basket for good measure, the perfect drink for the cold weather. If she remembered rightly, she had some mini marshmallows in the cupboard. She'd sprinkle those on top with squirty cream.

At the counter, she placed the basket down and snatched a newspaper from the stand beside her, thrusting it at Wasti.

"Ah, yes," he said. "I see we have a star in our midst. I have read that this morning. I knew you did not kill the baby." He got on with ringing her things up.

God, that carrot cake looked so good it could get in her belly anytime.

"Of course I didn't kill him, but with Fay gobbing off at every opportunity, saying I did, I needed to get it out there that I didn't."

"Fay is gone. Is it not wicked to speak ill of the dead? That is six pounds fifty-two."

Florrie's happiness got pricked by Wasti's comment, deflating her a bit. She took a tenner out and handed it to him. "Just because someone's dead, doesn't mean they're not a fucker. A git in life, a git in death, that's what I say. Death doesn't mean you're instantly a new person, absolved of all the horrible things you said and did."

"I see what you are saying. I had not looked at it that way." He prodded the till to open the drawer.

"Well, now you have." She waited for her change and took it. "Ta. What's your next set of BOGOFs and when do they start?"

"Monday, and it's litre bottles of Coca-Cola, Animal biscuits, and raspberry ripple ice cream sundaes."

"No good to me. I'll give them a miss." She dropped her things and purse in her bag. "Have a nice day."

"And you. Will you be going to Fay's funeral?"

Florrie thought about that. For a second. "No."

She walked out and legged it home as much as she was able, grimacing at Karen and Ray in their front garden yet again. She hadn't noticed it on her way out, but someone had sprayed SCUM on their front door in black.

At her gate, she pushed it open and waddled up her path.

"Was this you, you old bitch?" Karen shouted, her face scarlet, fist up.

"No, but I wish it bloody was."

"You cheeky fucking cow."

Florrie went inside, ignoring the stupid woman. She put her shopping away, stuck the kettle on, and hung her coat up. Tea made, pecan pastries on the table on one of her flower-patterned plates—all four of the buggers—she settled down to eat and read.

MRS DORCHESTER IS INNOCENT!

Katie Violet – Crime Reporter

For years, Florrie Dorchester has walked around with a mantle draped over her, the threads of it made from sorrow and false accusations, a heavy burden indeed. Her cousin's baby died of SIDS in the sixties. Fay Williams, the mother of the baby, allegedly told everyone that Fay was a murderer. Proof has come to light that this isn't the case.

Florrie found a diary, written by a Beryl Williams, Fay's mother, and it states that she, Beryl, procured poison to kill the child, disguising it as gripe water.

Florrie nodded to herself. "That's right, you tell them, Katie." She read on to near the bottom of the article, which explained the tragic circumstances, and anger flared at the final paragraph.

Fay was attacked recently in her own home, her fingers and tongue chopped off. We are unaware of why this happened at present, but it's a disgusting act against the vulnerable. Fay then took her own life, for reasons unknown. Such a tragedy that our elderly aren't safe. More to follow.

Why did Katie feel the need to taint the article with compassion towards Fay, who had been nothing short of a bitch for most of her adult life? Why couldn't this be focused on Florrie alone?

Where's my one moment in the bloody sun?

She scanned the page. Spied her photo. Well, that might make it a bit better.

She'd got her picture in the top-right corner after all, the one she'd wanted the fake Katie to take. Florrie looked suitably sad, a woman mortified by false accusations.

It was better than a poke in the eye with a sharp stick, wasn't it.

She grabbed a second pecan pastry and stuffed half of it in her mouth.

Delicious.

Chapter Fifty-Seven

Two days had passed since the monster had come back into his life, yet it felt like yesterday. Billy had gone to the police station the following morning to give his formal statement, along with Phil and Sherry. Billy had to go back soon, once they'd interviewed Noah, for him to give his account of the abuse.

The thing was, he didn't know if he wanted to.

He asked Sherry what she thought.

"Well," she said, "it might be like free counselling. You get to tell your story to a stranger—ask for a copper you don't know—and purge your mind of it that way. Cheaper than therapy an' all."

He knew she'd have the right answer.

Billy sighed and reached across to her from his favourite chair. "Thanks, love."

"Always here."

He marvelled at how this tragedy had brought them back together, no more griping, no more accusations. Sometimes, bad shit ended up okay.

He stared at the tonic water she'd recently poured him. The glass stood on the little table beside him, bubbles clinging to the inside, others streaming up in a line, popping when they broke the surface.

He thought of why he drank that stuff, and, of course, Mum jumped into his mind. She'd liked a vodka and tonic a couple of nights a week, and he'd asked her if he could have one.

"No, Billy, but you can have the pop that goes with it."

She'd poured him a glass, and he'd sipped, wincing at the sharpness, but he told himself to like it, because if Mum did, he did.

After her death, that drink had been a reminder of her every time he tasted it. He told himself she was still there if he had one, watching over him.

He took his hand from Sherry's and picked up the glass, sipping the clear liquid.

I'm almost free of the monster, Mum. Nearly there.

Chapter Fifty-Eight

Irritating Liz had come into Catherine's room yesterday and all but given Catherine a heart attack. *He* had been arrested. Again.

Later, Sarah had come and told her it was something to do with helping a man to kidnap a woman, plus he'd disposed of Ivy Gibbs' body with that awful Fay Williams.

Who had Catherine raised?

She was ashamed of herself for bringing such a wicked person into the world, one who'd gone on to hurt so many.

The little girl had stopped visiting since the medication change. Just one day with new tablets, and Catherine had been back to living her confusing existence as it had been before the child arrived.

Funny, but she missed her. She'd been a welcome change to the monotony of waiting to die. But that didn't matter anymore. The end was coming; she wouldn't be here for much longer, thank God. Her chest was heavy, see, and she was so tired, her breathing shallow. That had come on after hearing about that nasty boy of hers, and the need to give up and get away from this world took hold.

Maybe she wouldn't have to wait for long.

Maybe she'd go to sleep one night and just not wake up.

That would be lovely, wouldn't it?

Chapter Fifty-Nine

The past two days had been non-stop interviews. Shaz and Nigel had dealt with Mask, Shaz admitting she'd wanted to punch him every time he smiled regarding the boys, Nigel fighting tears over Mask's new confession.

The night Morgan had stayed on to search the missing person database, he'd found the four lads' names. John, seven; David, nine; Harry, ten; Kevin, eight. All taken from their towns on Mask's day off from Arms, sometimes years apart, him using the care home's van. He'd travelled miles to snatch them from random places and bundled them into the back, saying they needed to come with him to Arms as they'd been naughty at home, their mummies had told him.

He'd done despicable things for the whole day to each of them, then choked them with their own socks pushed right to the backs of their throats, Mask pinching their noses shut. He was always in a woman mask for the grabs, driving to nearby woods, stopping and climbing in the back with them, whipping the mask and hair off to reveal his real self.

He wouldn't say where their bodies were. Nor would he explain what he'd done with other boys he'd pushed down alleys or dragged into remote fields while he'd toured with the troupe. His only regret? That he hadn't 'shut those particular little fuckers up', letting them live to tell the tale of a young man who'd abused them, not wearing masks when he'd abducted them.

Oliver's had been an easier confession to swallow. Although no less harrowing, he'd at least showed remorse, and his broken mind had convinced him that what he'd done was out of love, Ivy and the Pinstone girl future wives he wanted to cherish. He'd had therapy in Rushford and at least understood now that what he wanted wasn't legal or moral, so he'd made a concerted effort to hold his urges back. The ones with real girls at least.

His phone told the story of what he watched in bed at night.

Morgan had nearly been sick.

With the CPS prosecuting—how could they not?—and statements filed, evidence tested then packed away for court, there were only a few odds and ends to finish off. The clock at last read five, and Morgan walked out of his office and into the incident room.

"I'd say it's the end-of-the-road drink, wouldn't you?" he said.

Nigel nodded. "Yep. This has been a tough one." The poor bloke's face looked haggard, shadows sitting above his cheekbones, the whites of his eyes bloodshot. He powered down his computer.

Jane stood and stretched. "There are times when murder should be acceptable."

Shaz swung her legs off her desk and got up to grab her bag. "What the chuff are you on about?"

Jane walked round her desk and stood in the middle of the room. "If I had a knife, I could have gladly stabbed Mask."

Shaz nodded. "Oh. I see."

Morgan widened his eyes at Jane. "Not a good avenue to go down." But he'd had similar thoughts. If it wasn't illegal, he'd have kicked the shit out of the man. Rushford would have to do, though, be the punishment Mask received. It wasn't nearly enough, and Morgan had an idea Mask would taunt him every so often by saying he'd reveal where he'd hidden those bodies, only to change his mind at the last minute.

Morgan had passed the information on to Tracy Collier, head of Serious Crimes, and she was dealing with the forces where John, David, Harry, and Kevin had lived. With Mask at least admitting he took those lads to the woods, the police had locations in their areas to go on now.

He prayed the bodies would be found so the families had closure.

"Come on, off to The Tractor's." He walked past the chief's office, glad he'd already given his update. He couldn't be doing with working anymore today.

Jane bagged a lift with Nigel—she wanted a drink tonight, she said—and Shaz got in with Morgan. He'd park outside the pub and just have one pint, in no mood to get rat-arsed. A bit of dinner wouldn't go amiss, though. Maybe the lasagne and garlic bread with a side of chips that thankfully wouldn't be nudged off his plate this time.

In the pub, they snagged their usual table, and Morgan ordered the first round.

"I hear you found Noah then," Heidi said.

"His name's Mask now."

"Mark. Right."

"No, *Mask*."

"You what?"

"You don't want to know, trust me."

Once she poured the drinks, he carried them over on a tray and placed it on the table. He sat to the sound of much male laughter and turned to look over his shoulder. Emma Ingles sat with the residents of Halfway House, all of them with meals in front of them and a couple of beer pitchers to share. She waved, looking so much more relaxed now, and he raised a hand to her, smiling, glad she was happy.

Terry brought a large cake out, candles alight, and stood beside Emma's table. A burst of *Happy Birthday* rang out, and Emma's teary eyes shone from the light of so many flickering flames, her face glowing from them. She let the emotion out, crying, and Lenny gave her a sideways hug. She rested her head on his shoulder, and it was so very clear this job was her life and she cared about the people she looked after.

The world needed more people like Emma.

Morgan turned to face his team, choked up, and coughed to clear his throat.

"Aww, have you gone soft on us?" Shaz asked.

"Nah, just glad it's over. For all involved. Come on, glasses raised. We did a bang-up job and need to toast ourselves."

"It's bad luck to toast yourself," Jane said.

Nigel shook his head.

Morgan smiled. "Do I look like I give a fuck about that? Cheers!"

Printed in Great Britain
by Amazon